ChangelingPress.com

Scratch/Havoc Duet

Harley Wylde

Scratch/Havoc Duet
Harley Wylde

All rights reserved.
Copyright ©2019 Harley Wylde

ISBN: 9781690609285

Publisher:
Changeling Press LLC
315 N. Centre St.
Martinsburg, WV 25404
ChangelingPress.com

Printed in the U.S.A.

Editor: Crystal Esau
Cover Artist: Bryan Keller

The individual stories in this anthology have been previously released in E-Book format.

No part of this publication may be reproduced or shared by any electronic or mechanical means, including but not limited to reprinting, photocopying, or digital reproduction, without prior written permission from Changeling Press LLC.

This book contains sexually explicit scenes and adult language which some may find offensive and which is not appropriate for a young audience. Changeling Press books are for sale to adults, only, as defined by the laws of the country in which you made your purchase.

Table of Contents

Scratch (Devil's Boneyard MC 2)..................................4
- Chapter One 5
- Chapter Two..16
- Chapter Three 30
- Chapter Four 46
- Chapter Five 59
- Chapter Six 72
- Chapter Seven 91
- Chapter Eight 102
- Chapter Nine 112
- Chapter Ten 126
- Epilogue 137

Havoc (Devil's Boneyard MC 3) 141
- Chapter One 142
- Chapter Two...154
- Chapter Three 164
- Chapter Four 178
- Chapter Five 191
- Chapter Six 203
- Chapter Seven 216
- Chapter Eight 227
- Chapter Nine 236
- Chapter Ten 248
- Chapter Eleven..257
- Chapter Twelve...268
- Epilogue 277

Harley Wylde 282
Changeling Press E-Books 283

Scratch (Devil's Boneyard MC 2)
Harley Wylde

Clarity -- I've been on my own since I was sixteen, and I've fought tooth and nail to make a life for myself and the son I never planned to have. Caleb is my entire world, despite the circumstances of his birth. Being homeless a second time certainly hadn't been in my life plans, so when a gruff yet sexy biker offers a bit of help, how can I possibly say no? Doesn't hurt that the older man is easy on the eyes, and he's so good with Caleb. I'd thought I wasn't able to trust anyone ever again, but looking into his eyes, I know deep down he'd never hurt us. It just never occurred to me that I'd fall completely in love with him.

Scratch -- The young woman and kid I find sleeping outside my club's chop shop make me feel things I shouldn't. Hell, she's younger than my damn daughter, but it's obvious she's been to hell and back, and she's still fighting. There's fire in her soul, but the gentle way she treats her son leaves me wanting things I shouldn't. Like a new chance at a family. What the hell would she want with a man thirty years older than her? When I took her home with me, I never counted on wanting to keep her. I'll slay her demons, bury the monsters from her past, and then I'll do the one thing I thought I'd never do... claim an old lady, then make her my wife.

Chapter One

Clarity

I held Caleb on my hip while I dug through the trash behind the diner. I had a box of peanut butter crackers and a few packages of snacks in my backpack, but I was saving those for my son. They weren't nutritious, but at least they hadn't come out of the dumpster. I might eat whatever I had to in order to survive, but I refused to let Caleb do that. He was only two years old, and he needed real food. Hot food, and a clean table where he could sit and enjoy a meal. That wasn't going to happen, though.

Giving up on finding myself something to eat that wasn't rotten, I backed away from the smelly trash bin and headed back up to the street. It was late, and even though the diner, Laundromat, and a bar up the road were all still open, the sidewalks were pretty empty. Not that the sleepy little Florida town where I lived was ever truly busy. We were off the path a bit. Not close enough to the beach to get a lot of tourists, and too small for anything else.

I hitched the bag on my back and tried to find a relatively safe place to sleep for the night. We didn't have a local shelter, and while the churches would sometimes let people stay there, I couldn't ask every night. I worried they would take Caleb from me. Maybe I should have let him go, found him a home where he'd have clean clothes, a roof over his head, and food in his belly. But my heart ached every time I thought about parting with him.

I had no one. My mom had died when I was two, and when my dad remarried, he'd chosen a woman who liked to pretend I didn't exist. Soon enough, my dad decided I didn't exist either. Once his new kids starting popping out every few years, I was pushed to the side, and eventually I left. I'd been sixteen when I'd hit the streets, and no one had come looking for me. I was sure that my dad was relieved I was gone. It hurt, but crying over it wouldn't change anything.

I'd thought I was doing okay when I found a man about five years older than me who offered me a place to sleep and help getting a job. I should have known not to trust him. Things had been fine for a while, but then he'd started asking to be repaid for his kindness. Blowjobs mostly, except for the night he was high on who knows what and decided to take more than I was willing to give. Caleb was the result of that night. Once I'd found out I was pregnant, I'd taken off. Even though the man hadn't touched me again, I hadn't wanted to take any chances.

A women's shelter had helped at first, even found me a job and a place to live. Things had been going pretty well, until two months ago. The little thrift store where I'd been working shut down without notice. I'd had enough in the bank to keep our tiny apartment for another month, and then the money had run out and I hadn't been able to get another job. So we slept where we could, ate what we could, and just tried to survive.

The church over on Pine Avenue would let me take a shower and would give me a dress out of the donations to wear for interviews, and the nice lady who worked in the church office would watch Caleb for me. I'd applied to every place in town that was hiring, and no one had wanted me. Our situation was bleak, but as long as we had each other, then I'd keep fighting. If Caleb weren't with me, I might have given up by now. Or decided to join the ladies who worked the street corner on the other end of town. But I'd been a virgin when Caleb's dad had raped me, and I couldn't bring myself to take that step. Not yet. I didn't think badly of the women who made their living that way, but I didn't think I could do it.

An auto repair shop was just a few more steps away, with a large enough doorway that Caleb and I could hide in the shadows and get some sleep. I checked the hours on the window and saw it wouldn't be open for at least five more hours, which meant I could rest a little. I'd learned to sleep lightly, so that I'd wake up at the first sign of trouble, or whenever Caleb stirred. I was always scared I'd sleep so hard that he'd wander off and I'd never see him again. Hunkering down into the corner of the doorway, I settled Caleb on my lap and used my backpack as a pillow. My son snuggled against me and closed his eyes.

I didn't think I'd been asleep for more than an hour when I heard a loud rumble. My eyes opened as a single headlight focused on us, making it hard for me to see. I held a hand up to my face, and shielded Caleb with the other. The light stayed on, but I could barely make out a shadowy figure dismounting from what I'd figured out was a motorcycle. The man approached and loomed over us.

"This is private property," he said, his voice deep and raspy.

"I'm sorry. We'll go," I said, struggling to stand.

I could feel his gaze raking over me. I managed to get to my feet without stumbling, got my backpack straps over my shoulders, then hefted Caleb into my arms.

"Where are you going to go?" he asked.

"Doesn't matter. I'm sorry we trespassed," I said. I hitched my backpack a little higher over my shoulder and clutched Caleb to me. I tried to step around the large man, but he reached out and placed a hand on my shoulder.

I froze under that touch, tensing and waiting to see what would happen. Is this where he offered me a place to sleep in exchange for the use of my body? Wouldn't be the first time I'd had that offer made to me, and I doubted it would be the last. I would do anything for my baby to have a place to rest and food to eat, or nearly anything. We'd struggled and things were bad, but I didn't think I could handle having strange men touch me. Not after Caleb's dad, or more like sperm donor. I didn't think he would come after Caleb, even if he knew my baby existed, but I'd decided not to take any chances. Thankfully, I hadn't seen him since we'd left. For all I knew, he wasn't even in town anymore.

"Christ, you don't even look old enough to have a kid," he muttered.

My chin raised a notch. "I'm nineteen. Well, almost nineteen. Not that it's any business of yours."

I saw a flash of white teeth as he smiled in the darkness. "All grown up then, aren't you? Eighteen, nearly nineteen, and think you know everything I bet. Why are you sleeping in the doorway of my business?"

I glanced behind me before facing him again. "I told you we didn't mean to trespass."

"That doesn't answer my question."

"We didn't have anywhere else to go," I admitted softly, my arms tightening around my son.

"There's a lot of expensive equipment in there. Going to steal anything?" he asked.

I felt fire ignite inside me and I clenched my teeth a moment. I might be broke, but I wasn't a thief!

"No!"

"Come on." He walked up to the doorway I'd just vacated, then he unlocked the front door and pushed it open.

I hesitated. I didn't know if I could trust him, and figured my chances were better out here in the open than inside, but what if he was going to offer food for Caleb? Or maybe there was a couch in the waiting room and he'd let my baby rest there for an hour or two. It was an opportunity I couldn't pass up, but at the first sign he was going to be a perv, I was out of there.

I stepped inside as he flipped on the lights, and I blinked at how bright they were. There was a beat-up leather couch with duct tape holding it together, and a scarred table with a few magazines on top. But the man didn't stop in the front room. He kept going, so I followed at a slight distance. If I needed to run, I wanted a head start.

He entered a small, cluttered office and turned on a lamp. It glowed softly, the light dim, but there was a huge couch on one wall that looked a little too inviting with its overstuffed arms. It was leather, but unlike the one out front, it didn't have so much as a scratch on it that I could see. The man pulled a blanket off the back and motioned toward the couch.

"You can rest here a while. I can either lock you in and reset the alarm, or I can stay until you've had a chance to rest. I'll leave it up to you. But know that if you steal so much as one thing, I will track you down," the man said.

I focused on him and noticed he wore one of those black leather vests I'd seen the local bikers wearing. *Scratch -- VP* was stitched on the front. He was an older man, a bit of gray at his temples and in his beard. I was horrible at guessing ages, but if I had to, I'd place him in his late forties or early fifties. He had the kind of eyes that looked like they had seen far too much, like he'd fought wars I could only imagine but was still standing. He was strong, his muscles stretching the sleeves of the T-shirt he wore, and his jeans encased muscular thighs. He could easily overpower me, and yet he hadn't come close to me since grabbing my shoulder earlier.

"You can lock us in," I said. "We won't take anything."

He nodded and looked at Caleb, who was yawning on my shoulder.

"When's the last time the two of you ate?" he asked. "And I mean real food, not something you've scrounged from somewhere."

"A while," I admitted.

"There's not much here. Some bottles of water in the mini fridge," he said nodding to a small black one in the corner I hadn't noticed. "I'll bring you something to eat when I get back. He allergic to anything? Are you?"

"No, we're not allergic to any food, but you don't have to get us something. Just giving us a place to sleep for a while is more than enough."

He grunted and looked around the room a moment before locking his gaze on me again. "We'll talk when I get back. For now, get some sleep. Both of you. There's a bathroom through there," he said pointing to a door behind his desk.

"Thank you," I said grudgingly, still not knowing what this would cost me. Or rather what he'd demand. Didn't mean I'd give it to him.

He turned to leave but paused in the doorway. "I have a daughter, a bit older than you. And a grandson close to your son's age. She was in trouble a while back and someone helped her. Just think of this as my way of paying it forward. If you're worried I'm going to ask for some sort of repayment, you don't have to be concerned about that."

My cheeks warmed and I wondered if I'd been transparent.

His lips twitched as if he fought back a smile. "Pretty thing like you, I imagine you've had a lot of assholes try to get into your pants. Didn't want you anxious I would be the same. When you wake up, you can tell me how you came to be on the streets, and maybe I can find a way to help you in a more long-term way than loaning you a couch for the night. The bathroom has a small shower if you want to clean up. Use whatever you need in there. Towels are in the cabinet and there are a few new toothbrushes in there too."

"You loan your couch out to people often?" I asked, wondering why he'd have spare toothbrushes at his work of all places.

"No, but I've crashed here a few times. I keep a lot of toothbrushes on hand for the guys who work out in the shop. They've come in one too many times with their breath smelling like they last used a toothbrush a decade ago. No one wants that in their face all day."

I bit my lip so I wouldn't smile and just nodded.

"Get some sleep, sweetheart. You can lock the office door if it makes you feel safer. I have a key, but I won't come in without knocking first." He gave me a searching look. "You're safe, all right?"

"Thank you," I said again. "I mean it. No one's..."

He held up a hand. "I'm not a saint, but I don't like thinking about what could happen to a pretty thing like you and that sweet little boy out there on the streets. This might be a small town, but bad shit still happens."

I nodded and eyed the couch. As much as I wanted to sleep, Caleb and I were both rather dirty. After Scratch left, I locked the door behind him, then pulled out a clean outfit for both of us and carried Caleb into the bathroom. Tiny was right, but it would be heavenly to have a hot shower and get clean. I tried not to abuse the kindness of the local churches by asking for things too often, so it had been a few days since we'd had a chance to get clean.

I stripped us both down, made the water just the right temperature for my sweet boy, then climbed in with Caleb splashing at my feet. I washed him first, then wrapped him in a towel I'd found in a cabinet, letting him sit on what looked to be a clean bathmat. Then I scrubbed myself until my skin turned red. I kept a disposable razor in my backpack for the times I was able to shower and I shaved as best I could since the blade was getting a bit dull.

Once we were both clean and dressed in fresh clothes, I bundled up our dirty stuff, pulled a plastic bag out of my backpack and put the dirty things in there. I tied it off and shoved it into my backpack before curling up on the couch with Caleb. I put him between me and the back so he wouldn't fall off while he slept, then covered us with the soft blanket. Once my baby was breathing evenly, I let myself relax enough to fall asleep.

My eyes popped open every now and then as I looked at our surroundings, making sure were still alone and still safe. There wasn't a window in the room and I didn't see a clock anywhere. I had no idea how much time had passed since Scratch had left us, but it felt like hours. Caleb still slept soundly, and I eventually went to sleep again. The next time I opened my eyes, I heard loud noises from the other side of the office door.

I held Caleb a little tighter, wondering if someone would try to come in. What would they do if they found me in here? Scratch had been nice, hadn't demanded anything for his kindness, but it was my experience that most men didn't act that way. The ones I'd been around had thought they could have whatever they wanted from me, even if I didn't agree.

I curled into a ball in the corner of the couch, Caleb clutched in my arms. There was a loud knock at the door and I fought back a whimper.

"It's just me," said a gruff voice I recognized. "I'm coming in."

I heard the rattle of keys, then the knob turned, and Scratch stepped into the office. There was a paper sack clutched in one hand and a plastic bag hanging from the other. His eyebrows lifted when he saw me cowering on the couch, and he glanced over his shoulder before focusing on me again.

"Anyone bother you?" he asked.

"N-no. It was just really noisy out there. I didn't know who…" I trailed off.

He nodded. "It's all right. I picked up some breakfast for both of you. Probably not the most nutritious meal, but this early in the morning it was either the diner or the only drive-thru open this time of day. I got both of you a chicken biscuit."

He handed the paper sack to me and the smell made Caleb's eyes pop open, his little nose twitching as he looked for what smelled so good. His eyes went wide when he saw the bag in my hand, and he slowly reached for it, then jerked his hand back at the last minute, looking up at me for permission.

"It's okay, baby," I assured him. I reached into the bag and took out a sandwich, unwrapping it for him.

Scratch handed me a bottle of orange juice and a bottle of milk. I assumed the milk was for Caleb and opened it for him. I watched as he devoured his sandwich then gulped down his milk. My heart ached that I hadn't been able to give him something this simple in quite a while.

"You need to eat, sweetheart. If he's still hungry, I'll get him something else, but you can't starve yourself."

"Clarity," I said. "My name is Clarity."

He smiled a little. "Nice to meet you, Clarity. People around here call me Scratch."

"You're part of the biker gang in town," I said as I unwrapped my sandwich.

"Club. We're a club. The Devil's Boneyard, but don't let the name scare you. None of us would ever hurt a woman or child."

"So, Scratch as in…"

"Like Lucifer, but I promise you're safe with me."

I nodded and finished my sandwich slowly so I wouldn't get sick. It had been a really long time since I hadn't had to share my food with Caleb, and I wasn't sure how my stomach would handle it. I managed to eat the entire thing and slowly sipped my juice. When I was finished, I tried not to fidget. Scratch had said he wanted to talk to me this morning and I didn't know what to expect.

He was leaned back against his desk, his arms folded, and one booted foot crossed over the other. While he appeared relaxed, there was a coiled tension in his muscles that probably came from years of having to watch his back. Just looking at him, I could tell he was completely in tune with everything around him. It made me feel safe, something I hadn't felt in a while. I relaxed back against the couch cushions and Caleb rested against my side.

A knock sounded at the door and it pushed open, a mechanic covered in grease stepping inside. His eyes widened in surprise as he saw me and Caleb, then he focused on Scratch.

"Sorry to interrupt, but there's some guy out front causing trouble. I'm surprised you didn't hear him shouting all the way in here."

"I'll be out in a minute, Killian," Scratch said.

Killian looked at me again, swallowed hard and looked back at his boss. "Um, he's armed, and I don't think he's completely stable if you know what I mean."

Scratch nodded and pushed off the desk. I saw a flash of a gun under his vest and my heart nearly stalled in my chest before it took off at a gallop. Scratch looked at Caleb before meeting my gaze. He didn't say anything, but he didn't have to. There was a promise in that look, one that said he would keep us safe.

"Be careful," I said softly.

He smiled faintly, then followed Killian out of the room. He shut the door behind him, and I was left with my chaotic thoughts, trying to figure out if I'd just landed myself in even more trouble than when I'd accepted help from Caleb's sperm donor.

Chapter Two

Scratch

"Sorry," Killian said again as we walked toward the front. "I didn't realize…"

"It's fine, but whoever is out front isn't getting down this hallway. Understood?"

Killian nodded. "Yes, sir."

He was a good kid, and I had no doubt he'd patch in before long. He'd been prospecting for the Devil's Boneyard nearly two years and proven himself again and again. He and Seamus were the youngest in our crew, but they'd seen more shit than most men their age, both having enlisted in the military when they were young. I'd trust either of them. A lot of clubs patched in after six months or a year, but our Pres, Cinder, wanted to make sure they had staying power and could stomach whatever we threw their way. He didn't give a shit about length of time and more about what they'd done to earn their name and patch.

Just as Killian had said, there was a man in the front lobby, waving a gun around and screaming at anyone within hearing distance.

"I want it back! You stole it and I want it back," the man yelled again and again, like he was stuck on repeat.

"Calm the fuck down and tell me what you think we stole," I said, my hand resting on my gun in case I needed to pull it.

"My pig!" the man screamed. "You stole my pig!"

My eyebrows went up and I looked at Killian who shrugged. Yeah, he'd been right. This man was batshit crazy and had either taken something he shouldn't have, or he was off his meds. Either way, he was a danger to the woman and child down the hall in my office. I had to be careful getting that gun from him. If it accidentally went off, it could easily penetrate the office door and hit either Clarity or her son.

Neither was going to happen if I had any say in the matter.

There was something about that young girl and her boy, something that pulled at my heart and made me want to take care of them. I hadn't quite figured out yet what I was going to do with them, but I wasn't letting them back out onto the streets. That was for damn sure.

"You can either calm down and put your weapon away, or we'll have to do this the hard way," I told the crazy man. "There are innocent people in this building. You shoot them, and your pig will be the least of your worries."

Not that I thought for a single moment the man actually had a pig.

I saw Seamus ease into the front lobby through the front door. The man was so quiet the crazy guy in front of me hadn't even noticed the ex-SEAL. In a blur of movement, Seamus disarmed the crazy person and had him pinned to the ground, his arms pulled behind his back. Seamus dug his knee into the center of the man's back and looked up at me.

"How are we handling this one?" Seamus asked.

"Let the cops take care of it. The man's crazy and clearly in need of treatment of some sort," I said. "There's nothing in the shop right now they would consider suspicious."

Seamus nodded and I saw Killian pull out his phone to make the call.

"I'll be in the office if you need me. Try not to need me."

Killian smirked and humor lit his eyes. I knew the moment I was out of earshot he'd be telling Seamus all about the woman and child in my office. And as damn young as Clarity was, she definitely had the curves of a woman. Even as malnourished as she was, the woman still had a body that most men would beg to touch. I wasn't blind, and despite the availability of club pussy, it had been a while since I'd been with a woman. After finding my daughter, Darian, my life had changed. Seeing her, and watching the way the Dixie Reapers and her old man, Bull, treated her had me realize I was missing something in my life.

Finding a woman around here wasn't that easy, though. Not the kind of woman you kept, the kind who would be a good mom. Even though my daughter was a grown woman now, I'd missed out on her childhood, and I wanted to experience all those firsts. Hell, at my age, it was probably stupid to even think about having more kids. I was a grandpa for fuck's sake.

When I entered the office, Clarity had her body wrapped around her son, and she'd made herself as small as possible in the corner of the room. I hated that she'd been scared, but it couldn't be helped. At least the threat was neutralized and no one had gotten hurt. Regardless, the two of them couldn't stay here, not long-term. I had to find a spot for them, other than letting them roam the streets again.

I shut the door and twisted the lock. Clarity slowly rose and lifted her son into her arms. I took a moment to study her. While her hair was a cloud of dark corkscrew curls, now that it was clean, her son's was such a light blond it was nearly white. I rubbed a hand across my beard and wondered what the next move should be.

"I think it's safe to say that staying here isn't in your best interest," I told her.

She nodded. "We'll just get our things and head out."

I held up a hand to stop her. "Just wait a minute. I didn't say I was throwing you out, just that staying at the shop isn't the best idea. There's no way I'm letting you go back out on the streets."

Her back straightened and she pushed her shoulders back. "Let me?"

I had to fight not to smile. Tiny little thing like her acting all big and tough. It was cute as hell.

"Put the claws away, kitten. It's not safe for you out there and you know it. How many times have you been propositioned just for a hot meal or place to sleep?" I asked.

"Maybe a few," she said unconvincingly.

"Uh-huh. And what are you going to do when someone doesn't take no for an answer?" I asked.

She glanced at Caleb quickly before looking at me again. It wasn't much, but it was something. The way the color drained from her face and her eyes got a haunted look, I knew that she'd already faced that horror head-on, and if I were a betting man, I'd say that her son was the result of that altercation. It made my blood boil to think of someone hurting her, especially since she had to have been a kid when it happened.

I moved closer, but went slow so I wouldn't spook her. "I want a name."

Her eyes went wide and she swallowed hard. "A name?"

"The man who hurt you," I said, looking from her to the boy and back again.

Her shoulders slumped and her gaze dropped to the floor. "It doesn't matter. It's over with, and I haven't seen him since I walked out."

"You're going to tell me that story one day. For now, the two of you will come home with me. And no, I don't mean for you to sleep in my bed, or offer sexual favors of any kind to me or anyone else."

"Then what am I going to do?" she asked. "I can't stay with you free of charge."

I tipped my chin up and thought about it a moment. "You keep the house clean, do the laundry and crap, then we'll call it even, and I'll throw in some extra cash so you can start saving up. It's the only way you'll ever get back on your feet."

"Scratch, I…"

I placed a finger over her lips to silence her. "If you won't do it for yourself, do it for your boy. You'll each have a room of your own. Plenty to eat. No more finding doorways to sleep in, and you'll both be safe. You have my word, kitten. No one will hurt you while you're under my roof. They wouldn't dare."

"For how long?" she asked.

"As long as you want," I said. "I live alone. Don't have a steady woman in my life to cause trouble. You'll have free run of the house."

She looked at her son, then slowly nodded. Her gaze met mine. "We'll come with you, but we can't ride on your bike to get there. Is it a far walk?"

"I'm not going to make you walk. Give me a few minutes and I'll have someone bring my truck." I paused and looked at Caleb. "And maybe have them stop and pick up a car seat. It's not safe for him to ride around without one."

"We don't want to be any trouble," she said.

I took her chin between my thumb and forefinger, tipping her head back. "You're not any trouble. Neither one of you. I promised to keep you safe, and putting your boy in a secure seat in the truck is part of that."

"All right," she said.

I released her and pull my phone from my pocket. I shot off a message to one of the prospects with instructions to bring my truck here and pick up a car seat on the way. I'd learned a lot about kids just from spending time with my grandson, Foster. I'd never had the chance to raise my daughter, but she'd turned out to be a strong woman. And thankfully, she had a good man watching out for her. I might not have chosen Bull for her, but I had to admit the guy loved her and treated her like a queen. That's all any dad could hope for his little girl.

I wished Darian were here now. Maybe she could set Clarity at ease. Foster was close to Caleb's age, and the two of them could play together. The problem was that while my house was big enough for all of them, I didn't have all of the bedrooms furnished. Darian had never come here to see me, and I wasn't sure about uprooting Foster even for a short stay. Bull would likely insist on coming too, and then I'd have to clear it with Cinder, my club President. Asking permission was only a formality, as the Reapers were like family. In the case of Bull and Tank, they *were* family. With my daughter married to Bull, and Jackal married to Tank's sister, we were one big happy family.

I watched the little boy clutched in Clarity's arms and I wondered when he'd last had a normal day-to-day routine. My daughter was always telling me how important it was for my grandson to have a routine. I figured that must apply to all kids. Did Clarity have toys hidden in her backpack for Caleb? They were going to need some things, but I had a feeling I'd have to fight Clarity to get her to accept them. She seemed like a proud young woman, and I didn't think she trusted easily.

I'd noticed in the early hours this morning that she'd followed me at a distance. It had been a smart thing to do since she didn't know anything about me. The fact she'd accepted my help at all was a miracle. My phone dinged a little while later. I pulled up the text from Seamus and tried not to laugh. He'd sent a picture of about six different car seats asking what the fuck he was supposed to get.

I was momentarily distracted by the sound of the man in the front lobby screaming and I figured the cops must have arrived. I listened harder and heard him being dragged away, which set me at ease. I hadn't liked that man being so close to Clarity and Caleb.

"Clarity, which one of these would you like to have for Caleb?" I asked, showing her my phone. I knew two of them weren't the right size, but the others would be okay.

"Whichever one costs the least amount," she said, not even looking at them.

I narrowed my eyes a moment, then sent a message back to Seamus with my selection. It was by no means the cheapest, but it looked the safest. I hesitated a moment, then sent another message asking him to pick up a stuffed bear and a few toddler toys for a little boy. I bit my lip to stop from laughing when I saw his response.

What the fuck is a toddler toy?

"How old is Caleb?" I asked Clarity, wanting to make sure we got the right toys.

"He's two," she said.

I nodded, then responded to Seamus.

Get toys for a two-year-old little boy. You were a boy once, right?

I smiled, knowing that he was probably cussing me out, but would never do it to my face. Not until he'd patched in. Now that I'd taken care of that, I figured we had a little time to kill, and there was no way the chicken biscuits I'd brought with me had satisfied two people who hadn't had a real meal in who knew how long.

"Are you up for a walk?" I asked.

"To your house?"

"No, kitten. We'll drive to the house, but it might be a little bit before my truck gets here. I thought we'd head over to the diner and get an early lunch."

She nodded and reached for her backpack, but I stopped her.

"You won't need that right now. No one will mess with your things. My boys wouldn't dare come in this office when I'm not here."

She looked tired, despite the fact I'd left her here for hours to get some rest, and Caleb looked like he was weighing her down. I held out my hands and waited to see what she'd do. I might be offering my help, but I was still a stranger, and she likely had some reservations about me. From what little I'd witnessed, she seemed to be a good mom, and was likely very protective of her son. She stared at my hands, then her son. Reluctantly, she handed him over.

"I'll protect him with my life," I told her.

Caleb pulled at my long hair and looked up at me with curiosity in his eyes. I wondered how many men he'd been around during his short life. As skittish as his mother was, I didn't see her as the type to bring a lot of men home, when she'd had a home anyway. If she'd been raped, there was a chance she'd never trust another man to get that close to her, which broke my heart. She was young enough that someday she'd find a good man, someone who would love her and protect her. If she gave him a chance. There were still good men out there, good role models for Caleb.

I led the way out of the office and down the hall. I could feel the gazes of the boys on the shop floor through the large window as I headed out the front door with Caleb in my arms and Clarity one step behind me. I pushed open the door and waited for her to walk through.

"You know, you can walk beside me," I said.

Her cheeks flushed and she fell in step with me. The diner was only a few blocks away. We got a few looks from people passing by, but I figured it had more to do with my cut than anything else. Clarity's clothes might be worn, but they were clean. She looked cute in the shorts and tee she'd put on. Hell, maybe they thought I was out with my daughter and grandkid. Probably feared for the safety of the kid in my arms, what with me being a big, bad biker who did horrible things. It wouldn't take long for someone to warn Clarity to stay away from me and the Devil's Boneyard. I wasn't a saint by any means, but I'd never hurt a woman or kid. Well, not a woman as innocent as the one next to me. Some of the poisonous bitches who hung around the club would be a different story. I wouldn't hesitate to end their miserable lives if they crossed the club.

When we entered the diner the bell over the door jingled.

"Sit anywhere you want," said a waitress as she passed by with a tray of drinks.

I picked a table at the back and snagged a highchair from along the wall near the hall to the restrooms. I put Caleb in the chair and buckled him in. Clarity took the seat next to him and I sat on the other side. The little boy slapped his hands on the table, a big smile on his face.

"Thank you," Clarity said. "It's been a while since he's been able to sit at a table like this and have a real meal."

"You don't have to keep thanking me for things, Clarity. I want to help. I don't know what happened to put you out on the streets with a small kid, but I won't let you come to any harm. And staying out there? That way lies trouble."

She reached over and placed her small hand over my larger rough one. "You're a good man, Scratch. Caleb and I have been homeless for two months. You're the first one to truly try and help us."

"Don't read too much into it, kitten. I just don't want anything bad to happen to either of you. There are men in this world who do horrible things, as you've already found out the hard way. But that's just the tip of the iceberg. You could have landed yourself in a much, much worse situation."

"I know." She glanced down at the table. "It's not like I asked to lose my apartment. The place I worked closed up, and I was unable to find another job."

"The local churches wouldn't help you?" I asked.

"They do what they can, but I can't exactly ask to just move in. We stay there some nights, and they feed us a hot meal once or twice a week. Usually soup and some bread. The nearest women's shelter is too far for me to walk to, and… well, there just aren't many options here for homeless people."

"Especially ones with small children, I would imagine."

She nodded.

"Well, you'll have a place to stay for as long as you need one. I keep some odd hours, but I'll try not to wake you up if I come in really late."

"I don't expect you to change your life for us, Scratch. Don't worry about waking us up. I haven't slept the night through in the last two months. Maybe one day I'll be able to relax enough to do that."

I hated that she'd been through so much in her short life. But there was one thing I needed to ask before I took her home. If she had family out there looking for her, the last thing I needed was them showing up on my doorstep, irate that I was corrupting their daughter. Not that I intended to do any such thing, but it was how most of the citizens here saw me. Biker filth. If only they knew…

"What about your parents? Or Caleb's dad? Will either of them come looking for you? You said you hadn't seen Caleb's dad, but do you think he's ever tried looking for you?" I asked.

Her eyebrows rose and she looked like she was trying not to smile. "Why? Are you planning to kill me and want to know how well you should hide the body?"

I narrowed my eyes at her. "Funny."

She shrugged. "I ran away from home when I was sixteen and made my way here. I only lived one town over, but as far as I know, my family never tried to find me. They didn't want me anyway. But maybe if I'd known how rough things would be on my own, I'd have stuck around long enough to finish high school and moved out the right way and not snuck off without a penny to my name."

"And Caleb's dad?" I asked. "You're positive he's out of the picture?"

She looked at her son, her expression softening. "He doesn't know I was pregnant, so he's not looking for his son. Like I said, I haven't seen him since the day I ran off. For all I know, he isn't even in town anymore. As small as this place is, I would imagine I'd have seen him by now."

"I still want a name, kitten. I can't protect you if I don't know who could come knocking on the door."

"Why do you call me that?" she asked, tipping her head to the side as she stared at me. "I don't mind it, but… no one's ever had a nickname for me before and we just met."

"Because you're tiny but fierce." I smiled. "And I have no doubt that when you're angry the claws will come out. I've seen a hint of that side of you already, and I'd imagine the more comfortable you are around me, the more you'll let that side show. I like that you have some fire in you. Without it, the world would swallow you whole."

A waitress came over, pad in hand, and harried look on her face. "What can I get y'all?"

"Menus?" I asked.

Her cheeks flushed. "Sorry! I'll be right back with those."

She scurried off and returned a moment later with three rolls of silverware and two menus. Then she ran off again while we decided what we wanted to eat.

"I think she likes you," Clarity said.

"What?" I looked at the waitress who was sure enough casting a glance my way. "Huh. I wonder if she's done that before and I never noticed."

"Yeah. I'm sure men like you don't notice when a woman likes them." She shook her head. "I have no doubt you have to beat the women off with a stick."

I couldn't hold back my laughter.

Clarity rolled her eyes, which showed she was getting used to me. Or at least I hoped she was.

"Kitten, in my world, I can have a woman with the snap of my fingers, but it doesn't mean I want them. They're… well, they're not like you or our waitress. Good girls like the two of you tend to stay clear of me."

"That's kind of sad," she said. "There's no reason you can't go out with a nice woman. Maybe you should ask the waitress out on a date."

"Not my type." I smiled. I wasn't entirely lying. The woman seemed nice enough, but looking at her I didn't feel a thing. She didn't stir even a tiny bit of interest, above or below the belt. "You ready to order?"

She nodded and I waved the waitress over. Her nametag said Helen, and her eyes were bright as she smiled widely at us. I hoped like hell she didn't do something awkward like ask me out on a date. It had happened a time or two, just not with a nice woman. Club sluts were more my norm, and I was tired as hell of their shit. Nothing but drama with the whores who spread their legs for the club.

"Ready to order?" Helen asked.

Clarity gave her order, and I made sure she got Caleb his own plate of food, then I told Helen what I wanted. We ordered drinks and I got a coffee on the side since I had a feeling I was going to need a good bit of energy to keep up with the two people sitting with me. Especially the smaller of the two. If he was like my grandson, once he had free run of the house, he'd be hell to keep up with.

As Clarity watched me talking to Helen, there was something in her eyes I couldn't quite discern. I had a feeling I'd want to analyze it more later, but right now, I just wanted to get them fed, then get them settled at my house. Shit. Caleb wouldn't be able to sleep in the big beds I had. I pulled out my phone and sent another message to Seamus, in hopes he was still at the store or close enough to run back inside.

Get a toddler bed and some sheets and blankets for it too

What the fucking hell is a toddler bed? Jesus. Kids need to come with an instruction manual. And apparently a money tree. Do you have any idea how much I've spent?

I tried damn hard not to laugh. Seamus was one of the biggest, toughest men I knew. But ask him to get some things for a small kid and he didn't know what the fuck to do. It was fucking hilarious and I had no doubt the club and I would have a good laugh over it later. As for the cost, I wasn't worried. It wasn't like my bank account couldn't handle it, and he was likely using the club money. I'd just put it back once I had the receipts from today.

And get anything else he'll need for a bedroom

This is fucked-up. I don't know shit about baby stuff

Aren't there any cute sales associates? Just ask one of them… Knowing you, you'll walk out with her number as well as the shit I need

Well, there is a blonde up by the register

I snorted. Yeah, figured he'd already scoped the place out. The man couldn't go anywhere without landing dick first in some pussy. One of these days, that shit would catch up to him. Either he'd get some woman pregnant, or he'd find himself a sweet girl who turned her nose up when she found out about the countless women in his past. Either way, I wanted a front row seat when that shit went down.

Chapter Three

Clarity

My eyes had to look like they were going to fall out of my head as I looked at Scratch's home. I had been expecting something small, or at least modest. The house in front of me was a sprawling Victorian in mint green with white gingerbread trim. I'd never seen anything like it before, and it didn't even remotely look like a home owned by a biker. I should have known he had some money when he'd helped me into the shiniest, prettiest truck I'd ever seen. It even smelled like new when I climbed inside, and I could tell the car seat he'd bought for Caleb was far from cheap.

As my son kicked his feet against the leather seats, I winced, hoping Scratch wouldn't get mad if my son scuffed his truck. The man turned to look at Caleb and just smiled. Then he gave me a wink before getting out of the truck. Before I could offer up a word of protest, he'd pulled Caleb from the car seat and was carrying him toward the house. I scurried to follow him up the front steps of the large home, and came to a halt as I went through the most gorgeous door I'd ever seen.

"I… Um…" I looked around at the maple-colored hardwood floors and the pristine white woodwork and doorways. "Maybe this isn't such a good idea."

He turned to face me, my son still clutched in his arms. I think I swooned a little. Scratch was a big, tough man in jeans and a black leather vest, and my son looked so damn small in his arms. And yet, they looked incredibly right together. I had to swallow hard and look away. He was being nice and helping me out, nothing more. Not once had he touched me inappropriately or made any advances. The man probably just saw me as a kid. He'd even said he had a daughter close to my age.

"Why are you worried, Clarity?" he asked.

Was it wrong that I was disappointed he hadn't called me kitten again? No one had ever given me a pet name before, and every time he'd said it, I'd felt all warm and gooey inside.

"What if Caleb messes up your floors or walls?"

Scratch came closer, and his woodsy scent wrapped around me. Now that I wasn't quite so scared, I was noticing more things. Like the way his eyes crinkled at the corners when he smiled. Despite the tough overall appearance of the biker, he seemed to have a heart of gold. Or at least, that was the side of him I'd seen.

He reached out and gently cupped my chin. "Kitten, it's just a house. If he scratches the floors or draws on the walls, I'm not going to get mad or throw the two of you out. A house is meant to be lived in, not kept as a display."

"I just..." I bit my lip. If he wasn't worried about Caleb messing up his house, then maybe I shouldn't either.

He smiled softly, then nodded his head toward the stairs. "Come on. I'll show you where you'll be staying. Caleb's room isn't put together just yet, but I have two guys coming over to take care of it."

"He can just stay with me," I said. The last thing I wanted to do was make him go to any trouble for us. What if he changed his mind and decided not to let us stay? It had been so long since I'd felt safe, or we'd have a nice place to stay, that I was worried it would all be taken away just as quickly as I stumbled into the situation.

"Kitten, I already bought stuff for him to have his own room. If I make Seamus take it all back, his head will likely explode."

"I can't pay you back," I said, worrying at my lower lip.

Scratch froze at the top of the stairs and turned to look down at me. "Have I asked you to pay for anything?"

"No."

"Then don't assume I expect payment. Of any kind."

"I'm sorry." My cheeks flushed with embarrassment. I'd learned early that you didn't get something for nothing, and while he'd offered to let me clean his house in exchange for a place to stay, all this seemed like too much.

With Caleb still on his hip, he reached for me with his other hand and tugged me down the hall. All the doors stood wide open, and the room at the far end of the hall looked like it might be his bedroom. We drew closer to it, and I saw a massive bed with rumpled sheets. Scratch stepped into the room next to his, dragging me in behind him. My breath caught when I saw how pretty the space was. The walls were a pale lemon and what looked like a queen-size bed was pushed against one wall. A white eyelet cover was on the bed, and sheer curtains hung from the windows flanking the headboard.

"It's beautiful," I said.

"Once I found out my daughter was still alive, I set up this room in case she ever came to visit. So far, I've always gone to see her, which is fine. It's nice to get out of town now and then."

"Still alive?" I asked.

"Her mother lied and said my daughter was dead. I'd had no reason not to believe her. My daughter ended up getting claimed by a man in another MC and that's how I found out she was still alive. I'd missed out on her entire life, but I see her as frequently as I can, and I mentioned my grandson earlier. He's about the same age as Caleb."

"I still can't believe you're a grandpa." I knew he was older, but he didn't seem old enough to have grandkids.

He nodded. "I'm hoping they'll have another one sometime. I like kids, and since I never got to spend any time with Darian when she was growing up, I feel like I missed out on a lot. At my age, it's not likely I'll have more kids."

"You make it sound like you're ancient," I said.

"I'm fifty-one, kitten. A hell of a lot older than you."

Right. Maybe that's why he hadn't made a move on me? Then again, some of the guys who had propositioned me were even older than Scratch. It wasn't that I wanted him to hit on me, but a man like Scratch falling for me wouldn't exactly be a hardship. I'd never met anyone like him before.

He tipped his head toward the hall. "I'll show you where Caleb will sleep, once his things are brought in and set up."

We passed the door next to mine, but I peered inside. The walls were blue and the furniture was darker and heavier than in my room, but I could see why he didn't want to put Caleb in there. It wasn't a room for a little boy for certain.

The room on the other side was empty and the walls were a soft gray. Darker gray curtains hung from the window, and Scratch gave them a tug.

"I'll have the guys take these down. Don't want Caleb pulling on them and getting hurt if the curtain rod comes down," he said.

"The members of your... what's it called?" I asked. I'd seen them around town before, but their name escaped me.

"Devil's Boneyard MC, but you can just refer to it as the Club if you want. And the men coming are prospects. They want to be members, but they have to put in the time to prove themselves first. We don't take just anyone," he said.

"And they'll be wearing a vest like yours?" I asked, remembering seeing some around town before. I'd never paid the men much attention, though, other than staying out of their way.

"It's called a cut, kitten. And yeah, they'll be wearing one, but theirs will say Prospect on it under the Devil emblem on the back."

He turned and showed me the back of his, with a horned skull over a set of bones. There were wings coming out from either side, but they were leathery like a demon's wings and not angelic by any means. It was a rather sinister image, but the man wearing it was the kindest, gentlest person I'd ever met. I didn't think he'd appreciate me saying that to his face, though.

The doorbell rang downstairs, and I tensed for a moment. It was silly because Scratch had protected us when trouble had come to his shop earlier. After that, I didn't see him letting someone come to his house and hurt us. He still held Caleb as we went back downstairs. When he swung the door open, there were two men on the other side. They both looked like they were maybe around thirty, and they wore equally shocked expressions when they saw Caleb, and then their gazes landed on me.

"Holy hell, VP. Seamus said he'd been out buying baby shit, but I'd thought he was just yanking my chain," one of them said. "When I saw them in the office this morning, I didn't realize you were bringing them home with you."

"Knock it off, Killian," Scratch said. "The stuff in the bed of my truck needs to be hauled upstairs and put into the gray room. You'll have to put the furniture together. Toolbox is in the workshop out back."

"Told you there was a kid here, smartass," the second one said. "Need us to do anything else while we're here, VP?"

"Not right now, Seamus. The room will need to be set up, but make sure Cinder doesn't need you for anything first."

Both men eyed me with curiosity blazing in their eyes, but Scratch didn't introduce us. He shut the door and I followed him into the kitchen. The double ovens and counter space nearly made me sigh with pleasure. Back before I'd run away, I'd enjoyed cooking. When I'd gotten my own place, the kitchen had been so small that making anything in it had been difficult at best. But in here? The possibilities were endless. He even had one of those fancy stainless-steel refrigerators with the bottom drawer for a freezer and some sort of screen on the door. I'd seen an advertisement for them on TV once.

"I know we just had lunch not that long ago, but I thought Caleb might like a cookie. They're just store bought, but I keep a package on hand," Scratch said.

"You don't strike me as the type to have a sweet tooth."

He smiled and winked. "I like all kinds of sweet things."

My cheeks warmed, but I figured it was just a little harmless flirting that he likely did with all women. Not once had he given me the impression he was attracted to me. I sat down at the kitchen table and Scratch placed Caleb in my lap. Then he disappeared into a small room off the kitchen, which I figured must be the pantry. I'd never been in a house with a pantry before. It made me feel completely out of my depth. My family had been far from rich, and I'd certainly not achieved anywhere near the amount of wealth Scratch must have.

He came back and set a package of chocolate chip cookies on the table, then got some milk from the fridge. He started to reach for a cupboard and then stopped.

"I don't have any of those sippy cup things like my grandson uses. I noticed Caleb drank from a straw at the diner, but I don't have any of those either," he said.

"Oh, well. We can try using a regular cup, but maybe a plastic one? He did okay with the small bottle of milk this morning."

He nodded and took down a plastic cup, then poured milk into it. After putting the carton back in the fridge, he carried the cup over and set it on the table in front of us. I helped Caleb take a drink, grimacing as it dribbled down his chin. Scratch just handed me some napkins, but didn't utter a word of complaint as the milk splashed onto the table from Caleb's chin. I tried to clean up the mess we were making, but as Caleb bit into a cookie, crumbs fell everywhere and I pretty much gave up. Scratch didn't seem to mind, if the smile on his face was any indication.

It was sad that he hadn't been able to raise his daughter. From what I'd seen so far, he probably was a great dad. Caleb trusted him, and that was saying something since he seldom trusted anyone. Scratch shoved his hands into his pockets and leaned against the kitchen counter.

"At the risk of you hissing at me and showing your claws, we need to talk," he said.

"About what?" I asked, wondering if I'd been wrong all along and he was going to ask for payment of some sort.

"There's not much room in the backpack you carry around, which means the two of you don't have many clothes."

"We'll get by with what we've got for a while longer. We each have three outfits in there. I just roll them tightly to make them fit, and it keeps them from wrinkling much." As if wrinkles really bothered me when most days I couldn't even shower.

His jaw firmed and the muscles in his arms bulged as his body tensed.

"You've spent too much on us already," I said, trying to make him see reason. "I can never repay you for all this."

"And I didn't damn well ask you to, now did I?" he asked.

"No, but..."

His eyes turned frosty as he pushed away from the counter. When he came closer, his gaze softened, but I could tell he was frustrated. He leaned in closer and lowered his voice to a whisper.

"I'm not the man who took advantage of you and left you pregnant and alone on the streets. I'm not one of the men who offered you food or shelter in exchange for sexual favors. I have not done one damn thing to make you fear me or think for a moment that I want anything more than to help you."

I swallowed hard and dropped my gaze. He was right. He'd been nothing but kind to us, and hadn't once tried to grab my ass or my breasts, hadn't tried to get in my pants. But trust didn't come easily to me. I probably trusted Scratch more than I had anyone else in a really long time, but he didn't know that.

I glanced at Caleb, but he was busy with his snack and wasn't paying the least bit of attention to us. He hummed as he chewed on his cookie and sipped his milk. The table was a mess, but Scratch didn't seem bothered by it.

Scratch's touch was gentle as he tipped my chin up, forcing me to look him in the eye. I expected anger or resentment, but all I saw was a man who seemed to care what happened to us, even if I didn't understand why.

"As long as you're under this roof, you have nothing to fear from anyone," he said. "Not even me. I will lay down my life if that's what it takes to keep you and your boy from harm. Despite everything you've been through, when I look in your eyes, I see innocence. You are the sweetest woman I've ever met, and I refuse to let anyone ruin that part of you."

My throat burned with unshed tears and I did something I shouldn't have. Leaning forward, I pressed my lips to his. I felt him stiffen almost immediately and I pulled away, my cheeks burning with embarrassment. His thumb stroked my cheek.

"Why did you do that?" he asked.

"I don't know. It was impulsive, but I… I wanted to know what it was like to kiss you. I've never known a man as good as you are, and I wondered if kissing you would be different from the others."

His thumb pressed to my lower lip. "Kitten, that wasn't a kiss. This is a kiss."

When Scratch claimed my lips, he didn't do it gently. His kiss was harsh and demanding, his tongue sliding into my mouth as if he had every right. If I hadn't been sitting down, my knees would have buckled. Never in my life had I been kissed so thoroughly. He slowly pulled back but didn't release me. I found myself leaning toward him, wanting more. In that moment, I wasn't a mom. I was a woman who desired a man. Something I hadn't ever experienced before.

"That's a kiss, kitten. And it was the best one I've ever had."

I smiled faintly, then touched my fingers to my lips. They tingled and I still felt the pressure of his mouth on mine.

"But you need to stop thinking I'm some saint," he said. "I'm not a good man, and I've done some seriously bad shit. I'll never hurt you, but don't think for one second that I'm some tame, sweet old man."

"I never called you old," I said. "Or tame. But you are sweet. At least, you are to me and Caleb. No one's ever treated us so good before."

"Then the people in your life were complete idiots."

"Scratch?"

"Damon," he said. "When we're alone, you can call me Damon."

"Damon," I said softly. "Will you kiss me again?"

"I don't think that's such a good idea." He drew away from me. "You're far too tempting, Clarity, and too damn young for me."

My back straightened. "I may be young, but I've lived through more than other women my age. I lived on the streets twice now, had a kid when I was seventeen, I've been raped and propositioned like I'm a whore all because I don't have money. I've seen the ugly side of life, Damon. Watched people get killed just for a few dollars or a handful of drugs. You don't have to sugarcoat things for me. I'm a big girl, and I can handle whatever things in your past you think should scare me."

His lips twitched like he was fighting a smile. "All right, kitten. But let's table the discussion for now."

My sweet boy finished his snack and Scratch put the cup in the sink, then wiped down the table and swept up the crumbs. Caleb began squirming and whimpering. I knew what that meant and shot up from my chair before he had an accident.

"Bathroom?" I asked, hauling Caleb up against my chest, hoping he didn't pee on himself and me.

Scratch pointed to a door behind me. I hurried through it and barely got Caleb onto the toilet in time. He was still too small to learn to pee standing up. I'd left the door open and Scratch peered around the doorframe.

"Everything okay?" he asked.

"Yes, he just needed to go pretty bad."

"He's not in pull-ups?"

I shook my head. "We had to learn to potty train pretty quick the last two months. It's hard to get diapers or pull-ups when you're living on the street. He's been a good boy, though, and picked it up pretty quick. Getting him to hold it until I find a bathroom isn't always easy, though."

"What about at night now that he'll have his own room?" he asked.

I hadn't thought of that. "I don't know. He hasn't slept by himself since he potty trained."

"When he's done, we're going to go shopping for some stuff. And don't argue with me, kitten. You may have claws, but I'm bigger and meaner. There's shit you both need and you're damn sure going to have it."

Part of me wanted to argue and tell him we'd be fine with what we had, but at the same time it was really nice that someone wanted to take care of us. No one had given a shit about me in a long time, and no one had ever cared about what Caleb needed or wanted except me. I didn't care what Scratch had done, or would do in the future. He was a good man when it came to me and my son, and that meant the world to me.

"Okay," I said. "I'll let you buy some stuff for us, but not too much. We've made do with the few things in the backpack for the past two months. I don't need material things to make me happy, Scratch. They're nice and all, but I've found that what's important is my son and the fact that we're together. I could have given him up, found him a stable home with a loving couple, but I couldn't handle parting with him. And I'm glad because if I didn't have him, I'd have given up."

I helped Caleb wash his hands, and then to my surprise, he lifted his arms for Scratch to pick him up. The man smiled at my boy before lifting him, and I swear it was the sexiest thing I'd ever seen. I felt my heart thaw a little more and my throat tightened with emotion. I wanted that for Caleb, for both of us. A man who cared, who could smile at us like that. Didn't hurt that his kiss had damn near turned me into a puddle of goo. I'd never in my life been kissed like that.

"Come on, kitten," he said. "Let's go shopping, and then I think this little guy could use a nap."

Caleb yawned as soon as Scratch said the word nap, then laid his head on the big man's shoulder. Yeah, I was in trouble. The big, tough biker holding my sweet baby boy did strange things to me. I'd never been the type to swoon, but that's how I felt watching Scratch with my son. If ever there was a man who was meant to be a father, it was him. It didn't seem right he'd been robbed of taking care of his daughter when she was little. I didn't know what had happened with the mom, and I was scared to ask. He's said she'd lied to him, and if there had ever been a trace of her in this house, it was long gone. No pictures, no womanly touches.

The upstairs hallway held a few photos. I'd noticed a woman who looked close to my age, and I'd assumed that was his daughter. There'd been others of a cute little boy near Caleb's age, and an older man with long blond hair and a beard. He'd been wearing a cut like Scratch so I assumed he was either in Scratch's club or another one. I didn't really understand this world, but I was willing to learn. I'd seen a few episodes of *Sons of Anarchy* so I wasn't completely in the dark, but it hadn't really been my type of show so I hadn't stuck it out past the first three episodes.

I followed them out to the truck, and Scratch opened my door before buckling Caleb into his seat. I'd expected him to just stop at one of those twenty-four-hour stores that carried a little bit of everything, but instead he took us to the mall. I wanted to protest but bit my lip instead. Accepting a place to stay had been hard enough, but all this? It was too much, but telling him that didn't seem to do anything.

"First thing we're doing is getting this little guy a stroller," Scratch said. "He'll enjoy the mall a bit more if he can ride through it, and if he gets tired he can sleep."

"Not an expensive one," I said.

He smirked and something told me that my son was about to own the priciest, fanciest stroller in the mall. Scratch reached for my hand and clasped our fingers together, then led the way. He bought Caleb a big padded stroller that probably weighed a ton, then he grabbed a diaper bag and anything he seemed to think my son needed for our outing through the mall. After he'd paid, he put everything into the new diaper bag, then stuck it in the basket under the stroller seat.

I apparently wasn't the only one who found the biker hot while he was pushing the stroller. I swear I heard women sighing as we passed by, and I couldn't blame them. There was just something about seeing a rough guy like Scratch being so damn gentle and caring with a small child. I think ovaries were exploding all over the mall as we went from store to store. Eventually, he let me push the stroller so he could carry our purchases, and there were far too many sacks in my opinion. He definitely bought way more than we needed, but he couldn't be deterred. If I tried to object, he just arched an eyebrow and stared me down until I relented.

Probably a good thing we weren't in a relationship. It would be far too easy for him to get his way all the time. When I couldn't walk another step, I convinced him it was time to head home, but he stubbornly herded me into a Bath and Body Works store. Everything smelled so good, and I migrated over to the aromatherapy selection. I'd never been someone who enjoyed wearing perfume, but the eucalyptus and mint bodywash, lotion, and spray weren't overpowering, and I ended up with all three.

I wandered the store with Caleb while Scratch paid for my things, except he had a much too large bag when he made it back to my side. I eyed the sack, then him, but he just smiled and tipped his head toward the door. I had no idea what else was in that bag, but I had a feeling he'd spent way too much. The man had easily spent over five hundred dollars on us today, and if I added in the furniture and toys at his house, it was well over a thousand. I couldn't even imagine having that kind of money, much less spending it all in one day. I didn't think for one minute that his little shop paid enough to cover all that, but I wasn't about to ask how he earned his money. There were whispers around town about his club, and some of them were probably true. Not the sacrificing of virgins, though, unless the poor girls died from too much sex. Every member that I'd seen of the Devil's Boneyard was sexy in some way or another, and I doubted any of them lacked for female companionship.

Scratch loaded our bags into the back floorboard of his truck, then put Caleb in his seat. The stroller went into the bed of the truck, and he stood there frowning at it. I went to stand beside him and placed my hand on his arm, drawing his attention.

"What's wrong?" I asked.

"Need a bigger vehicle."

"Bigger than a truck?" I asked, my eyebrows shooting upward. "This thing is massive."

"It needs more space inside. Maybe a big SUV."

"Are you trying to tell me that you're going to buy a new car just because Caleb and I are staying with you right now? You know that's insane, right?"

He muttered something that I didn't quite catch.

"What?" I asked.

He sighed and ran a hand through his hair. "What's insane is that I want to keep the two of you. Get in the truck, Clarity."

He wanted to keep us? I wasn't entirely certain what he meant by that, but the kiss we'd shared in the kitchen gave me an idea. I didn't think us being a permanent part of his life would include me sleeping in a separate bedroom, and for the first time in my life, the thought of sharing a bed with a man was… exciting.

"Make me," I said, folding my arms.

He bit the inside of his cheek, but the humor shining in his eyes told me he wasn't mad at me for defying him.

"Make you? Are you three? Get your ass in the truck, kitten."

I shook my head.

Scratch placed his hands on my shoulders, turned me around and marched me to the passenger door of the truck. He pulled it open, then swatted my ass hard enough that it stung. I gasped and jerked my gaze up to his. That evil smirk was back in place, the one I wanted to kiss, the one that made me want to get naked. He placed his hands at my waist and lifted me into the truck, his hands lingering on my body.

"You're playing with fire, kitten, and you're going to get burned."

Maybe, but I had a feeling it was the good kind of burn. The kind that left you satisfied and achy the next morning. The kind I'd only read about in books. He clicked my seatbelt into place, gave me a heated look, then shut the door. I fanned myself as he walked around to the driver's side, and I wondered if it was possible to combust from sexual tension. The swagger in his walk was quite a sight to behold, and I wasn't the only one noticing. Two women on the next aisle were checking him out and I stared them down. It wasn't like I had a claim on the man, but maybe I wanted to? I felt so confused.

Maybe I just needed a few good nights of sleep, then whatever I was feeling would die down. The last thing I needed was to get involved with Scratch. He'd said himself that he was too old for me. If he kept kissing me, though, all bets were off. The way his lips devoured mine, I knew I wouldn't be able to remain strong. I'd end up throwing myself into his arms and begging him to show me what it was supposed to be like between a man and a woman. Something told me that if I took that step, if I went to his bed, I'd never want to leave. Scratch was the kind of man who ruined you for anyone else. I didn't have to be experienced to know that. The way my body reacted to him gave me that message loud and clear.

Chapter Four

Scratch

What the fuck are you doing, old man? She's younger than your damn daughter. Giving myself a pep talk didn't stop my dick from getting hard when I was around Clarity. I'd managed to think of her as just some helpless waif who needed some assistance. Then I'd gone and kissed her. Biggest fucking mistake I'd ever made because now all I wanted was another taste.

Caleb was upstairs in his new bedroom sleeping, and Clarity was putting her things away in the bedroom I'd given her. Fuck if I didn't want her things mixed in with mine, though. It was completely insane, and I felt like a pervert for wanting in her pants. It was more than just that, though. I enjoyed the time we'd spent together today, liked talking to her, and just something as simple as holding her hand. I'd never felt like that about a woman before, which meant I was in deep shit.

The doorbell rang and I went to get it, not wanting it to ring a second time and wake up Caleb. Poor kid probably hadn't had a decent nap since they'd been out on the streets. I pulled open the door and stared at the President of my club. Cinder tossed down his cigarette and put it out with his boot before pushing past me into the house.

"Well, come in," I said.

"What the fuck, Scratch?" Cinder asked. "Half the club is talking about some woman and kid you moved into your house. Did you knock up some club slut?"

"Again, you mean?" I asked, thinking about my daughter's mother. "Clarity is so far from being a club slut the mere thought of that is laughable."

"But you aren't denying knocking up some woman?" he asked.

I crossed my arms and knew I needed to make a decision. I could claim Caleb as mine, and get shit for supposedly being with a seventeen-year-old girl, which is how old she'd been when she was raped, or I could tell the truth. Then again, I didn't know shit about genetics. Could two dark-haired people have a kid with white-blond hair? It was possible no one would believe me anyway, just from looking at the kid, but I didn't like the thought of the club thinking badly of Clarity, and I didn't want them to know she was raped, not unless she wanted to tell them. That shit was personal, and I knew most women didn't exactly want to scream something like that from the rooftops. I remained mute as I stared at my Pres, but I heard the soft tread of footsteps and knew Clarity would be here any second.

"All you need to know is that they're under my protection," I said.

"Jesus Christ," Cinder muttered. "First you knock up some club slut, then Jackal knocks up a Reaper's sister, and now this? Why can't any of you do things the normal way?"

I felt Clarity's small hand on my back. "Everything all right?"

"It's fine, kitten. My Pres was just stopping by to say hi. Isn't that right, Cinder?" I asked the man who was still shaking his head in disbelief.

"She doesn't even look legal. Are we going to have to worry about cops?" Cinder asked.

"I'm nineteen," Clarity said. I wasn't going to correct her, since she'd told me was *nearly* nineteen. Still way too fucking young for me, and I knew it.

"And your boy is how old?" Cinder asked.

"Two," she answered.

Cinder let out a slew of cuss words and began pacing my living room. Clarity's hand wrapped around my bicep, and she gripped me tight. I felt a slight tremor and knew she was scared. Wrapping an arm around her waist, I pressed a kiss to the top of her head. "Kitten, why don't you go check on Caleb? I'll be up in a few minutes."

She nodded and slipped out of the room, casting one last nervous glance at Cinder.

"Calm the fuck down," I told him. "You may be the president of this club, but you're also my best friend. Do you think I'd do anything to hurt her? That woman is the sweetest thing I've ever met, and I'd sooner cut off my balls than harm her in any way."

"She was seventeen when that kid was born," he said, his voice a near growl.

I sighed and knew I'd have to tell him the truth, but I didn't want it spread around the club. "This stays between the two of us," I said. "I won't have anyone looking at her differently because of what happened to her."

Cinder stopped and faced me. "What the fuck does that mean?"

"Some asshole raped her when she was still a kid herself. Knocked her up and she took off. I found her living on the streets with a little boy clutched in her arms. Something about them…" I shook my head.

"So this is you being a knight in shining armor?" he asked, seeming a bit calmer. "You're not fucking her?"

I shrugged. I wasn't. Not yet, but after kissing her and the way she'd responded to me, I had a feeling if she stayed in my home it would happen sooner or later.

"This is fucked-up," Cinder said. "I won't tell the club, but they won't be happy with the idea of you sleeping with a kid, especially at your age."

I snorted. "You're older than me."

"Yeah, and I keep my dick in my pants if they aren't over thirty. Even then I feel like a dirty old man since I could easily be their daddy. Why do you think I don't get laid as much as I used to? It's not because I can't get it up. It's hard to find a club slut who isn't some naïve kid wanting to claw her way up the ranks and thinking she'll get there by spreading her legs for anyone in a cut."

He wasn't wrong about the club whores.

"Just be careful," he said. "When Darian finds out, she's going to blow a gasket, and I can only imagine how her husband will react. We have peace with the Dixie Reapers. They're like fucking family, and I don't want to wreck that."

"They *are* family," I corrected. My daughter was property of a Reaper, and Jackal was married to a Reaper's sister. Hell, one of our prospects had met the daughter of another Reaper and had enough of a reaction to the girl it scared the shit out of him. Ever since Janessa had been here, Seamus had gone around fucking anything that would hold still long enough, like he was trying to prove something to himself. I had a feeling that was going to be a shitstorm one day.

"They could stay at the compound," Cinder offered. "I know it's not big and we only have a few homes there and the rooms in the clubhouse, but we could make it work. They'd be safe and you'd be free to carry on as usual."

"I want them here," I said. "They're under my…"

"Protection," he finished for me. "Yeah, I heard you. You going to claim them? Do I need to prepare for that?"

"Don't know what the future will bring, but I wouldn't entirely rule out the possibility."

He nodded ran a hand through his close-cropped silver hair. "Fine. Just let me know if things change."

"You still looking at that property out in the county?" I asked. A larger compound farther outside town could mean big changes.

"Yeah, why?"

"I know you wanted to hang onto our compound before, because of the history of the place, but if we sell our current location and set up a new, larger compound, I'm not selling this house. I know you like the way the Reapers have their shit set up, but we're not them. I like living in town."

Cinder shrugged. "We can talk about it if we move forward with a bid on the property. If you get an old lady, she may have her own opinion on where she wants to live. She'd be safer behind a fence. Her and the kid."

He wasn't wrong, but I'd cross that bridge when I got to it. I saw him out, and then went to find Clarity. She was pacing the hall upstairs while Caleb slept soundly in his room. I wrapped my arms around her when she came barreling into me. She trembled and I hated that she'd been scared. If she was going to stay here, though, she'd have to get used to my brothers dropping by, even if they asked questions she might not like.

"Do I have to leave?" she asked. "I don't think he liked me."

"Kitten, it's not that he doesn't like you. He was concerned that Caleb might be my son."

She looked up at me. "Why would that be a bad thing?"

"You're obviously young, and you were still a kid when you had Caleb. Even if it had been consensual, it still would have been statutory rape. Cinder was worried the cops might come down on the club. I would be honored to be Caleb's dad, but he's right to be worried," I said.

"I hadn't thought of that," she admitted. "I don't want you to get into trouble. Maybe we should go?"

"Kitten, I'm sure it's going to be fine. Most people go out of their way to avoid my club. Cinder just wants to be cautious in case someone tries to start shit. All it would take is one phone call to arouse suspicion and bring the cops to the door. Even though a blood test would prove that Caleb isn't mine, it could bring the club under scrutiny, and that's the last thing we need."

I smoothed the wrinkles between her eyes as she frowned at me, then did the only thing I could think of to get her mind off it. I leaned down and kissed her. It was getting to be a habit, but she tasted so damn sweet. Her body melted against mine and she clutched my shirt. My cock pressed against my zipper and I knew I needed to put a stop to whatever was going on between us before it was too late. She wasn't ready for this. We barely knew each other, and she wasn't the type of woman to fall into bed with a stranger. I might not know her well, but I knew enough to discern that much.

I tried to pull away, but her grip tightened on my shirt and she wouldn't let go. It was damn good for my ego, not that I'd ever lacked female company. A woman like Clarity, though? That was new. She was good, sweet, and if she hadn't had her innocence stolen, she would likely still be a virgin. The exact opposite of the type of women who flocked to me and my brothers.

"Kitten, we shouldn't do this," I said before kissing her again briefly, unable to resist the temptation.

"Caleb will sleep for a while," she said.

I smiled and smoothed back her hair. "That wasn't my concern. I'm more than thirty years older than you, and I haven't exactly led a law-abiding life. You can do a hell of a lot better than me. Hell, I'm old enough to be Caleb's grandpa and your dad."

She arched a brow, but didn't move away.

"I'm not calling you Daddy," she said.

I gave a bark of laughter and tightened my hold on her. Some men might be into that shit, but I certainly wasn't. I didn't want a little girl in my bed, I wanted a woman. And despite Clarity's young age, she was certainly all woman.

"If you did, I'd have to spank your ass. I'm too damn old for those games."

"I know I'm young," she said. "But I had to grow up fast. I'm not some kid who doesn't know what she wants. No matter how many times you say you're a bad man, I'll never believe it. You've been wonderful to me and Caleb."

"If we go down this path, it changes things, kitten. I don't think you're ready for that. There's too much about me and my life that you don't know."

"What are you worried about?" she asked.

"You're different. It's not a bad thing, but it means that once I get you in my bed, I'm not going to let you leave. The last thing you need right now is a commitment. And if I claim you, make you my old lady, there's no going back. You'll be mine until one of us dies. Focus on you and your boy, get adjusted to life here and to me, and then if you still think you want me, we'll talk about it."

"Why do you have to go and be all reasonable?" she asked.

I smiled a little. "Comes with having lived so damn long."

She snuggled closer; then she yawned.

"You should rest while Caleb is down for nap," I said. I doubted either of them had slept well the months they were on the street. It would probably take a few days before she looked and felt well rested.

"I don't want to be alone," she mumbled.

I lifted her into my arms and carried her down the hall to her bedroom. Even though she was a little on the curvy side, she was too damn light. It made me wonder just how badly she'd been starving herself to make sure her son had food. I left the bedroom door open and eased her onto the mattress, but she refused to let go. It took me a minute to get my boots off while she clung to me, but then I climbed onto the bed with her and held her close. She curled into me and rubbed her nose against my chest. After her third deep breath, I had to fight back a laugh.

"Are you smelling me?" I asked.

"Maybe," she said, pressing her nose closer to me.

I rubbed my hand up and down her back. "Go to sleep, kitten. I'll stay right here."

Once her breathing evened out and her body relaxed, I eased out of the bed and went to check on Caleb. He still slept soundly, his tiny body sprawled across his toddler bed, one foot hanging off the edge. The bear I'd asked Seamus to purchase was clutched in the little boy's arms, and he looked completely at peace. I looked in on Clarity once more and then decided to do something about the problem I'd had since I kissed her in the hall.

I left my bedroom door open a crack in case Caleb woke up and needed something, but I went into my bathroom and stripped my clothes off. It took a minute for the shower to heat up, then I stepped under the spray and closed my eyes as I wrapped my hand around my cock. I'd been fucking hard since my lips had touched Clarity's. Club sluts could plaster themselves to me and I didn't get hard -- most of the time -- but that sweet woman in my arms made my dick stand at attention.

I soaped my hand and started stroking. Long, hard tugs that felt damn good, but not good enough. I tried to picture her, naked and kneeling at my feet, those pouty lips of hers parted. Would she let me grip her hair and fuck her mouth, take complete control of her? Her mouth would probably feel like heaven wrapped around me, sucking me off. I stroked faster and harder, my other hand braced on the wall.

My breath sawed in and out of my lungs, and when I imagined her hands on my body, I could feel them, like she was standing in the shower with me. I felt her lips trail down my spine, her small hand slide around my hip and cover my hand and cock. It was when her thumb stroked over the slit at the head of my cock that my eyes jerked opened and my body went tight. I looked over my shoulder and the little angel was smiling at me shyly.

"Clarity, what the fuck are you doing?" I asked, my voice harsher than I'd meant it to be.

She didn't flinch, or draw away. If anything, she came closer, pressing her naked body to mine. She slipped under my arm and faced me as her hand gripped my cock again, sliding up and down my shaft.

"Clarity…"

"You might think we shouldn't have sex, and I understand your concerns, but at least give me this much. Let me make you come."

My eyes closed tight and I gave a slight nod, having no doubt I was going straight to hell for allowing her to do this. Fuck, I already had a seat reserved. But all the bad shit I'd ever done didn't compare to giving into her when I knew it was wrong. One of us needed to be the voice of reason, but with her small, soft hand stroking my dick, any sense of self-preservation I'd had was long gone.

Her lips touched my chest, then she gently bit down on my nipple. It was enough to send me over the edge and I came, spurts of cum coating her belly and breasts. When my balls had been drained, a shudder raked my body. It was the hardest I'd come in a while and I stared down at her, trying to figure out what she was thinking or feeling. Her body was flushed and the look in her eyes was pleading with me to touch her.

"Kitten… you shouldn't have come in here."

"I want you. I've never wanted anyone before, and while it's a new and scary feeling, I know that I'll regret it if I just sit back and do nothing. I don't care if you're older than me, or that your club does illegal stuff. You make me feel things no one has ever made me feel before, treat Caleb like a treasure, and I…"

I cupped her cheek and ran my thumb along her skin. "You what?"

"Well, we aren't technically in your bed, so if anything happens here in the shower…" She shrugged.

I bit my lip so I wouldn't laugh. "Found a loophole, did you? Maybe I should have been a bit clearer. Once my dick is inside you, you're mine, Clarity. You and Caleb. That's a big fucking step to take, kitten, especially since you don't know shit about me."

She opened her mouth, probably to protest, and I silenced her.

"You trusted Caleb's dad and look what happened. Just because you think you know me, that you think I'm a good man, it doesn't mean we should do this. I'm not who you think I am, kitten."

She ran her hand across my chest, tracing the lines of my tattoos. "The fact you keep pushing me away tells me enough. Anyone else would have had me naked within minutes of letting me into your shop, or pushed me to my knees and ordered me to suck them off. You didn't do any of that."

The fact I'd just tried to be a decent human being and she acted like I'd made the sun rise and set told me quite a bit about everything she'd been through. The things I'd done were things any person should want to do for another, without expecting repayment. Maybe not all the shopping I'd done for them, but giving them a safe place to sleep, feeding them? It was just human decency to do those things. Even a bad man like me wouldn't let a little kid starve on the streets.

"Please," she said softly. "No one's ever touched me the way you do. I want to experience it all. With you. I want to know what it should have felt like the day Caleb was conceived, what it would have felt like if I'd been with a man I'd chosen and not one who took what he wanted."

Christ! She was fucking killing me with her big eyes and her soft pleas.

"Kitten, I doubt that you're on birth control, and I don't keep condoms at home because I never bring women here. I'm clean. I get tested every month, and I always use protection, but you could get pregnant. If only took the one time before…"

"Then pull out."

"That's not foolproof, Clarity. You could still get pregnant."

"Are you going to throw me out and make me leave?" she asked. "I don't mean out of your shower, but if we… if we're intimate, will you change your mind and make us leave?"

"No, baby. I told you, once I'm inside you, I'm not letting you go. You'll be mine, both of you. I've lived long enough to know that a woman like you is one in a million. I'd be stupid to let you go."

"And if I got pregnant, you'd want the baby, wouldn't you?"

"Of course, I would, but I'm not taking that chance, kitten. You're still vulnerable and shouldn't be making that kind of decision right now. I'll make you feel good, but we aren't taking this any further until I've picked up some condoms. And before you argue, I'm doing it for you. I'd love nothing more than to be inside you bare, but I don't think that's what you need right now. After you're more rested and have had a few more meals in your belly, you'll likely see that I'm right. We don't have to rush things."

She wound my hair around her hand and pulled my head toward hers. "Then make me feel good. No one's ever made me come before. I've never even come by my own hand."

My lips crashed against hers as I kissed her hard and deep. I reached between her legs, stroking the soft hair covering her pussy before seeking out her wet heat. She was so slick and more than ready to be fucked. I thrust a finger inside her, then added a second. I groaned at how fucking tight she was. Just two of my fingers barely fit inside her, and I wondered if I'd split her in two if I did claim her the way I wanted. If I hadn't just come, the feel of her around my fingers would have made me hard as a fucking post.

I thrust my fingers in out and of her while I brushed over her clit with my thumb. She made soft sounds and her pussy squeezed tight. I could tell she was already close, and I wanted to push her harder, make her fall and scream out my name. I drew back a little so I could watch her, the cream coating my fingers making me wish it was my cock inside her. She looked fucking beautiful as she panted and sweetly begged me for more.

"I… I feel…" she stammered and bit her lip as she moaned.

"That's it, kitten. Come for me. Let go."

"I… I…" She screamed as her hips bucked. "Damon!"

Fucking hell! A woman had never said my real name as she orgasmed, and even though I'd thought I was too damn old to get hard again so soon, my dick seemed to have other ideas. I slid my fingers out of her pussy, then sucked off her cream. Her eyes dilated as she watched me.

"I didn't know men actually did that. I thought it only happened in books," she said.

"You taste so damn good, kitten."

Her gaze dropped to my cock. "You're hard again."

I rubbed the back of my neck. "Yeah. Seeing you come seems to affect me that way. I'll be fine. You should get dressed and check on Caleb."

She kissed me sweetly, then got out of the shower. Once she had a towel wrapped around her and was gathering her clothes, I turned the hot water all the way off and tried not to curse as the icy water beat down on me. It took a few minutes, but my dick finally deflated and I was able to get out.

Something told me that my life was about to get a hell of a lot more complicated. Now that we'd crossed a line, there was no going back. I only hoped that she didn't regret it after she'd had some time to think things over. Clarity was the first woman I'd ever invited into my home, other than the invitation I'd extended to my daughter, and she was the first woman who had ever screamed my name like that.

No matter what she decided, I knew this moment was a life changing one for me. After being with her like that, someone as sweet and innocent as she was, club sluts would never do it for me. I leaned against my dresser and crossed my arms as I stared at the opposite wall. Logically, I knew I shouldn't have touched her, should have never shared that moment with her. But I also knew I'd never regret it. Not even if she walked away and didn't look back. It would be a memory I'd cherish the rest of my life.

Fuck. I was turning into a goddamn sap in my old age.

Chapter Five

Clarity

It was both frustrating and touching that Scratch had held back in the shower. I wanted him more than I'd ever wanted anyone before, but the fact he was thoughtful enough to consider protection and insist on using it kept me from being mad. The fact he'd given me my first orgasm, and it had completely rocked my world, definitely hadn't hurt. My body was still humming. I had to wonder if he'd been able to make my knees turn to jelly just with his fingers, could I handle being in bed with him? If sex between us got any better, I wasn't sure I'd survive it.

By the time I'd dressed and run a comb through my hair, Caleb was already awake. His blond hair stood every which way and reminded me a little too much of his father, but his dark eyes were definitely mine. Even though I'd inherited my father's pale white skin, I'd gotten hair and eyes from my mom. I'd sometimes wondered if that was why my stepmom hadn't seemed to want me around. She'd made racist comments on more than one occasion, and it had to make her burn that her stepdaughter was mixed race. Or maybe she'd just been embarrassed by me, since she'd always asked me to stay in my room when her friends came over.

I picked up a still somewhat sleepy Caleb, made sure he used the bathroom, then carried him downstairs. He'd never been around a staircase before, and I didn't want to take a chance on him falling on the way down. If we were going to stay long-term, maybe I could talk Scratch into putting a baby gate across the top and bottom. Caleb was my entire world and if anything happened to him, something I could have prevented, I would never forgive myself.

Scratch was in the living room with his feet up in a recliner. He was flipping through TV channels when he saw me lingering in the doorway. He gave me a wink and smiled at Caleb.

"Hey, little man. Do you like watching TV?" Scratch asked.

Caleb shoved his fist in his mouth and nodded. My boy could talk, but he seldom did. If I'd had the money for a specialist, I'd have asked them to test him, make sure he didn't have a learning disability or hadn't been traumatized in some way that would make him go silent. He'd been a real chatterbox when he'd first learned to talk, then about six months or so ago, he'd suddenly stopped. I'd thought it was strange, but he'd seemed perfectly healthy. We'd gone to the free clinic the church hosted once a month and they'd assured me he was perfectly healthy.

I eased onto the couch, nearest to Scratch, and held Caleb in my lap. I was a little surprised when Scratch put an animated movie on TV, something Caleb hadn't seen since it was still fairly new. Glancing his way, I found him watching me. Or maybe it was more that he was watching both of us.

"You watch cartoons often?" I asked.

His lips twitched and he smiled a little. "I added a bunch to my digital movie library in case the grandkid ever came to visit. So far, he hasn't. I see him often enough, though."

"Where does he live?" I asked.

"Alabama. His daddy is a Dixie Reaper, and our clubs get along just fine, but Bull would technically need permission to be in our territory. I have no doubt that Cinder would give it to him and it's not a complicated process or anything, but it's just easier for me to go there.

I'm on good terms with their Pres and everyone knows me. Besides, routine is good for Foster. Maybe when he's older they'll come for a visit."

"How often do you go visit?" I asked, hoping I wasn't prying too much. I figured if I crossed a line, he'd let me know.

"Sometimes I'm over that way once a month, other times it's a few months between visits. It depends on what's going on with my club, their club, or my business. I usually head over there for a long weekend, or occasionally I'll stay for a week. It's nice getting to spend time with Darian after missing out on so much."

I wanted to ask about Darian's mom, but I didn't dare. If she'd made Scratch think his daughter was dead, then I had a feeling she would be a sore spot with him. I was more than a little curious, though. What type of woman had he cared enough about to have a child with her? He'd said he'd never been with someone like me, but he must have cared about her at least a little. Unless his daughter had been a mistake, which was possible. Caleb had been the result of a rape, but it didn't mean I loved him any less, and I could tell that Scratch loved his daughter, no matter who her mom was or how she'd been conceived. He definitely seemed crazy about his grandson. His eyes lit up every time he talked about the little boy.

"What about your parents?" he asked. "What made you run away from home?"

"My mom died when I was younger, and when my dad remarried, he picked a woman who seemed to hate me. My dad is white and so is my stepmom."

"But your mother wasn't," he said.

"No." I shifted Caleb onto to the sofa. "Wait right here."

I shot up and ran up the stairs, going for the backpack I'd stashed in my room. I hadn't had a chance to wash it yet, and I had to admit it was making the room smell a little funky, but it held my most prized possession. I hadn't been able to keep much when we'd been evicted, but I did have a picture of my mom I'd salvaged from our stuff on the street and kept it in the front pocket.

I carefully took the picture out and carried it downstairs. Standing next to Scratch's chair, I showed it to him.

"This is my mom. My dad told me it was taken around the time she found out she was pregnant with me. It's the only one I have of her."

He took the picture from me, holding it gently, and he grinned. "You look like her. Your skin might be lighter, but you have her eyes, her hair, and you definitely have her smile."

I took the picture back from him, looking at my mom. She'd had such pretty skin, a light mocha that I'd often wished I had too. Anyone who'd seen a picture of my mom always asked how I could be so pale. If it weren't for my decidedly non-white hair, no one would ever know my mother was African American.

"I have my dad's nose," I said, wishing I didn't look anything like him. Once upon a time, I'd loved him and I'd been convinced he loved me too. You didn't throw away the people you loved, and as easily as he'd pushed me aside I had to wonder if he'd ever felt anything for me, or if he'd just been going through the motions.

"You're beautiful, kitten, and so was she. I'm sorry you lost her and that your dad turned out to be an asshole. If you ever want to talk about her, or about how your dad made you feel, I'll always listen." He reached for my hand and tugged me down across his lap. "I can promise you right now, if I make you mine, I will treat Caleb like my own son. It doesn't matter how he was conceived or who his birth father is, that boy will be mine and he will be loved."

"If you make me yours?" I asked.

"Going slow, remember? Or trying to." He smiled. "You seem to want to run full steam ahead."

I curled against his chest and grabbed onto his shirt. I felt his heartbeat and let his scent surround me. If I could spend every night for the rest of my life just like this, curled up in his lap, then I would be happy. I'd never felt so content, so at peace, as I did right that moment. We watched the movie, and eventually Caleb came over, lifting his arms up.

Scratch helped him onto the recliner and I worried the chair might break with all three of us in it, but he didn't seem to mind. He wrapped his arms around us. For a moment, I could picture Scratch as my husband, Caleb as our son, and us having a happy family. I didn't think everything would always be all sunshine and roses if he did decide to keep us, but it would be the first time my son had been part of a complete family unit. I wanted that for my sweet boy, and I wanted it for me too.

When it was time for dinner, Scratch ordered some pizza and breadsticks. Caleb's eyes went wide when he saw all the food and my heart hurt, knowing I hadn't been able to do something like this for him. Even when I'd been working, our meals had been inexpensive but filling. Eating out had been a treat, and usually meant ordering off the dollar menu, or getting the special at the diner.

Caleb ate an entire slice and then reached for a breadstick, but his hand froze partway and he looked at Scratch. The fear in his eyes nearly took my breath away, his small hand trembling as if he'd done something wrong, and I didn't understand what was happening. I'd always given Caleb as much as he wanted, often going hungry myself to make sure he was full. Not once had I disciplined him for wanting more food, or for helping himself to whatever was on the table.

Scratch met my gaze before looking at Caleb, and I knew he'd seen it too.

"It's okay, Caleb. Take as much as you want," Scratch said, his voice low and soft.

My throat tightened and my heart raced as I wondered what had happened to my small boy to make him that scared. Caleb ate his breadstick, eyeing Scratch as if the man might snatch it away at any moment. After dinner, we cleaned up and I bathed Caleb, then tucked him into bed. I shut off his light and pulled his door partway closed, then met Scratch back down in the living room. He was standing in the center of the room, his expression fierce and his arms folded.

"What the fuck happened to make him think he'd be punished for eating?" Scratch asked.

"I don't know. He's never done that around me before, and I always give him as much as he wants."

I was wringing my hands and shifting from foot to foot, scared about what might have happened to my son, and not knowing who was responsible. There was only one person I could think of, but it scared me. My gaze met Scratch's and told him my fears.

"When I was working, I would have to leave Caleb with a sitter. There was a woman two doors down who had a few kids. She said watching him wouldn't be any trouble, and I paid her twenty dollars every shift I worked to make sure he stayed safe. No one else had access to Caleb, unless it was through her," I said. "What did she do to my baby?"

His stance softened as did his expression, and Scratch came toward me, pulling me into his arms. "Did you notice any behavior changes in Caleb at all?"

"He stopped talking about six months ago. He talks, just not nearly as much. I wondered what would have caused it and had thought he was sick, but the doctor at the free clinic said he was fine."

"I want the name and address of that woman," he said. "I think I need to pay her a visit and find out what she did to that boy."

"I'm scared," I admitted. "I'm terrified you'll find out something horrible, and I'm responsible for putting him in that situation. It's my fault someone hurt my baby."

I couldn't hold back my tears and sobbed against his chest. Scratch rubbed my back and tried to soothe me, but my heart was breaking. I was supposed to protect my child, make sure he didn't come to any harm, and I'd left him with someone who had possibly abused him. What kind of mother did that make me?

"Kitten, I'll figure out what's going on, and I will keep the both of you safe. Whatever it takes. Understand?"

I nodded and tried to dry my tears, but more kept coming.

"I failed him," I said, sniffling.

"No, you didn't. You left him with someone you thought you could trust, so that you could work and earn money to keep a roof over his head and food in his belly. No one is going to fault you for that. There are bad people in the world, and sometimes they wear really good disguises. Did her children ever look like they'd been abused? Were there any warning signs?" he asked.

"No. Her kids were always clean, looked healthy, and seemed well mannered. I'd thought maybe she was one of those super moms who had kids who always behaved."

He chuckled. "I don't think there's such a thing as a kid who always behaves, but I get your point. Now understand mine. There was no way you could have known that she would do something to scare Caleb. If she never left a mark on him, and he couldn't tell you what was happening, how would you have known? When he stopped talking, you took him to the doctor like any concerned mother would. It's not your fault, kitten."

I clung to him, wishing there some way to rewind the last hour or so, turn back time to when I didn't know someone had hurt my little boy. I had suspected something was wrong, something that had made him feel like he couldn't speak anymore, but maybe I hadn't wanted to know what happened. If I knew, then it was real and someone had harmed my sweet little boy, and I wasn't sure I could handle that knowledge.

"Can I stay with you tonight?" I asked softly, not daring to look up at him. If he rejected me, my heart might completely shatter.

"Do you just want to be held? Because I can do that if that's what you need right now."

I shrugged. "Yes, and no. I want that, but what if I decide I want more than just holding?"

"Then I'd better have a Prospect bring me a box of condoms."

I tried to remember the biker show I'd watched a while back, but the word Prospect was drawing a blank. Scratch had told me before what he'd meant by calling them that, but I must not have paid close enough attention. "What's a Prospect?"

"It's someone who wants to join the club. They have to do whatever jobs we give them, have to prove themselves as loyal to the club, and after a while the members vote and decide who is allowed to patch in and who isn't. We only have a few of them because our Pres is rather selective."

"Like the men who put Caleb's stuff together?" I asked. I remembered them wearing a cut like Scratch, but theirs had been different.

"Yes, those two were Prospects. Why don't you go soak in the tub and change for bed? I'll wait down here for him to bring the condoms, and then I'll come up and we can go to bed. And if sleep is all you want to do, then I'm perfectly okay with that. You never have to do something you don't want, and I don't want you to feel obligated to have sex with me. Or with anyone for that matter."

"I don't feel obligated." I looked up at him. "But I'll go up and run a bath like you suggested. Maybe it will make me feel better, but I doubt it."

He kissed the top of my head. As I walked out of the living room, I saw him pull his cell phone from his pocket, and I heard him speaking to someone as I went up the stairs. Butterflies swarmed my stomach at the thought of sharing a bed with him, but they were quickly squashed by the horrid feeling someone had abused my child. No matter what Scratch said, I still felt responsible. I'd given that woman permission to care for him, paid her to do it for that matter, and it made me feel like I'd condoned her behavior. I knew deep down that wasn't true, that I hadn't known and couldn't have known that there was something wrong with her. It didn't ease my guilt any.

I soaked in the tub until my fingers and toes began to prune, then drained the water and dried off. As I looked around, I realized I hadn't grabbed any clean clothes from my room, so I wrapped the towel around my body and walked down the hall to the spare room Scratch was letting me use. I pulled on some of the new things he'd bought me, a silky pair of panties with a cute shorts set that had stars on them. Then I padded into his bedroom. He'd removed his cut and shirt, and stood barefoot in nothing but his jeans.

My breath caught in my throat as I stared at him. In the shower, I hadn't really taken the time to admire the scenery. He wasn't overly bulky with muscle, but his abs were defined and biceps were still large in my opinion. The ink that swirled across his chest traveled along his shoulders and down his arms. He watched me, but didn't make a move to bring me farther into his space. I put one foot in front of the other, until I stood right in front of him.

"Feel any better?' he asked.

"Not really. I don't think I'll be able to relax until I know for sure what happened to Caleb, and even then I can't guarantee it will change anything. I might actually feel worse depending on what you find out."

"Whatever it is, I'll handle it. If she hurt that boy, I'll make sure it doesn't happen again."

My stomach clenched, and I wasn't sure I wanted to know exactly what he meant by that. He'd said that he'd done things I didn't know about, bad things. I still didn't think that made him a bad man. If he did something to the woman who hurt my kid, it wouldn't make me see him any differently. I wouldn't fault him for wanting to protect innocent children, no matter how he went about it.

I noticed the box of condoms on the nightstand. Instead of the fear or revulsion I'd always felt when sex came up with other men, it just felt right when I thought about doing those things with Scratch. I didn't care about our age difference, or that he thought he was all wrong for me. No one had ever looked at me the way he did, ever treated me as good as he did, and they certainly hadn't made me feel the things he did. Once I'd let down my guard even a little, I'd realized that I felt safe with him. When I looked into his eyes, I just knew that he would protect me, and maybe even love me one day if things went that far. As broken as I was, I had a feeling he was a little bit broken too, or had been at some point. The strong man holding me right now wasn't broken anymore, but maybe just a little damaged. Whatever he'd been through, it had made him into the man he was today, a man I would be proud to call mine.

"Make love to me," I said. "Show me what my first time should have been like."

"Remember what I said?" he asked.

"That if we do this, then I'm yours, and Caleb is yours."

He nodded. "I shouldn't want you, should send you back to your room and stay the hell away from you. But I don't know that I'm strong enough to do that. You make me feel..."

"Complete," I said, because that's how he made me feel. "It feels like you're the piece that's been missing from my life. Do you believe in soul mates?"

"People destined to be together?" he asked. "Always thought it was a bunch of crap."

"Oh." I nibbled my lower lip, but he reached up and pulled it from my teeth, smoothing his thumb across it.

"Until I met you," he said. "I tried to tell myself I just wanted to help out a single mom who was struggling, but I think it was something more. I've never loved a woman before, Clarity, and I may not be capable of it. I love my daughter, and I already love that kid of yours. But women..."

"Someone hurt you," I said.

He shrugged. "Everyone gets hurt at some point, but yeah. I've had some women fuck me over in the past. I won't promise you love, but I can promise that I will respect you, I will take care of you, and that I do have feelings of some sort for you even if I don't have a label for them. Which is insane since we've only known each other for about a day. It doesn't feel like that, though."

I smiled a little. "I know. When I look at you, when your eyes lock onto mine, I feel like I've known you forever. Like maybe we knew each other in past life or something."

He chuckled a little. "Now you believe in past lives too?"

"Don't you?" I asked. "Haven't you ever had something happen and it felt like you'd been faced with that situation before, even though you knew you hadn't? Or maybe you heard about something that happened long enough and you could vividly picture it your mind, even smell the scents that would have been there? I think it's memories of what happened in a life before this one."

"Maybe you're right. Never really thought about it that way."

"I won't hear that often, will I?" I teased.

"Hear what?"

"That I'm right."

He grinned and then leaned down and kissed me hard. "Kitten, I will always admit when you're right and I'm wrong. Just not in front of my brothers. I have a badass image to uphold after all."

"I think we're wearing too many clothes," I said, reaching for the button on his jeans.

"Caleb?" he asked, nodding toward the hall.

"He'll sleep for at least a few hours. Even on the street he'd doze off for three or four hours at a time. Now that he has a home to sleep in, a place to feel safe, maybe he'll sleep longer. With that episode at dinner, I can't guarantee it, but I think we have time."

He pressed his forehead to mine. "Then get naked, kitten."

I took a step back and slowly removed my clothes, loving the heat that flared in his eyes as he watched me. I didn't feel nervous or scared like I'd thought I would. I just felt desirable and wanted. He removed his jeans and boxer briefs, his cock already hard. When he pulled me into his arms again, I felt like I'd come home, like I was exactly where I was supposed to be.

We toppled to the bed as he kissed me, his hands sliding up and down my sides, then gripping my hips. His cock pressed against me and I felt a thrill run through me. He took his time, tasting me, licking along my collarbone before taking my nipple into his mouth. I sank my fingers into his hair, wishing we could stay in this moment forever. My body came alive, every nerve ending humming as he lovingly traced my curves with his lips and hands.

Pleasure consumed me, and I gladly gave myself over to Scratch. I was his. His to touch, to protect… And my heart felt full.

Chapter Six

Scratch

Her skin felt like silk and she tasted sweet as honey. She had the prettiest nipples I'd ever seen, and I loved the way she shivered when I sucked them into my mouth, then lightly bit them. I stroked the curls between her legs, feeling how wet and ready she was for me. Her clit was swollen and I lightly rubbed it. Not enough to get her off, but just enough to have her begging for more.

"Feel good, kitten?" I asked.

"So good," she murmured, her eyes fluttering as she tried to keep them open. A soft smile curved her lips.

I remembered how tight she'd been in the shower and used my fingers to stretch her a little. My cock wasn't fucking huge, but I was bigger than average and could hurt her. If she didn't have a son, I'd have sworn she was a virgin.

"I can't wait to feel this pussy wrapped around my dick," I said as I kissed along her neck. I added a second finger as I worked her pussy, and the soft moans coming from her damn near made me come.

"Damon, please," she begged.

"Please what, kitten?"

"I need… I need…"

I knew exactly what she needed, wanted, and drove my fingers in and out of her harder and faster. I pressed down on her clit with my thumb. Her hips bucked against me and I could feel that she was close. Sucking her nipple into my mouth again, I lashed it with my tongue before biting down just hard enough that she came.

"Damon!" She shuddered and trembled as her pussy gushed around my fingers.

Before she had a chance to come down from her high, I slipped my fingers out of her, sucked her juices from them, then ripped open a condom. It had to be the fastest I'd ever put one on, then I braced my weight so I wouldn't crush her and I slowly eased into her tight little pussy.

"Fuck, Clarity! So damn tight!"

I used short thrusts to work my way inside her, and when she'd taken all of me, I knew I wouldn't be able to hold back. I wanted to make it perfect for her, to take my time, but I felt like a randy teenager with her lying under me, looking up at me with wonder in her eyes.

I fucked her hard and deep, taking her like a man possessed. Her hands clung to me and her passionate cries spurred me on. It didn't take long before she was coming again, and as her pussy clamped down on me, my balls drew up and I came so fucking hard. I growled as I kept stroking in and out of her, our hips slapping together. When every drop of cum had been wrung from me, I stilled with my cock buried inside her. My chest heaved like I'd run a fucking marathon and I felt sweat slicking my skin.

Clarity smiled up at me with a dreamy expression, then she ran her fingers through my beard.

"Sorry that didn't last very long," I said. Embarrassment made my cheeks warm. I hadn't come that fast in a long fucking time, but being with her… Damn. There were no words to adequately describe the way she made me feel.

"Don't apologize for one of the greatest moments of my life," she said. "Did you hear me utter a single word of complaint?"

"No," I admitted.

"That's because I didn't. I was too busy screaming because of how good you made me feel."

I kissed her, wondering what I'd ever done to deserve such a sweet woman in my bed. When I pulled away, I gripped the condom and slid out of her. I stepped into the bathroom to throw the condom away and wash up, but I froze as I looked down. Holy shit!

My heart pounded in my chest as I stared at the broken condom. I'd been fucking girls and later women since I was fifteen years old. Not once in all that time had a condom ever broken. I pulled it off and tossed it into the trash, then rinsed my dick off in the sink before walking back to the bedroom. Clarity had curled onto her side, the sheet pulled over her body. She gave me a contented smile that quickly slipped away as she looked at me.

"What's wrong?" she asked.

"Condom broke."

Clarity sat up, the sheet falling to her waist. I was momentarily distracted by her rather perky breasts, but I snapped back to reality when she gripped my hand.

"Damon, it's okay."

"You don't need a pregnancy to deal with right now," I said. "I promised to protect you, and that means from me too."

She bit her lip and I could tell she was fighting not to smile.

"What?" I asked, my tone gruff as I sank onto the bed next to her.

"Did you not say that I'm yours now?" she asked. "That you were keeping me?"

"Yes."

"And you're going to love the baby if we have one?" she asked.

"Of course, I will."

"Then what would be the harm in expanding our family?" she asked. "I'm not a naïve young girl, Damon. I've faced more in the last three years than a lot of thirty-year-old women have dealt with. Don't let a number on a piece of paper fool you into thinking I'm some silly girl who doesn't know what she wants."

I wrapped my hand around the back of her neck and kissed her softly. "I know you're not. You're a strong, capable woman. It's part of what I like about you."

"Part? What's the other part?

"Your perky breasts, obviously." I grinned and she playfully smacked my arm. "I like the way you care for your son and put him first, I like that you don't see the world through rose-colored glasses. You left a bad situation and forged a life of your own through hard work and dedication. And when everything was yanked out from under you, you still protected your son and did your best to keep him safe. You're an absolutely amazing woman, Clarity."

Her eyes misted with tears and one rolled down her cheek. I wiped it away before kissing her again. From what she'd told me, I knew that no one had ever shown her any appreciation, had ever really noticed her. I didn't want to make the same mistakes everyone else in her life had made. I wanted her to know that she was special, and that I could see how strong and capable she was, not only of caring for herself but her son too. I wasn't trying to rescue her and dictate her life, I just wanted to give her the tools she needed to get where she was going… as long as it ended with her in my bed every night.

"I'm claiming you," I told her. "I'm not putting it to a vote, not asking anyone for permission. Not even you, and if that makes me a Neanderthal, then so be it. But having said that, I'm not going to lock you away or keep you in a cage. If you want to work, I'll support your decision. If you'd like to go back to school, I'm okay with that too. Or if you want to stay home and be a mom to Caleb and any other kids we might have, then I'll do whatever I can to help you."

She tugged on my beard. "Are you real? I didn't think a man like you existed."

"I'm real, kitten. And I admit that I can be a real asshole sometimes, but I'll try not to be that way with you. I'm old and set in my ways so you'll have to stand up to me every now and then. Just don't do it front of my club. That's the one thing I can't allow. You want to get sassy around the house when it's just us, I have no problem with it."

"Right now, I just want to curl up in your arms and go to sleep." She yawned so wide her jaw cracked. "It's been a while since I really and truly slept, but I feel safe with you holding me."

"Before you go to sleep, there's one thing I need."

"What?" she asked, sounding drowsy.

"The name of Caleb's father. And your dad's name too. I'm not backing down on this one, kitten. They hurt you, and I'm not going to sit back and let them get away with it." I paused a moment. "And I need the name of the neighbor who watched Caleb."

"Caleb's dad is Damon." She smiled up at me. "But his sperm donor is Ryan Peterson."

"And your dad's name?" I asked, trying to ignore the warmth spreading through my chest when she'd called me Caleb's father.

"Heath Davis. And the neighbor who watched Caleb was Mary Hurst."

"So you're Clarity Davis and your son is Caleb Davis?" I asked, needing to know if she'd given Caleb his daddy's name. Since she'd claimed Caleb's dad didn't know about him, he couldn't have signed the paternity papers required to be on the birth certificate. I did remember that, even if I couldn't remember much from the day my daughter was born, probably because I'd likely been drunk off my ass.

She nodded, but I could tell she was mostly asleep already. I retrieved my phone from the pocket of my jeans and texted Shade. He was our club wizard when it came to anything electronic, and could probably hack into government files without anyone even knowing he'd been there. If anyone could find information on those men, it would be him. And once I knew where they were, I was going to pay them a little visit.

See what you can find on a Heath Davis, daughter's name is Clarity, and a man named Ryan Peterson who was in the area about two or three years ago. And look for a woman named Mary Hurst here in town.

Is this club business or personal? Heard you had a woman and kid at your place

Both. She's my old lady and those two men hurt her, and the woman might have abused Caleb.

When there wasn't an answer right away, I started to wonder if maybe I'd killed him with shock by saying I had an old lady. The proper way to do things was to put it to the club during Church and let them vote. Fuck if I was going to take even the slightest chance they'd say no. Kitten was mine, and I wasn't letting her go. If the club didn't like it, too fucking bad. I knew they'd love her once they got to know her. Being their VP had to have some sort of perks.

I'm on it. And congrats. Can't wait to meet her. If the bitch, Mary, hurt your son, there's nowhere she'll be able to hide

I snorted and put my phone away. Yeah, I'd just bet he couldn't wait to meet her. Shade was a good guy, a great brother, but when it came to the ladies he was like a natural disaster that left chaos in his wake. He'd probably broken the heart of nearly every female under the age of fifty in a ten-mile radius. As for Caleb... it made me smile that he'd called the boy my son, and same for Clarity. I'd be honored to be considered that boy's father.

I shut off the light and then pulled Clarity into my arms. It had been a long fucking day, but I just couldn't sleep. I could hear Caleb rustling around in his bed, and I wondered if he was having a bad dream or if he was awake. I pressed a kiss to Clarity's forehead, then got back out of bed. After I pulled on some boxer briefs and a tee, I headed down the hallway to check on the boy.

Caleb was lying on his side with his thumb in his mouth, but his eyes were wide open. He blinked and stared at me as I stepped into the room, but I didn't see even a hint of fear in his gaze. If he was confused about where he was, he didn't show it. I moved farther into the room until I was standing next to his little bed. Kneeling down, I refrained from touching him in case it made him feel afraid. He hadn't been leery of me so far, but it was dark and it was his first night in a new place.

"Hey, little man. Can't sleep?"

He shook his head.

I held my hands out to him, letting him decide if he wanted to come to me or not. If he didn't, then I'd back away and figure out some other way to soothe him. I wasn't going to press him for more than he was willing to give. Caleb looked at my hands, then pulled his thumb out of his mouth and launched himself at me. I caught him against my chest, then stood.

I didn't want to take him to my room since his mom had fallen asleep naked, so I went downstairs to the living room. I turned the TV on low, then stretched out in the recliner with him sprawled across me. His fingers tangled in my hair, and he held on, like he was scared I was going to leave him. Rubbing his back, I hoped he'd go back to sleep so he wouldn't be tired and cranky tomorrow.

"I know being in a new place can be scary, but you're safe here, Caleb. And so is your mom. I won't let anything happen to either of you."

He picked his head up and looked at me, staring hard, almost like he was trying to see into my soul. I briefly wondered if he was able to actually do that. I didn't get unnerved by grown-ass men, but the toddler lying on top of me looked like he'd seen too much already in his young life.

"I wish you'd tell me what happened to you." I ran my hand over his head. "I know the lady who was taking care of you did something bad. I'm going to find out what it is, and I'm going to punish her for hurting you."

Probably not something you should tell a toddler, but his body relaxed a little more and he laid his head back down. I flipped through the channels until his breathing evened out, but every time I shifted to get up and carry him back to bed, he'd wake up again. I ended up staying in the recliner all night, dozing off and on, until the sun started streaming through the living room windows in the morning.

I was getting too damn old for this all-nighter shit, but if Caleb felt safe and was well rested, then I'd give up a few nights of sleep. I turned on the morning news but only half paid attention to it. When I heard movement on the stairs, I watched for Clarity. She stood in the entryway, rubbing her eyes, and looking completely adorable. She'd put on her pajamas again and looked around as if she didn't quite know where she was.

"In here, kitten," I said loud enough she could hear but not so loud I'd wake up Caleb.

She padded into the room, then stopped and smiled when she saw her son sprawled across me. "I wondered where you were when I woke up this morning. I see I lost you to our son."

Our son. My throat tightened and I felt like a sentimental fool.

"He couldn't sleep last night so I brought him down here. Every time I tried to get up and put him to bed, he woke back up. Figured it was better to just sit here and let him sleep."

"Want me to take him?" she asked.

"I've got him. If you'll get my phone off the nightstand upstairs, I'll have a Prospect bring us some breakfast."

"Or I could cook something for us," she offered. "I'm not a gourmet chef by any means, but I won't give you food poisoning."

"If you want to cook, you certainly may. But don't cook because you feel like you need to."

She stretched and I shifted in my seat when my dick started to get hard. Her breasts pushed out against her thin pajama top, and strip of her belly showed as her shirt lifted. She looked really damn good in the morning, but I wasn't surprised. Even covered in dirt, she'd been pretty irresistible.

When she was finished tormenting me, she stepped out of the room and I heard her going upstairs. Guess having breakfast brought in won over cooking. I smiled, wondering how many mornings we'd have like this one. If I'd known that something so domestic would be this appealing, I may have considered having an old lady a little sooner. Then again, no one had tempted me to make that kind of commitment, not until Clarity showed up on my doorstep. She was different from anyone I'd met before, and in a good way. There was an innocence to her, even though I knew she'd seen more shit than most women her age.

There was a strange look on Clarity's face as she came back into the room, my phone clutched in her hand. I instantly went on alert, my body tightening. She came closer and set the phone on the arm of my chair before sinking down onto the couch. When she didn't say anything, I started to worry even more. There wasn't anything in the bedroom that should have put that look on her face, and my phone was locked so she couldn't have seen any messages from the club.

"Kitten, the look on your face is scaring the shit out of me."

"I think your daughter might be on her way here," she said.

"Darian? Why the hell is Darian coming here?" And how the hell had she come to that conclusion? I unlocked my phone and saw a recent call from my daughter, and that it had lasted roughly three minutes. My gaze locked on Clarity. I had nothing to hide from her, except club shit she didn't need to know about. Didn't really bother me she'd answered my phone, but something must have transpired between the women in my life, and I doubted it was a happy occurrence.

"Your phone was ringing when I went upstairs. I saw Darian's name and remembered she was your daughter, so I answered, thinking maybe it was important." Her hands fidgeted in her lap. "She, um… she didn't handle it well when I picked up your phone."

"I don't think anyone has ever answered my phone but me. Doesn't explain why she'd be upset over it, though."

"She asked who I was and why I had your phone."

My eyebrows went up. "And you told her what?"

"That you'd claimed me and I was living here with you." Her cheeks warmed. "She said I sounded like a teenager. I assured her I'm an adult, but she's convinced I did something to force you into claiming me. She wasn't very happy when she hung up."

"Shit," I muttered. The last thing I needed was my daughter on my doorstep, irate over the woman I'd chosen, and she'd likely have that hulking husband of hers with her. The bright side would be seeing my grandson.

"Yeah, so…" She chewed on her lip. "I'm sorry I answered your phone. I won't do it again."

"Kitten, it's fine that you answered it. I just didn't want to deal with my daughter right now, especially if she's worked up. I'll call my Pres and give him a heads up in case her husband asks permission to come with her. It's just a courtesy thing for Bull to check with Cinder, but I want to make sure the Pres knows what's going on. We'll deal with it, and once she calms down, the two of you will get along fine."

I knew my daughter, though, and she was going to have a shit fit when she realized Clarity was only eighteen. Yeah, she was a legal adult, but compared to my advanced years, she was still a kid. Younger than my daughter, and younger than any of the old ladies with the Dixie Reapers. I was going to catch some serious shit for this, but I wouldn't give up Clarity and Caleb. There was a sense of rightness that I felt bone-deep when they were with me.

I sent a text to Reed, one of the Prospects, and asked him to pick up three breakfast specials from the diner and bring them by the house. I'd have to take Clarity grocery shopping later. I had some food in the house, but I didn't know their favorite meals, or if they even had favorites. There was still a lot we needed to learn about one another, but we had a lifetime to figure it out. Well, my lifetime anyway. With thirty-two years between us, I didn't doubt for a moment I'd kick the bucket before she would, especially if my club got mixed up in any dangerous shit again.

Clarity still looked freaked out over her talk with Darian, and I hoped I wouldn't have to kick my daughter's ass whenever she showed up. I stared at my phone, knowing I needed to give Cinder a heads up, if it wasn't too late already.

Claimed Clarity as my old lady. No, I'm not putting it to a vote. Darian found out and she's pissed. Bull might need permission to come with her when she shows up to give my woman a piece of her mind.

I can deny both of them permission. I'll let them know it's not safe right now. That should keep them away.

I stared at my phone. What the fuck did he mean it wasn't safe? Or was he just trying to find a way to give me more time with Clarity before subjecting her to my daughter and son-in-law? I'd have thought if anyone would understand, it would be my daughter. Hell, she'd been twenty-one to Bull's forty-nine when they'd gotten together. Maybe it was just hard for her to picture her daddy with a woman, especially one as young as Clarity.

Get your family settled for the morning. I'm sending a Prospect to watch over them. Then get your ass to the clubhouse. We have shit to discuss.

Well, that was cryptic as fuck and didn't sound the least bit promising. I sighed and set my phone down, not quite sure what to tell Clarity. I didn't know if the things being discussed were about her, or if something else was going on. The last thing I wanted was to drop her and Caleb into the middle of a war. I'd thought all that was behind us, that it was safe for us to have families now. Had I been wrong?

"Kitten, it seems I have some club business to deal with this morning. I'll have breakfast with the two of you, then I need to leave for a little while. Someone will be out front to make sure you're safe, and you can tell them if you need anything."

She stared at me a moment, then nodded. I'd expected some questions, but if she had any, she was keeping them to herself. I let Caleb sleep until the food arrived, then I transferred him to Clarity's arms and went to answer the door. No way was I letting her get it while she was dressed in her pajamas. Her curves were only for me to enjoy.

Reed looked about half-asleep as he stood on my doorstep. I took the food from him, then watched as he stumbled down the steps and climbed into one of the club trucks. A tarp was pulled over the back, and I wondered what was under it. I shut and locked the door, then took our food to the kitchen. There was some thumping around upstairs and I figured Clarity had tried to put Caleb back to bed. When she came back down, she'd put on the robe she'd bought at the store yesterday.

I set her breakfast in front of her, then poured us each a glass of juice while I brewed some coffee. I put Caleb's food in the oven so it would stay warm. Whenever he woke up again, he'd likely be hungry. The coffee finished brewing and I pulled down my largest mug and filled it, then fixed a regular-size cup for Clarity. If I was going to sit in Church, I needed to be clear-headed, and I had a feeling she would need the caffeine to keep up with Caleb once he woke up.

I didn't have a fucking clue what Cinder wanted to discuss, and I knew I needed to be prepared for anything. I only hoped it didn't take me away from Clarity and Caleb all day. I wanted to introduce them to Jackal's family. Allegra was close to Caleb's age and I hoped the two would become friends. Hell, Josie was pregnant with another one and was due within a few months. It made me wonder what Clarity would look like pregnant with my kid.

My phone dinged and I picked it up to check the display.

Church in twenty.

Fucking hell. So much for enjoying breakfast with my woman. I shoved a few bites of food into my mouth, drained my coffee, then stood. Clarity blinked up at me, and I gave her a smile.

"Sorry, kitten. I have to go for a bit. Make yourself at home." I paused a moment, realizing she didn't have a way to reach me. "We'll get a phone for you when I'm finished with club business."

"You don't have to…"

I held up my hand. "No arguments. You need a phone."

She sighed and nodded. I knew it was hard for her to accept all the things I was buying for her and Caleb, but they were mine to take care of, and I was going to make sure they had everything they needed. I pressed a kiss to the top of her head, then went upstairs to shower and dress. I scrubbed my skin until it turned pink, and took the time to use the conditioner Darian had talked me into buying during my last trip to visit her. I hadn't really given a shit about my appearance in a long ass time, but I combed out my beard and added a little oil to it, then pulled my hair back in a ponytail.

I dressed in my usual black tee, jeans, and my Harley Davidson boots, then pulled on my cut. When I got back downstairs, Clarity had finished her meal, and Seamus was standing in the front entry. My eyes narrowed as I remembered locking the door, then I sought out Clarity. She was nervously twisting her hands in front of her, and I wondered if Seamus had said something he shouldn't have.

I pulled Clarity into my arms. "Everything all right, kitten?"

She nodded. "Was it all right that I let him in? I could see his Devil's Boneyard patch through the peephole in the door."

"It's fine, but in the future, you should probably leave his ass outside. Or anyone else for that matter. I want you to stay safe."

"I'll make sure her and the kid are okay while you're at Church," Seamus said. "Don't worry about them, VP. I'll protect them with my life."

"See that you do."

I gave Clarity a quick kiss, nodded at Seamus, then went out to my bike, grateful a Prospect had brought it to the house. The compound wasn't too far from my home, but I was still running a little late. In all the years I'd been with Devil's Boneyard, I couldn't remember ever being late for Church before. My brothers would likely give me shit about it, but I knew they'd understand. I clomped up the steps of the clubhouse and went inside, then down the hall. Two wooden doors at the end of the hall had the Devil's Boneyard symbol burned into them, and I pushed them open.

Cinder looked at me with raised eyebrows, but didn't make a comment. I made my way over to my seat on his left, and the second my ass hit the chair, he called the meeting to order. I noticed all of our patched members were present, and one Prospect. Killian.

"I'm sure word has spread that our VP claimed a woman and kid," Cinder said. "We're not putting it to a vote. They're his and if anyone at this table wants to say otherwise, I'll have someone on standby to clean up the blood."

There were a few snickers around the table.

"It seems his woman, Clarity, has come with a bit of trouble on her heels. I had a few people picked up this morning for questioning based off facts that Shade dug up on his computer. The boy, Caleb, was left in the care of a neighbor and it seems he was abused," Cinder said.

My gut clenched and I wondered what Shade had discovered. He hadn't gotten back to me, but whatever he'd found, he must have turned the info over to Cinder. I looked down the table where he was sitting. He glanced at me, but didn't give anything away. Something told me that I was going to hear some shit I wouldn't be able to forget.

"The neighbor, Mary Hurst, had a boyfriend who was into some bad shit," Cinder said. "She didn't protect the kids in her care, which makes her just as guilty. When we picked her up, she wasn't even remorseful over what happened, just begged for her worthless life. Didn't think of her kids once."

"Where is she?" I asked.

"In a building out back, along with her boyfriend. Danny Simmons is wanted in several states for child pornography. Shade hacked the man's files. I know you don't want to see that shit, Scratch, but if you'll provide the club with a picture of Caleb, we'll go through every damn bit of that crap and make sure he's not in there. From what we can tell, the clips seem to go back further than when Caleb would have been anywhere near the asshole, but we want to make sure."

I'd done some fucked-up shit in my lifetime, but the thought of child pornography made me want to puke. Part of me wanted to get up and walk out, not listen to another word, but I needed to know just how bad it had been. What had Caleb been exposed to while he was with that woman? And more importantly, how did I keep this shit from Clarity? If my kitten thought for a second she'd put her child in that situation, I worried what she might do. I knew she'd blame herself, that it would possibly even break her.

"I'll take a picture when I get home," I said.

"Until we know more, we're going to hold on to Mary and Danny. If Caleb is in any of those files, we'll let you take whatever justice you want. Otherwise, the club will handle it. The cops aren't going to dig too deep when a child pornographer shows up dead in a ditch," Cinder said.

"And Clarity's dad?" I asked. "Or Caleb's father?"

"That man was never a father to the boy. Caleb's sperm donor is dead," Shade said. "Overdose a year ago. And I checked. He was never listed on Caleb's birth certificate. Your woman put *father unknown*."

I nodded.

"As for Clarity's dad, he's a piece of work. Just like she said, he remarried after her mom died and they have several kids. He's never so much as looked for her after she ran away. Their lives carried on as usual. I can't find any illegal dealings surrounding her family, they're just assholes," Shade said.

"Leave them be," I said. "But if he ever comes knocking, I'll be having a conversation with him that might require a little cleanup."

"No one would fault you for that," Cinder said.

Shade cleared his throat. "There's one other thing that you may or may not know."

"What's that?" I asked.

"Clarity's birthday is tomorrow. But there's something I found when I was digging through her background." He lifted a hand before I could say anything. "I only checked to see if there were any skeletons that could bite the club in the ass. Didn't find anything quite like that, but I did discover a hidden paper trail. And it's a bit... strange."

"What kind of hidden trail?"

"She's not turning nineteen tomorrow," Shade said.

"Not turning..." My stomach felt like it might revolt. "Then how old will she be? Do I need to worry about the cops showing up on my doorstep? Christ! I knew she looked too fucking young."

"Quite the contrary. Clarity's daddy isn't really her daddy. Her mom had her before she even met Heath Davis. For whatever reason, they had a document forged that made Clarity younger than she really is and claimed Heath as her birth father. I'm still looking into her real daddy to see what's going on there," Shade said.

"Tell him," Cinder said. "All of it."

"Her real name is Clarity Jane Parkhurst, daughter of Tamara Clarke and Scott Parkhurst. Her momma was married to Scott Parkhurst a year before Clarity was born, and then her daddy disappeared when Clarity was just a baby. From what little I've been able to find on Scott Parkhurst, he was a philanthropist who met Tamara on a trip through Mexico, South America, Haiti, and Jamaica," Shade said.

"I don't understand. Why lie to her and forge new documents?" I asked.

"I'm looking into it," Shade said. "But the good news is that your girl just ages really fucking well. Probably helps that she's the size of a pixie. I bet she was a really tiny kid. She's going to be twenty-two tomorrow, not nineteen. How the hell her mom ever convinced her that she was three years younger I don't know. None of this shit makes any sense."

"But if Heath wasn't really her daddy, then that would explain why he didn't seem to give a shit about her," I said. "Maybe knowing that will give her closure, even if it does bring up some other questions."

"There are quite a few pictures of Tamara and Scott in the early part of their marriage. I printed them off," Shade said, sliding a folder down the table to me.

I flipped it open, but what I saw made me freeze. I stared at the woman in the picture, and there was no doubt she was related to Clarity, but it wasn't the woman in the picture Clarity had shown me. They looked similar enough, maybe sisters? And the man... Clarity definitely had his eyes, and his hair was nearly white blonde just like Caleb's. They were definitely related. But why was this woman different from the one Clarity thought was her mother?

What the fucking hell was going on?

"Find out everything you can on Tamara's family, and then find out what happened to Tamara." I looked up at Shade. "Because this woman isn't who raised Clarity."

I didn't know how Clarity was going to handle this information, or if I should even tell her until I knew more.

She'd have questions I wouldn't be able to answer, and the last thing I wanted to do was stress her out. The least I could do was tell her that Caleb's father wasn't going to be an issue. The pornography bit… I was keeping that to myself for now too. If Caleb hadn't been exposed, then there was no sense in torturing Clarity with the knowledge her son could have been in that sort of danger.

I ran a hand down my face and tried to focus as the club discussed other business, but my mind was on the woman and boy at my house. I wanted to protect them from all the horrid things in the world, but I knew that wasn't possible. Not without placing them inside a bubble, and neither of them would appreciate that. Once I knew all the facts, I'd sit down with Clarity and we'd figure everything out. Until then, I just had to hope that Shade would work fast, and that he didn't dig up anything too horrible.

Chapter Seven

Clarity

Seamus hadn't talked much since Scratch had left. Mostly, he prowled around the house, peeking out the windows and tensing at every sound. Who the hell did he think was going to come after us? I was a homeless woman with a family who didn't give a shit, and I didn't have so much as one friend in the world. I hadn't exactly made a bunch of enemies during my short life. Of course, I didn't know anything about the Devil's Boneyard except the rumors around town. For all I knew, the club was into something bad and Seamus had a right to be overly cautious.

I'd gone upstairs to change, but I still wasn't quite comfortable around the Prospect. He didn't look at me inappropriately or make me feel unwelcome, but there was a predatory air about him. I'd gotten a quick look at some ink on his bicep that made me think he'd been in the military. I wondered how he'd gone from serving his country to being part of a motorcycle club, but not enough to ask.

Caleb was still asleep upstairs. I'd checked on him a few times, but he must have been completely exhausted. His chest rose and fell evenly so I left him rest as long as he wanted. He'd likely be hell to get to bed later tonight, but it had been a long time since he'd felt safe. I'd done my best, but he couldn't hide the fear I'd sometimes caught in his eyes while we were on the street.

"You aren't worried about people thinking you're too young for our VP?" Seamus asked out of nowhere. He wasn't looking at me, though. He was still watching out the window.

"He's said several times he's too old for me, but no one has ever made me feel so safe, or cared for. Not since my mother died. If other people have a problem with our age difference, that's on them."

He nodded, but there was a tenseness in his shoulders and back.

"Someone special out there you like who is maybe younger than you?" I asked.

He snorted.

Interesting. I moved a little closer. "Maybe she likes you too?"

He finally looked at me. "She's a kid. A sixteen-year-old kid and I don't… it's not like that. But there's something about her. She has this magnetic personality and when you look into her eyes, it's like…"

"Like you're free falling?" I asked.

He nodded.

"You going to wait for her to grow up?" I asked.

"Maybe. It's complicated. Her dad is a Dixie Reaper. Pretty sure he'd kick my ass for dating his daughter even if she was legal." He shook his head. "Best if I stick with women my age, or at least over the age of twenty-one."

"Do those women make you happy?" I asked.

"Happy enough," he muttered, and I knew he was damn well lying.

It was a slippery slope that he was on. Yes, the girl was underage, but he made it sound like he wasn't thinking of her sexually. I wondered if he felt drawn to her like I did with Scratch. More a sense of rightness, like two puzzle pieces that fit together perfectly. I truly did believe in soul mates and I thought maybe Seamus had met his, even if fate was a cruel bitch and the girl was too young for him. For now, anyway. She'd grow up in a few more years, and I couldn't wait to see what happened between them.

"You know, I really do believe that there's someone special out there for each of us, someone we're destined to find. Maybe she's yours and you just have to be patient while she grows up. There's thirty-two years between me and Scratch. Do you have a problem with that?"

"No," he said quickly.

"Are you saying that so Scratch won't kick your ass? Or because you really mean it?" I asked.

"Can it be both?"

I bit my lip so I wouldn't laugh. "You're at least twenty years younger than him. Don't think you can take him?"

"No way in hell. He's the boogeyman. Maybe he's a cuddly teddy bear with you, the rest of us? None of us want to meet him in a dark alley, unless we're on the same side."

I could kind of see that. I didn't know anything about Scratch's background, but when he said he'd take care of us, protect us, I knew he'd do whatever it took. If someone told me the man had left a trail of bodies in his wake, it wouldn't surprise me. Wouldn't bother me either, since those people were likely bad men and women.

"He's a good guy," Seamus said. "The kind you want to have your back in a bad situation."

"He's the kindest man I've ever met," I said. "No one's ever treated me or Caleb the way he does. He makes me feel special, and he gives me hope for the future."

Seamus smiled faintly.

I heard the rumble before the bike pulled up out front. Seamus peered out the window again, then gave me a wink.

"Looks like your man is home."

Butterflies rioted in my stomach and I went to the front door, pulling it open just as Scratch stepped up onto the porch. There were shadows in his eyes, but he pulled me against his chest and held me tight. I clung to him, breathing in his scent.

"Hey, kitten. Miss me?"

"Yes." I looked up at him. "Caleb is still asleep."

He nodded, then looked over my head. "Seamus, you can head out. Stop by the clubhouse and see if anyone needs help, then you're free until someone calls."

"Yes, sir," Seamus said as he brushed past us and down to his bike parked in the driveway.

After Seamus had pulled down the driveway, Scratch led me into the house, then locked the door behind us. He cupped my face with both of his hands and leaned down to kiss me softly. It surprised me every time such a big, gruff man was tender and sweet. It wasn't something I was used to, but I liked it.

"Caleb is a pretty sound sleeper," I said.

He arched an eyebrow, a smirk playing along his lips. "Is that right?"

I nodded.

"Is there something in particular you'd like to do while he's asleep? Clean the kitchen? Play a board game?"

"Not unless it's Twister, and we're in the bedroom."

Scratch burst out laughing, then led me up the stairs and down the hall to our room. I hadn't moved my things in yet, but I knew he'd want me to. Right now, my new things were all still in the guest room. He shut the door and twisted the lock, then turned to face me with a predatory gleam in his eyes. I licked my lips as he shrugged out of his cut and tossed it onto the dresser. The hem of his shirt lifted and he pulled it over his head, letting it fall to the floor. Scratch stalked closer and I backed toward the bed.

"Think you can handle me, kitten? All of me? No holding back, just the two of us, and my cock as deep and hard as you can take it?"

My knees trembled and my panties grew damp. Oh yeah, I wanted that. I felt my nipples harden, and he prowled even closer. He settled his hands at my waist and tugged on my shirt. In a matter of seconds, he had me completely naked and at his mercy. Scratch dropped to his knees, then gave me a gentle shove so that I sprawled across the foot of the bed. He pressed his palms to the insides of my thighs and spread me wide open.

"So pretty," he murmured, running a finger down the lips of my pussy. He held me open with his fingers and brushed my clit with his thumb. My body trembled and I fought to hold still. "Does my kitten want me to make her feel good?"

"Yes. Please, Damon. I need you."

"You come for me, then I'll fill this pretty pussy with my cock."

His beard tickled my thighs as he rubbed his face against one leg and then the other. He kept rubbing my clit, his gaze dark and hungry as he stared at my pussy. I was close to coming, but couldn't quite get there. Lifting my hips, I wanted more but wasn't brave enough to ask.

He sank two fingers inside me and I couldn't hold back my cries of pleasure. I nearly came off the bed when I felt his tongue swipe across my clit, then he was sucking it into his mouth as his fingers worked my pussy. Waves of ecstasy rolled over me, making my thighs shake and my heart race. I fisted the bedsheets and nearly sobbed, I wanted to come so badly.

"Damon, I… please…"

He lashed my clit with his tongue and drove his fingers into my pussy harder. I saw stars as I came so hard it left me breathless. I could hear my heart thundering in my ears and I blinked trying to clear my vision. Damon kissed his way up my body, pausing to suck and bite my nipples. Not hard enough to hurt, but it made my pussy clench and ache for more.

"You have on too many clothes," I said.

He smiled and pulled away, then kicked off his boots and stripped out of his jeans and boxer briefs. I locked my gaze on him as he came around the bed, but when he reached for the bedside table drawer, I reached out and stopped him.

"The last one broke," I reminded him.

He stared down at me a moment, then pulled the drawer open anyway. I wanted to scream in frustration. Didn't he understand that I wanted to feel him inside me without barriers? He'd already admitted he would love a baby if we had one, and I knew I would too. If we were together, the kind that lasted forever, then did it really matter if we used a condom? I could see the determination in his eyes, though.

He rolled the latex down his cock and crooked his finger at me. I crawled to him, placing my hands on his chest and leaning up for a kiss. He tangled his fingers in my hair as he kissed me long and deep, his tongue stroking mine. When he pulled away, he gripped my waist and flipped me onto my belly. I squealed in surprise and looked at him over my shoulder. The sexiest smirk I'd ever seen was on his face, and he looked like he was ready to devour me.

I got my knees up under me, then he spread my thighs wide. With his hands holding my hips tight, I felt him slowly sink into me, his cock stretching me in the most delicious way. I pressed my forehead to the bed and nearly moaned with how damn good it felt. He started to stroke in and out of me, and fuck if it didn't feel like he went a little deeper each time!

I clenched on his cock and I heard him curse.

"Fuck, kitten! You're going to make me come if you keep doing that."

"Please, Damon. Harder. Take me harder."

He growled softly and gave me exactly what I'd asked for. Our bodies slapped together as he pounded into me. I felt his cock swell and I knew he was close. I slid my hand down between my legs and rubbed my clit.

"That's it, baby. Make yourself come," he said.

No matter how fast or slow I rubbed, I wasn't getting any closer and it was leaving me frustrated. I whined and pulled my hand away.

"I'll get you there, kitten," he said.

His fingers spread my pussy open and he teased and tormented my clit as he thrust into me hard and deep. When he pinched down, I screamed out my release, feeling like I was flying. He kept toying with me, even as he came. His cock jerked inside me and he soon had me coming again. Damon's body slumped over my back, but he held most of his weight off me.

I felt his lips trail across my shoulders, and then he was pulling away and slipping out of my body. I collapsed onto the bed and watched him through blurry eyes as he went into the bathroom. When he came back out, he was rubbing his hand down his face and looked unsettled.

"I think that punk ass Prospect gave me a faulty box of condoms," he said.

"Did that one break too?"

"Yep. In over thirty years of fucking, I've never had one break. Until you. So either you have a magic pussy that destroys condoms, or there's something wrong with that box."

"Or maybe it's the universe telling us that we don't need condoms," I said.

He snorted, then crawled into bed with me. He wrapped an arm around my waist and kissed my forehead. I loved the way he smelled and I pressed my nose against him, breathing him in.

"All right, kitten. We'll do this your way. No more condoms. If you end up pregnant, then we'll just get a nursery set up and prepare Caleb for being a big brother." He sighed. "I don't like denying you something you really want, and I have to admit that the thought of taking you bare is pretty fucking tempting."

"I think Caleb would be a good big brother," I said.

"There are some things we'll need to discuss in the upcoming days, but I want all the facts first. But one thing I found out today is that it's your birthday tomorrow. Why didn't you say something?" he asked.

I rubbed my face against his chest. "Didn't seem important. I haven't celebrated a birthday in a really long time."

"Well, we're going to celebrate this one. We'll have a small party at the clubhouse. You can meet my brothers and Jackal's wife, Josie. They have a daughter about Caleb's age. Doesn't talk much, but she's a sweetheart."

"Wife? Not his old lady?" I asked.

"She's both."

"Oh." I thought that over for a minute. When he'd talked about making me his old lady, I'd thought maybe bikers didn't get married. Now that I knew one of them was, I had to wonder if maybe Scratch just didn't believe in marriage. Or maybe he just didn't want that with me.

My stomach cramped at the thought and I hoped he didn't sense my agitation. If all he was willing to give me was status as his old lady, then I'd take it and be happy. I'd try to bury my fear that him not wanting to marry me meant he didn't really want me forever. The little devil on my shoulder wasn't making it easy to ignore that feeling though. I didn't want to fall for him, for Caleb to love him, and then have Scratch ask us to leave one day. I'd rather live back out on the streets than put either of us through that kind of heartache.

"We should probably rinse off in the shower, get dressed, and check on Caleb," he said. "If he sleeps all day, we'll all be up into the wee hours of the morning."

"I'll check on him if you want to go ahead and shower," I said, moving to rise from the bed, but he wrapped his fingers around my wrist and held me still.

"Kitten, what's wrong?"

"Nothing." I couldn't bring myself to look him in the eye, though.

He pulled on me until I was lying next to him again.

"Don't lie to me," he said, his voice stern and deeper than usual. "Never fucking lie. About anything."

I swallowed hard and felt my eyes sting with unshed tears. I slowly nodded, but didn't know how to tell him what I was feeling. That I was scared he'd change his mind and ask us to leave one day. I knew a marriage license didn't mean forever would really happen, but it would make me feel more secure.

"Why are you trying to put distance between us?" he asked.

My throat grew tight and I didn't think I could answer without crying.

"Look at me, Clarity."

I took a shuddering breath and looked up, our gazes locking. I couldn't hold back the tears and they silently slipped down my cheeks. I wasn't this person, this weak woman who cried so easily. But as he stared at me, it felt like the wall I'd put up around my heart was cracking. The blue of his eyes darkened and the harsh lines of his face softened. Scratch cupped my cheek and wiped away my tears.

"Kitten, talk to me."

"I'm scared," I admitted.

"About what? The party? We don't have to have one, but I thought it would give you a chance to meet everyone."

"No. Not the party. I'm… I'm scared that you'll change your mind."

"Change my mind?" he asked.

"What if you decide not to keep me? What if you wake up one day and want us to leave?" I asked softly.

"Kitten, what made you think I'd ever want to get rid of you?" he asked.

"You said that Josie was Jackal's wife and old lady. I just thought…" I couldn't finish saying it.

"You thought because I hadn't asked you to marry me that I wasn't as serious about keeping you?" he asked.

I shrugged.

Scratch sighed and pressed another kiss to my forehead. "Kitten, I'm an old man and I'm set in my ways. I honestly never thought about getting married, or having more kids. If you want a ring and a piece of paper that says you're mine, then we'll talk about it."

"You're not old," I mumbled.

He chuckled and hugged me tight. "Only you don't seem to think so."

"I'm sorry I got emotional."

"Kitten, you've been through hell, and you've fought long and hard on your own. You were bound to break down sooner or later."

"We should go shower and then check on Caleb. You were right. He shouldn't be allowed to sleep all day. He needs to get into a routine now that we're not sleeping in doorways."

"I'll start the shower. Just lie here and relax a moment, give the water some time to heat up."

I watched as he walked into the bathroom, and a few minutes after I heard the shower running, I followed him. It hadn't escaped my notice that he'd said he'd give me a ring if that's what I wanted, but he hadn't said it was what he wanted. If he didn't really want to get married, then I wasn't going to beg him to do it. Maybe one day he'd want the same thing I did, but until then, I'd be content with what he was willing to give me.

Chapter Eight

Scratch

Caleb had played in the living room for most of the day, enjoying the few toys we had for him. The way his eyes lit up whenever he saw a train on TV, I knew that would be his next present. I'd downloaded a shopping app on my phone and had already started pricing them, along with a few other things I thought he'd like. When I finished browsing through the toys, I picked out a few things for Clarity and added them to my cart with overnight shipping. With some luck, they would arrive before her party. If we had one.

Clarity was in the floor with Caleb, pushing cars around, when my phone chimed with a message. I swiped the screen and frowned when I saw it was from Shade. I glanced at Clarity, but she wasn't paying me any attention, which was a good thing at the moment.

we need to talk
can it wait?
you'll want to see this. My house.

I closed out the messages and watched Clarity and Caleb for a moment. They both seemed content, and I didn't want to worry them, but if Shade said it was important, then I needed to go. I stood up and Clarity gave me a slight smile.

"I'll be back soon," I said. "We'll go out for dinner tonight since we didn't make it to the store."

"Be careful," she said.

I nodded, then went out to my bike. Shade lived on the other end of town, but the traffic was light and I made it in fifteen minutes. I knocked on his door, then turned the knob. It twisted easily and I pushed the door open, stepping inside.

"Shade!" I called out.

"Down the hall."

I went down to what he called his war room, and looked at the bank of monitors. There was a file folder on the edge of his desk and he picked it up and handed it to me. I hesitated only a moment before opening it and reading the contents. I blinked a few times and re-read the documents, certain that I was misunderstanding.

"You're not reading it wrong," Shade said. "Your girl was hidden to keep her safe. The mom she knew was really her aunt, her mother's half-sister. And her dad had a lot of enemies. He wasn't a bad guy, quite the opposite. Donated to charities, gave his time to mission projects, and would have given the shirt off his back to a homeless man on the street."

"So what kind of trouble was he in?" I asked.

"Parkhurst inherited a company from his father. It's what helped fund his philanthropy, but the board wasn't happy with the way things were being handled. I found some transactions between one of the board members and a hit man. It looks like Parkhurst was murdered, and Tamara was with him when it happened."

"So the sister took off with Clarity in hopes of keeping her alive," I said.

"Right. The original birth certificate is in there, along with Scott Parkhurst's will. In the event of his death, all his possessions were to go to his only daughter, his heir."

"Are you saying Clarity is well-off?"

Shade snorted. "Yeah, if you consider half a billion dollars as well-off. Once we prove she's the heir of the Parkhurst fortune, she'll have access to all that money. Downside is that it's been so long, the family home was sold and the business was run into the ground by corrupt board members. The money would likely be gone too, except Parkhurst had it well-hidden. Only his lawyer knows where it's located, and it looks like no one has touched the account."

"Half a billion?" I asked. What the fuck would she need me for once she had all that money? Right now, I offered her comfort and shelter, but she could buy the entire damn town several times over with all that money.

"A DNA test would be required. She should consider herself lucky. I don't believe the aunt ever told Heath Davis about the money, or he likely would have found a way to force Clarity into signing it over. If he didn't do something worse. From what I can tell, the aunt tried to cover her tracks. Only a hacker would have been able to find her, so the lawyer was unable to find Clarity. I'm a little surprised he didn't hire someone, unless he didn't feel it was safe."

"I'll take this home and show it to her." I stared at the file, wondering if the family I thought I'd gained was about to walk out the front door. Now I understood how Clarity felt earlier when she'd been afraid I'd kick her out, and I felt like a shit for the way I'd handled it. I didn't know how she'd gotten under my skin so fucking fast, but now that I had her in my bed and had claimed them both as mine, I didn't want them to leave.

"There's something else," Shade said. "I looked into the situation with the boy a bit more. I can't guarantee he didn't see what was happening, but he wasn't in the videos. I asked Seamus to come take a look since he'd seen him. Doesn't mean they didn't abuse him in some other way, though."

I nodded. "Or whatever he saw could have traumatized him, but it's the fact he thought he'd be in trouble for getting food that bothers me. Guess there's only one way to find out for sure what happened."

"You're going to pay them a visit?"

"Yep. Looks like I'm about to get dirty, and find out exactly what Clarity can handle. Maybe this inheritance is a good thing. She might see me covered in blood and take off."

Shade stared at me a moment. "You really think she wants to leave you? Even if she did inherit a shit ton of money? I may not have met her, but Seamus said that woman thinks you hung the moon."

"She's just grateful I'm taking care of her."

Shade arched a brow but didn't say another word. When he turned back to his computers, I knew that was all I would get from him. I took the file out to my bike and stuck it in a saddlebag, then I drove to the compound. The bitch who had been babysitting Caleb, and her fucked-up boyfriend, were still being held in a building out back.

Killian was guarding the building and gave me a nod as I approached. I pulled off my cut and handed it to him as I passed by and went inside. My clothes could be burned if necessary, but I didn't want my cut getting fucked-up. The building smelled like piss and shit, which meant they hadn't been released from their bonds for any reason. I smiled grimly as I approached the two figures hanging from chains in the center of the building. There was a drain directly below them for easy cleanup. I pulled out my knife and tried not to laugh as the woman started thrashing and screaming against her gag. Served the bitch right to be afraid. Anyone who allowed children to be harmed didn't deserve to fucking live.

I cut the gag away, and she started blubbering about how she hadn't done anything, it was all a mistake. Her boyfriend knew the score, though, and just eyed me, like he knew the end was coming. Man like that had to know his sins would catch up to him sooner or later. It just wouldn't be a prison cell he'd be living in, but a hole in the ground when I sent his black soul straight to hell.

I backhanded the woman. "Shut up!"

She whimpered and tears ran down her cheeks. Didn't fucking move me, not knowing she'd hurt Caleb either directly or by standing back and letting something happen to him. Either way, she would be joining her boyfriend in the fires of hell soon enough. I pressed the tip of my blade against her throat and her eyes went so wide all I saw were the whites of them. "I'm going to ask you once, and only once. What the fuck did you do to Caleb?" I asked.

"C-Caleb? I don't k-know a Caleb," she stuttered.

I pressed the blade a little harder and watched as blood started to run down her neck. Gripping her hair tight, I made sure she couldn't move away from the pain. "Let's try this again, before I lose my patience. You used to babysit Caleb while Clarity went to work. What the fuck did you do to him?"

She pissed herself and I knew I was right. She'd hurt the boy in some way, or allowed her boyfriend to do it.

"Why is that kid afraid to reach for food? Why doesn't he talk?" I asked.

"He was a greedy little bastard," she said. "I had to stop him from eating everything in my house. That's all."

I pushed the knife in a little more. "And how did you do that?"

The man next to her was trying to talk through his gag so I released the woman and moved over to him. If he wanted to talk, I'd let him. Wouldn't change his fate any. I cut off his gag and his hard eyes stared me down. "You obviously have something to fucking say, so say it." I waved my knife in front of his face. "Or do you need some encouragement?"

"She hit him, whenever he would try to get some food. And don't listen to her skank ass. She wouldn't even let him have one meal, much less go back for more."

My gaze slid to the woman, who had paled at least three shades. I looked back at the man and waited to see what else he had to say.

"She got off on it, you know. Watching me strip those kids naked and film them. Bitch enjoyed every second of it, got her all hot and bothered. The kid saw it all."

"Caleb wasn't in your videos," I said, my voice deceptively soft. "Why not?"

"None of my clients wanted a kid with white-blond hair. Guess he got lucky."

I leaned in close. "Just so there's no misunderstanding, you aren't leaving this building while you're still breathing. Can't let a sick, twisted fuck like you loose on the world, now can I?"

He smiled and it sent a chill down my spine.

"You give that sweet momma of his a kiss from me. I had plans for her, before she vanished. Bet she has the sweetest screams."

I had to fight for control. I knew what he was doing, trying to egg me on and get me to end his life quickly, but I wasn't going to fall for it. The man had tortured and abused kids, and I wasn't about to let him off the easy way. I backed up and faced the woman again. The fight had drained out of her and she stared at me with nearly vacant eyes. Yeah, bitch knew her time was up, but she didn't realize that I could make it last a while. I knew what my club called me. The Boogeyman. They weren't far off. Only Cinder knew the truth about my background, and he'd never asked for the details, and I knew he never would. Not unless my past came knocking at the clubhouse door.

I took my time over the next hour, inflicting as much pain on the bitch as I could and still keep her alive. I'd learned a few torture methods over the years and could get a person right to the edge of death, then back, and start over again. I toyed with her, leaving her a bloody, whimpering mess as I sliced at her clothes and skin, whispered dark taunts in her ears. My club didn't believe in harming women or children, but this bitch was barely human in my opinion. Carving her up and seeing the fear in her eyes didn't bother me in the slightest.

When I knew she'd had as much as she could handle and remain breathing, I stepped back and turned to the boyfriend. As much as I wanted to get a pound of his flesh, exact some revenge, I decided to let the club handle him. I knew some of them had been abused as kids, even sexually abused, and I figured they'd have fun with this one. Make him scream and beg, and I knew it would take a lot to make that happen. The guy was completely dead inside, evil to the core.

"My brothers will have their fun with you." I looked at the woman again. "And we're not done with you just yet."

She pissed herself again and I chuckled as I wiped my knife off on my shirt and backed away. It was already covered in her blood, so what was a little more? I pulled it over my head and tossed it into a metal barrel, knowing it would need to be burned later. Using the utility sink on the far wall, I cleaned myself up to get her likely tainted blood off my skin and out of my hair, then I left the building, knowing I'd never see either of them breathing again.

Killian handed my cut back to me, and Cinder stood with his arms folded, feet braced a shoulder's width apart. He tossed a black tee to me and I pulled it on, then shrugged on my cut. Cinder looked from me to the building, then back again. "They still alive?" he asked.

"Yep. I'd let the woman rest a bit before you work her over anymore. Otherwise, she won't last long. Found out what I needed to know, and now I'm going home."

Cinder nodded. "Take care of that woman and kid, we'll handle this shit. Shade called. I know what you found out, but don't go in half-cocked and determined you're going to lose her. I think that woman might surprise you."

"Her name is Clarity, not 'that woman,'" I said.

Cinder cracked a smile. "Clarity might surprise you. I know you think she's with you because she has security with you, money… but I don't think that's it."

"Let me guess. Seamus was running his fucking mouth to you, too."

"He's told everyone that woman -- Clarity -- is head over heels in love with you, and you're too damn stupid or blind to see it. Maybe you need to get your eyes checked, what with your advanced years and all."

I flipped him off. "Younger than you, asshole."

"Yeah, but I'm wiser. So listen the fuck up before you screw everything the hell up and lose something precious. It's obvious to all of us that you feel something for her and that kid, so man the fuck up and tell her how you feel."

"Too soon to feel anything."

"Bullshit! When you meet the right woman, you just know. It's a deep down, gut-clenching reaction. If she can walk away and you won't give a shit, then let her go. But if you're going to miss her and be a miserable fucking bastard, then convince her to stay."

Killian cleared his throat.

"Something to add?" I asked.

"Sometimes we're only given one great love," he said. "Don't lose yours because you can't admit you want to keep her. Some of us never had a chance to hold onto the woman we loved."

That was more than I'd ever heard the man speak about his past. There were shadows in his eyes, something we'd all noticed from the beginning, but now I understood a little more about what put them there. One day he'd tell us the entire story. "Fine. I'll go home and be a pansy ass and tell her how I feel," I said. "And when this all blows up in my face, I'm coming after you fuckers."

Cinder slapped me on the back. "It will all work out the way it's supposed to. And just because I'm such a nice guy, I'm going to let you in on a little secret."

"What?" I asked.

"Your daughter is at your house." He smirked. "Better hurry home before she runs off your woman and kid. The money won't matter much then."

I started cursing and ran for my bike, my tires spitting gravel as I revved the engine and took off. Why the fucking hell hadn't someone told me that sooner? Shit. If Darian was pissed and trying to protect her papa, there was no telling what the fuck she'd say or do. I broke every traffic law between the compound and my house, burning rubber as I came to a screeching halt in the driveway. I'd barely cleared my bike before the front door opened and Bull stepped out onto the porch.

"What the fucking hell!" I demanded as I stomped up the steps. "No warning what-the-fuck-so-ever?"

He shrugged. "You know how Darian can get, especially since she's hormonal as shit right now."

That made me pause. "You're making me a grandpa again?"

"Yep, and it's been a roller-coaster ride. One minute she's screaming and threatening to cut off my balls and the next she's sobbing and saying she's a horrible wife."

Fuck my life.

I went inside and listened to see just how far off the rails my delightful daughter was, but silence greeted me. And that scared me far fucking more. I peered into the living room and saw Caleb and Foster playing in front of the TV, and Darian and Clarity seemed to be having a civilized conversation. I cleared my throat and made my presence known, and Darian flew off the couch and into my arms.

"Daddy!"

"Hey, baby girl. A little notice next time would be nice."

"If I'd given you notice, then you might have run off with Clarity," she said.

"You're not wrong." I glanced at my woman and noticed that she seemed calm and perfectly fine. Maybe I'd been worried for no reason. Until I noticed the only breakable items in the living room were missing and a broom was leaning against the wall. I looked at Darian and she just smiled up at me.

Bull squeezed my shoulder. "I hope you weren't fond of the vase in the corner, or the two pictures frames you had in here, or the candy dish. They're in the kitchen trash."

"Fucking hell," I muttered. I looked at Clarity again, but she calmly stared back at me. "You okay, kitten?"

She nodded and the tension inside me loosened a little.

If she could handle Darian, then maybe she could handle anything. Including finding out she's rich beyond her wildest dreams, and that her boy had seen some shit that was going to require some trips to a therapist. It was a reminder that she was a strong woman, someone worthy of standing by my side. And fuck if I was going to let her go.

Chapter Nine

Clarity

Meeting Darian had been a bit... well, honestly, she'd scared the shit out of me. She'd just barged inside, pushing her way past me, and started screaming about how I was taking advantage of her dad. When I'd tried to explain things to her, the breakables had started flying, and I was grateful to her husband for keeping the kids out of the way. It hadn't taken long for her rage to turn into tears, and that's when I'd noticed her slightly rounded stomach and put a few things together. Like the fact Darian was a hormonal bitch because she was pregnant, and I was guessing that Scratch didn't know yet.

He didn't look convinced when I said I was fine, but he hadn't exactly let go of his daughter and come to me either. He rubbed her back and hugged her before greeting his grandson. When he came toward me, he took my hand and gave it a squeeze. I was about to say something with stray droplets of blood along the leg of his jeans caught my eye.

"Trouble while you were out?" I asked, staring at the stains.

"Shit. I didn't realize it got on my pants."

"Go shower and change. I'll keep everyone entertained," I said.

He nodded, pressed a kiss to my cheek, then left the room. Darian was gaping at me and Bull merely gave me an assessing look.

"What?" I asked.

"He comes in with blood on him and you just calmly tell him to shower and change?" she asked. "You aren't concerned about where it came from or if he might have killed someone?"

"If he did, I'm sure they deserved it," I said. "And since I didn't see any cuts on him, I'm assuming it's someone else's so I'm not too worried about him."

Bull smiled faintly. "I think you're just what he needs."

Darian elbowed him in the ribs. "Shut it. He's with a woman even younger than me."

Bull cleared his throat and gave her a pointed look. Darian's cheeks flushed.

"Right," she said. "And I'm younger than Ridley."

"Who's Ridley?" I asked.

"My daughter," Bull said. "I have two granddaughters who are older than my son, and Darian is a few years younger than my daughter. So if anyone shouldn't be throwing stones at you and Scratch, it's Darian. She's been in your position."

"You're right," she sighed. "You couldn't have started off with that before I lost my shit earlier?"

"Would it have done any good? You didn't seem to be in a reasonable mood," he said.

Darian snorted, then came and sat back down next to me. She held out her hand and I gripped it.

"Sorry. Truce?" she asked. "I guess I feel a little protective of my dad. I didn't even get to meet him until a few years ago, but we've gotten really close."

"I understand." Well, sort of. I couldn't care less if someone set my dad on fire, but I would do anything to protect Caleb, or Damon for that matter.

"So you and my dad," Darian said. "You aren't wearing a property cut, but you said he'd claimed you."

"Property cut?"

She turned so I could see the back of the cut she was wearing, and the stitching that said *Property of Bull -- Dixie Reapers*. Was I supposed to wear something like that? Scratch hadn't mentioned it to me, but we hadn't really had a lot of time either. We were still bonding, and there was the shit from my past to consider. Maybe he just hadn't gotten around to it yet.

"Have you met Josie?" she asked. "Her brother is a Dixie Reaper, but she's married to a Devil so she lives here now."

"No. Scratch has mentioned her before, but we haven't had a chance to meet. There are some things that have needed our attention."

"I knew it," she muttered. "A fucking damsel in distress. Figures. It seems to be every biker's kryptonite."

"She's not a fucking damsel in distress," Scratch said from the doorway, his wet hair in a ponytail. "That woman has been through hell and she's still standing, still fighting. Never met anyone stronger."

"So she doesn't need you?" Darian pressed. "Maybe need your money?"

I felt the blood drain from my face.

"Nope," he said. "She's a fucking heiress so the last thing she needs is the paltry amount in my accounts."

"Paltry?" Darian asked. "You have like half a million in the bank, Daddy. That's not paltry."

"Heiress?" I asked.

"We'll talk later," Scratch said. "Found out some things about your dad. Your real dad."

My real dad? That meant… Heath wasn't my father? My mom had lied to me? They both had? My mind was spinning and Scratch came over and picked me up, settling me across his lap as he sat in his recliner.

"There's some stuff we need to go over, things Shade found, but right now we're just going to have a family visit, okay? I'll answer all your questions later."

"We were hoping to stay here," Darian said.

"There's a perfectly fine hotel five minutes from here," Scratch said.

Darian's mouth dropped open. "I can't stay in my dad's house?"

"Not a good time, baby girl. You'd have known that if you bothered to call before you decided to come save me from this nefarious woman. You can tell she's a killer and I might not get out alive."

I bit my lip and choked back my laughter.

"Told you he was fine," Bull said. "Your hormones are going to get you into trouble."

She narrowed her eyes on her husband. "You mean my out-of-control hormones because *you* knocked me up? I'm pregnant, not irrational."

"Same difference," Bull muttered.

I was glad there weren't any more breakable items in the living room or I had a feeling she'd have launched a few at her husband's head. It would have been funny as hell to witness, but I didn't want to be searching for microscopic pieces of glass over the next several months. It made me nervous that the kids were playing on the floor when there could be some stray pieces still down there.

"We're going to get checked in at the hotel," Bull said. "Then maybe we can all meet up for dinner somewhere. If you're all right with it, we'll stick around a day or two so Foster can play with his new friend."

"You mean his uncle," Darian said with her lips twisting. "If my dad is claiming them, that makes Caleb his uncle. That's fucked-up."

"You mean like grandkids having an uncle who's younger than them? At least Foster and Caleb are about the same age. Stop being bitchy and get your ass out to the truck, Darian."

She rolled her eyes but got up and walked over to him.

"Foster can stay here," I said. "If you're all right with that. They're playing and having a good time. No sense in upsetting either of them."

Bull smiled and nodded. "If you're sure you want to watch him, that's fine."

"I'll call you after I've had a chance to talk to Clarity about a few things," Scratch told him. "Thanks for giving us some space."

I heard the front door close a moment later and focused on Scratch. "What do you mean I'm an heiress and Heath wasn't my real dad?"

"I have the papers out in my saddlebags."

"Just tell me. I don't have to see a piece of paper."

He rubbed his beard. "Well, your mom wasn't your mom. The picture you have? It's your mom's half-sister. Your parents were Tamara and Scott Parkhurst. Your daddy was a philanthropist who was worth a lot of money, inherited a big company. And it put a target on his back. Your parents were killed so the board members would have control of the company, which they ran into the ground. But your daddy's accounts are still intact, and with a DNA test, we can prove you're the rightful heir to his fortune. You'll have half a billion dollars at your disposal."

I blinked. Then blinked again, trying to process what he was saying. His words were ricocheting around my brain and nothing was making any sense.

"I'm not Clarity Davis?"

"No, kitten. You're Clarity Parkhurst. I have a copy of your birth certificate, which brings up another matter. Your age."

My breath stalled in my lungs. Oh God. If my age was wrong, did that mean I was even younger than I'd thought? If I wasn't legal, I couldn't remain with Scratch, and he could get into serious trouble for being with me.

"Don't tell me I'm younger than eighteen."

He smiled a little. "No. You're actually turning twenty-two tomorrow. I have no idea how your aunt convinced you that you were three years younger. Maybe they brainwashed you somehow."

I frowned, something pulling at my memories. No, not brainwashed, but… There were flashes of a man with a deep, soothing voice. Having to sit in a chair. But it wasn't anything I could completely grasp.

"Hypnotized maybe?" I asked.

His eyebrows shot up and he seemed to think about it. "That's possible I guess. Don't really know much about hypnosis, but I've heard it can make people stop smoking or lose weight, so it's certainly possible they could trick your mind into thinking you're younger, especially if they did it when you were just a little kid."

"What does all of this mean?" I asked.

He ran a hand through his hair. "It means you don't have to stay with me. You're rich beyond your wildest dreams and don't need anyone to take care of you. Not that you ever really did need that. You'd have gotten yourself off the streets sooner or later. I don't doubt that for a moment."

My heart fell like a lead balloon. "You don't want me to stay?"

His gaze locked with mine. "Kitten, I want you here, but I know you were only with me out of necessity."

"That's what you think?" I asked softly. "That I only agreed to be with you because of what you could do for me? For Caleb?"

"You'd do anything for that boy."

"Never once did I give my body away to keep him fed or a roof over his head. Do you really think so little of me? Am I just a whore now?"

I struggled to stand up, but he banded his arms around me.

"I have never, and would never, call you a whore," he said, his voice deep and gruff. "Fuck, kitten! You're the closest damn thing I've ever met to an angel. You really think I would ever believe you're a whore?"

"It's how you made me feel," I said, my throat growing tight as I dropped my gaze from his. "I didn't sell myself to you for a roof over my head or for money or anything else. I gave myself to you because I wanted you. You're the only man I've ever wanted that way. You make me feel special, like I'm important. Or you did until just now."

He cupped my cheek and forced me to look up.

"I'm not good with words, or expressing my feelings to a woman. Never had to do it before. I want you here, both you and Caleb. You're my family, my woman and son. It's what I feel here," he said, pressing his hand to his chest. "I know you can do better than an old man like me, and that money can give you a new life. You could move anywhere in the world, find some young man who wants to marry you and have a ton of children."

"I don't want some young guy, Damon. I want you. Only you. You're my other half, the man who makes me feel whole. Age is just a number. Are you going to stop wanting me when I get older and get gray in my hair? If I gain weight and no longer look cute and young?"

"Of course not," he said.

"Then why would you think I can't fall in love with you just because you're older than me? And yes, I'm falling for you. I know it's only been a few days, and it seems completely insane, but I know that you're it for me. Please don't push me away. It would break my heart."

"I'm sorry, kitten," he said softly, running his fingers down my cheek. "I wasn't trying to push you away. The second I heard about that money, I got scared. I'm man enough to admit it. The thought of you walking out was the most painful thing I've ever faced. Even when I'd thought Darian had died as a baby, I hadn't hurt like that."

"Do you think you could ever love me, Damon? Maybe someday?"

He smiled faintly. "Clarity, you're really damn easy to love. You said you're falling for me, but, kitten, I'm falling for you too. And I already love Caleb like he's my own. I'd like to adopt him, make it official."

"You want to adopt Caleb?" I asked, my eyes stinging with unshed tears.

"Yeah, baby. I want to adopt him." He took a deep breath. "And if you'll have me, I'd like to marry you. Make us an official family. My club already sees us that way, but I want everyone to know you're mine, and Caleb is too."

"You don't have to marry me," I said, remembering how he'd reacted before. "I'll stay even if we don't get married."

"I want to, kitten. And it's not about the money. I'll have the club lawyer draw up a prenup so that I won't have access to your inheritance."

"Do you really think I care if you use that money? What if I want to give part of it to the club? You mentioned something about a new compound. I'd imagine a million dollars would go a long way toward making that happen. Maybe it would even allow you to keep the one you have and buy some extra space?"

"Kitten, my Pres isn't going to take money from you, not even for the benefit of the club. But it was generous of you to offer. We need to have your DNA tested first. Don't spend the money before you have it."

"I want to make a difference, not just go crazy spending money."

"We'll talk about it later. Right now, I need to know if you're going to marry me."

"Yes," I said, smiling widely. "I would love to marry you, Damon. And nothing would make me happier than for you to adopt Caleb. I think he'd like that too."

"Then I guess we'd better go ring shopping later. We'll stop on the way to dinner with Bull and Darian."

I glanced at the boys who were still playing and ignoring us. "Um, we only have one car seat. Exactly how are we getting both of them to the restaurant?"

He looked at the boys, then back at me. "I have no idea. I guess it wouldn't hurt to get a Prospect to pick up another seat. Now that Darian has been here once, I'm sure she'll show up again."

"Yeah, with two kids in tow. Maybe you were right about needing something bigger. You're not going to fit your grandson, another grandbaby, Caleb, and any other kids we have into the back seat of your truck."

His gaze dropped to my stomach and I felt his cock harden under me. My cheeks flushed, and if we hadn't had both boys to watch, I had no doubt he'd have carried me off somewhere and made me scream his name.

I kissed him, his beard tickling me.

"After Caleb goes to bed, I'm going to do my damnedest to knock you up," he said, kissing me again. His voice dropped low so the boys wouldn't hear us. "Going to fill up that sweet pussy of yours until it's overflowing with my cum. Every damn night for the rest of our lives. Or until I can't get it up anymore."

I snickered. "They make little blue pills for that."

"Smartass."

"I thought you liked my ass."

He placed his lips against my ear. "I love your ass so much, one of these nights I'm going to fuck it. Can't wait to see that tight little hole stretched wide around my dick, and hearing you beg me for more."

My breath caught and my eyes widened. I swallowed hard as my panties flooded and my clit pulsed. He subtly slid his hand under my ass and squeezed. If we didn't have the boys, I'd have unbuckled his belt here and now, and ridden him until we both came. I didn't think it would take much for me. His words alone were enough to turn me on.

"Later, kitten. If you're really good, we'll see if this old man can get it up twice tonight. Maybe I'll fill up that pussy and your ass."

I clenched my thighs and knew I couldn't wait. Later wasn't going to get here fast enough. I frantically grabbed at his phone, but the damn thing was locked.

"What are you doing?" he asked, his voice laced with humor.

"Call a Prospect. Any of them."

"Why?"

"So he can take the boys out back to play."

Damon chuckled, but he unlocked his phone and made a call.

"Get your ass to my house. You're on babysitting duty while I make sure my woman is taken care of."

I didn't hear the Prospect's reply, but whatever it was made Scratch laugh.

"Just get here. And do it fast."

He hung up the phone and teased me with light strokes along my thighs and lower back. When the boys weren't looking, he ran his fingers across my breasts, making my nipples harden. By the time Seamus arrived, I was a quivering mess. I barely heard the instructions Scratch gave him before I was bolting up the stairs. He shut the door behind us, and I quickly removed my clothes.

"Eager, kitten?"

"You know damn well I want you. All that teasing and playing downstairs when I couldn't do anything but sit there."

He removed his clothes, then prowled closer. When he reached me, he slipped his hand between my thighs and stroked my pussy. I groaned as he flicked my clit, then thrust a finger inside me. My nipples tightened even more, and I was ready to spread my legs and take whatever he wanted to give me.

Scratch placed his other hand at my waist while he finger-fucked me. His thumb stroked over my clit, back and forth, in a slow lazy motion. When he took my nipple between his teeth and lightly bit down, I saw stars and my knees nearly buckled. He kept teasing until I wanted to cry in frustration.

"Damon, please."

"Please what, kitten?"

"Please fuck me," I said.

"You want me to fuck you here?" he asked, his fingers playing with my pussy. Then he slid them out and pressed against the tight hole between my ass cheeks. "Or here?"

It felt like the world was spinning and I could barely breathe. My gaze latched onto his and he smiled, then slowly turned me to face the bed.

"Ass in the air, baby."

I pressed my breasts to the bed and watched as he took a tube of something from the bedside table drawer. He lightly stroked my back before reaching for my hands. He placed them on my ass cheeks.

"Hold yourself open for me, kitten. Show me how much you want this."

I trembled at his words, but did as he said. The lube was cold, and I gasped as he started working it into me. It burned as he stretched me with his fingers, but it felt strangely good too. While he worked on loosening me up, his other hand played with my pussy, pinching and rubbing my clit.

"Come for me."

I whimpered and pushed back against him as he fucked my ass with his fingers. He put more pressure on my clit and it was enough to send me soaring. I screamed out his name and it felt like the world exploded around me. I was still disoriented from coming so damn hard when I felt his cock pressing into me. Biting my lip, I tried to keep still and quiet. It took a few thrusts before he'd worked his way inside.

"Fuck, kitten. You look so damn beautiful taking my cock like this," he said, fucking me with slow, long strokes.

I already felt another orgasm building. His hands spread my ass cheeks even wider.

"Please play with your pussy, kitten. Let me feel you squeeze my dick when you come."

I worked my clit hard and fast and soon I was begging him for more.

"Faster, Damon! Harder!"

He growled and slammed into me, again and again, until I was screaming out his name again.

"Damon! Yes! More! Don't fucking stop!"

He growled and I felt the splash of his cum filling me. When he stilled, buried in my ass, my heart started to slow and I was able to catch my breath. His hands ran along my sides and back, gentle strokes that were likely meant to soothe me. If I'd known it would ever feel that good, I'd have begged him to do this sooner.

"Don't move, kitten."

He pulled out and I winced at the momentary twinge. My ass was sore, but it was the good kind. I had no doubt every time I sat down for the rest of the day, I'd remember him taking me so hard and deep, riding me until we both came.

I heard the bathroom water running, then he returned a moment later.

"Fucking beautiful," he said. "Let me see."

I reached back and spread myself open for him again. He groaned and I felt the heat of his body as he came closer.

"Fuck. I don't think it would take much to get me hard again. No one has turned me on this much in a really long fucking time. And back then a stiff breeze was enough to get me hard."

I couldn't hold back my laughter at that. I rolled over and looked up at him, a smile curving my lips. "Maybe he just needs a little assistance?"

Before he could say anything, I dropped to my knees at his feet and took his cock into my mouth. I had no clue what the hell I was doing, but I hoped my enthusiasm made up for my lack of skill. I licked and sucked, and was soon rewarded when his cock hardened. I wasn't ready to let him go just yet, enjoying the taste and scent of him. Pre-cum hit my tongue and I sucked harder, wanting more.

"Enough, kitten," he said, pulling me to my feet. "If I come in your mouth, there's no way I'll get hard again fast enough to please you. Downside of being with a man my age."

"There aren't any downsides to being with you, except that you're stubborn."

He smiled. "I am that. How do you want me, baby? You want to lie on your back? Get on your hands and knees? Want to ride me?"

"You'd let me do that? Be in charge?" I asked.

He sat on the edge of the bed and motioned for me to come closer. "Put your legs on either side of my hips."

I put my knees on the bed on either side of him and felt his cock brush against me. Scratch gripped his shaft and I lowered onto it, my eyes nearly sliding shut in pleasure as he filled me. He helped guide me until I found a rhythm we both seemed to enjoy. Sweat slicked my body as I rode him harder, faster, chasing an orgasm I could feel was so close. I gripped his shoulders tight as the world spun around me and I came really damn hard.

Scratch clamped his hands tight on my waist and surged upward, thrusting until I felt the heat of his cum spurting inside me. I clung to him, slumping against his chest with my head on his shoulder. With his arms around me, I felt safe, happy, and like I was home. My heart rate started to slow and I lifted my head.

"Guess we'd better clean up and rescue Seamus from the boys," I said.

"The man could handle a platoon of Marines. I think two small boys should be a walk in the park."

"Do you not remember what toddler boys can be like?" I asked.

"Fair enough, kitten. We'll take a quick shower and go save Seamus. Then we'll figure out how we're taking the boys with us to go ring shopping and meet my daughter for dinner."

"After babysitting two toddlers, a trip to the store for a car seat should be easy enough for Seamus to handle."

He smiled. "I'll be sure to tell him you said that."

I kissed him hard, our tongues tangling as I pressed myself close to him. I wanted more days like this and wondered if I could put Seamus on speed dial.

Chapter Ten

Scratch

The ring Clarity picked out wasn't quite what I'd had in mind, but as long as she was happy that was all that mattered. She claimed the sapphire in the center reminded her of my eyes. It was just an average-size round stone with small diamond chips surrounding it, on a plain platinum band. I'd gone into the store prepared to spend a chunk of money and I'd walked out with my bank account only five thousand dollars less. I'd been assured there was a matching wedding band they could order when I was ready.

After we'd finished eating and had dessert, Darian noticed Clarity's ring and blinked at me like an owl. "You're engaged? To a woman you've only just met?"

Bull nudged her with his elbow, probably a reminder that they'd been all over each other when they'd first met. Darian pressed her lips together and looked from Clarity to me, then back again before giving a nod of her head.

"All right. As long as the two of you are happy, then I'll be happy for you. Besides, Foster likes playing with Caleb, even if it is a little weird that my son is the same age as my stepbrother."

Clarity snorted her water and started coughing. I patted her back and stared at my daughter. Darian just shrugged with a sheepish smile.

"Play nice," Bull murmured to her just loud enough for me to hear. "Or I won't do that thing you like."

And that was more than I needed to know about my daughter and son-in-law.

A basket of breadsticks was on the table between Caleb and Foster. When I saw Caleb reaching for a second breadstick, I watched and waited. He did the same thing he had at home, freezing with his hand partway to the food, then looking around nearly frantic.

Clarity tensed next to me and I reached for her hand. "That's the other thing I needed to talk to you about."

"What did she do to my baby?" Clarity asked.

"She was abusive, and he saw some things he shouldn't have. Bad things. She also forbade him from eating. We need to talk to a pediatrician and see what they recommend, but as he gets older, he might need counseling," I said.

"What kind of things?" she asked, fear blazing in her eyes.

I leaned in closer so I could whisper and not let the entire restaurant hear our business. "Mary's boyfriend was running a child pornography ring. He never filmed Caleb, but our boy saw some of it happening, and he saw that his babysitter got excited by it. We're going to have some damage to reverse, but he's going to be okay, kitten. And Mary and her boyfriend aren't going to be an issue ever again."

She looked into my eyes and nodded.

"I will always protect you. Both of you, no matter what it takes."

She cupped my cheek and kissed me softly. "Thank you, Damon. I only wish…"

"You couldn't have known, Clarity. Don't beat yourself up over something that's in the past. We'll make sure Caleb gets whatever help he needs, and we'll give him a good life. Now let me go talk to my boy a minute." I winked and pushed my chair back.

Caleb was still staring at the breadsticks with longing, but he'd put his hand back in his lap. I knelt by his highchair and got his attention.

"Hey, buddy. Still hungry?" I asked.

Caleb just stared at me.

"It's all right if you're hungry, Caleb. You can eat as much as you want, whenever you want. The bad lady can't hurt you anymore, all right? My family made sure she went away and won't ever come back."

I reached for a breadstick and held it out to him.

He wrapped his chubby hand around it, then grinned at me before taking a bite. I kissed the top of his head and went back to my seat. It would take time, but he would be fine, just like I'd told Clarity. I'd see that he had whatever he needed, and I'd make sure the club put those bodies where no one would ever find them. I'd also have Shade track down the kids were who exposed and make sure they were taken care of, in whatever way was necessary. Her kids would either go to family or they'd likely end up in the system. It sucked, but they would hopefully be better off than they were with her. There was too much evil in the world, and I hated that kids had ever been a part of it. They were to be sheltered and protected, not exposed for monetary gain.

My woman reached out and placed her hand on my thigh. I put my hand over hers and gave it a squeeze. We'd get through this, and whatever else life threw our way. I had a strong woman by my side, and I knew she could handle some serious shit if the need arose. Maybe she was right about the soul mate thing and she'd been chosen for me by the universe.

"You love her," Darian said.

"What?" I glanced at Clarity, but she was focused on Caleb and Foster.

"You love her," my daughter said again. "And I don't think you even realize it. You're different when you're around her. You've been protective of me and Foster, but with Clarity and Caleb you're like…"

"Like I am with you," Bull told her. Then he nodded. "I would have to agree, Scratch. I think it's obvious you're in love with her. And the deer in the headlights expression on her face tells me you haven't said that to her yet."

I looked at Clarity again and her eyes were wide.

"You love me?" she asked. "You said you were falling for me, but you never…"

"Never been in love before," I told her. "Maybe that's what I'm feeling and I just don't realize it, but I do know that you own my heart. I don't see any woman but you."

"Someone should tell the club sluts that," Darian muttered.

"What's a club slut?" Clarity asked.

"Oh my God." Darian cast an accusing glare my way. "You haven't even taken her to the clubhouse or told her about those women? When she buries you in a shallow grave, I'm not crying over your corpse."

"What's a club slut?" Clarity asked again, keeping her voice low enough the boys wouldn't hear.

"It's, um…" I glanced at Bull and Darian, but they weren't going to help me with this one. "There are some women who hang around the clubhouse and they…"

"They're whores who have sex with all the club brothers," Darian said. "And I'm sure Daddy Dearest hasn't exactly been a monk, so those women are going to think they have a prior claim on him and won't give a shit the two of you are engaged. They'll still try to get into his pants."

"Thanks, Darian," I said. I sighed and looked at Clarity, who didn't seem too pleased with this new knowledge.

"You've slept with random women who still hang around the clubhouse, and they'll expect you to sleep with them again?" she asked. There was a flicker of uncertainty in her eyes and it nearly gutted me.

"Kitten, I'm not going to touch any of them. I can't throw them out since most of my club are single men and they have needs. But yes, I've been with some of the club sluts. It didn't mean anything. It's never meant anything, not until you."

"But you have to go be around them?"

"Yes and no. There are times I'll need to be at the clubhouse and they'll be there, but my party days are over. I'd rather be home with you and Caleb."

"You're the VP, Dad. You can't just ghost on the parties," Darian said. "Don't lie to her because you think it's what she wants to hear."

"Darian, you might be a grown adult, but I will take you over my knee and beat some sense into you if you don't shut the hell up," I said casting her a glare. Bull merely raised his eyebrows, but stayed out of it.

"I don't want to take you away from your club duties," Clarity said. "But I won't lie and say I'm okay with you being around those women."

I looked at the clock on my phone. Our meal was over and we didn't have plans for the rest of the night. Maybe if Clarity saw the clubhouse, she'd understand that those women couldn't hold a candle to her. They were all used up and not the least bit attractive to me. Being with them had just been a way to find some relief, but it was just meaningless sex. They hadn't been more than a willing place to stick my dick.

I looked at Bull and my daughter. "Can Caleb go with the two of you for a little while? We can swing by the hotel and pick him up in about an hour."

"Sure," Bull said.

I tossed him the keys to my truck and he got up to go transfer the car seat. Darian studied Clarity, and I could tell she had questions. I also knew her pregnancy was making her batshit crazy and her emotions were all over the fucking place. She was supportive one second and a fire-breathing fucking dragon the next. I didn't envy Bull in the slightest.

"Caleb can stay the night, if you'd like," Darian offered. "He gets along really well with Foster and they're about the same size. I'm sure we have some pajamas that will fit him."

"You okay with that, kitten?" I asked.

"He's never stayed the night away from me before," she said.

"We can pick him up when we're done if that's what you want, or he can stay with Foster and they can have some more playtime until they go to bed. Up to you. Darian might be a hormonal witch when she's pregnant, but she's good with kids."

My daughter stuck her tongue out at me, which just made Clarity laugh.

"All right. He can stay the night," she said. "But call us if he wants to come home."

Darian nodded, then gathered the boys and took them outside. Caleb went without so much as a backward glance, which I was sure had to hurt Clarity. She'd been his entire world, and now he was opening up to new people and making friends. It had to be hard on her.

I paid for dinner, then led Clarity out to the truck. She was quiet on the way to the clubhouse, and I only hoped that I was right and she could handle this. If our roles were reversed, I knew I wouldn't be too happy right now either. The thought of her being in regular contact with men she'd slept with, had there been any, would have infuriated me.

The parking lot outside the clubhouse was pretty packed considering we weren't an overly large club. I parked the truck and went to help Clarity out. She smoothed her hands over her outfit and fidgeted.

"You look beautiful, kitten, and I'll be right by your side the entire time. If you're uncomfortable or want to leave, just say the word and we'll go home, or go get Caleb if that's what you want."

"All right."

I took her by the hand and led her up the steps and inside. Music was booming and smoke filled the air. A few brothers were already screwing the club sluts out in the open and I felt Clarity tense. We went to the bar and I ordered a beer, then got her a virgin drink. She stared at it with her brow furrowed.

"No alcohol. Just in case," I said, looking down at her stomach.

Her cheeks flushed, but there was a pleased look on her face as she sipped her drink. It didn't take long for Cinder to make his way over to us, and he looked confused as fuck.

"Thought you wanted to keep this one," he said.

"I do. We're engaged."

"Uh-huh. And you thought bringing her here was a good idea? Is this some sort of test?" Cinder asked.

"Not exactly. I tried to explain club sluts to her and didn't do such a great job."

Cinder looked over at Clarity, who was staring a little too hard at her drink. Maybe this wasn't such a great idea after all. Cinder shook his head and moved away, leaving us alone at the bar. I finished off my beer and was going to suggest that we leave when a hand wrapped around my arm and a naked body pressed up against me.

"I wondered when you'd come and have some fun with us," the whore said, her make-up so heavy it cracked at the corners of her eyes. She might have been attractive once, but hard living had aged her.

"Not tonight, Stella. Or any night." I removed her hand, but she wasn't deterred.

"Oh, come on, Mr. VP. You know we had us a good time. Wasn't all that long ago you were taking me up against that wall over there," she said nodding across the room.

I felt Clarity tense even more and I wondered just how fucked I was going to be once I got her out of here. Before I could open my mouth and say a word, my fiancée skirted around me and got right in Stella's face.

"He said to back off, bitch."

I put my hand over my mouth to hide my silent laughter as my little kitten showed her claws. It seemed I might have been worried for nothing. Well, maybe not nothing. When we got home, I might get an earful, but I'd gladly take a tongue-lashing from her as long as she was still speaking to me. I hadn't done the best job preparing her for this life, and if she needed to vent her frustrations I'd let her. In private. In front of the club was another matter, but watching her stand up for herself and claim me wasn't a bad thing. I was damn proud of her.

Stella flipped her hair over her shoulder and sneered at Clarity. "And who the fuck are you to talk to me that way?"

Clarity put her finger an inch from Stella's nose, her engagement ring shining under the lights. "I'm the woman he's going to marry, you whore. Take your sagging tits somewhere else."

Stella's lips thinned and she pulled back her hand. I reached out to catch her mid-slap, but Clarity didn't give me a chance. She barreled into Stella, knocking the whore down, then grabbed a handful of hair and slammed her head on the floor. My jaw dropped as my sweet little kitten stood up and started dragging Stella's naked ass through the club and out the front doors. I followed in their wake, along with half my brothers, and watched my woman kick the slut down the steps.

"Damn," Renegade said in a hushed tone. "Your woman is badass. Where can I get one?"

"Hands off, dickhead," I said, but I was smiling. It was kind of hot watching her take care of the club slut all on her own.

"You ever think of trying to fucking hit me, and I will beat your sorry ass," Clarity said. She pulled her foot back and kicked Stella in the stomach. "And keep your skank ass away from Scratch. He's mine and doesn't want a nasty whore like you."

I reached out and wrapped an arm around her waist. "Easy, kitten. I think she gets the message."

A woman snorted behind me and I heard a muttered, "We all got the memo. Hands off the VP."

Yeah, my fierce little kitten had made an impression. I was not only proud of her, but really fucking turned-on. I'd never had a woman fight for me before, not like this. Cat fights between the club sluts happened from time to time over any officer in the club, but Clarity claiming me like that? Big difference.

"You really fucked her? I hope you doused your dick in antibacterial soap." She pressed against me and fisted my cut, but I could feel the anger still simmering under the surface.

"Come on, kitten. We'll go home. I think you've made your point. No one's going to touch me."

She nodded and let me lead her to the truck, but a hand on my shoulder stopped me. I turned to look at Shade, Renegade, and Phantom.

"Mind if we welcome her to the family?" Renegade asked. "Mostly because I want to hug the fiercest woman I've ever seen."

I snorted and introduced Clarity to my brothers. They each hugged her, and Renegade gave her a kiss on the cheek. She stiffened for a moment, but as Renegade held her gaze, the tension drained from her. He reached out and squeezed her hand, and Clarity relaxed even more.

"You ever need anything and Scratch isn't available, you come find me," Renegade said. "I've got your back."

Clarity smiled a little. "Thanks. It was nice to meet all of you. Sorry about…" She waved a hand toward Stella, who was still crying on the ground.

Shade shrugged. "Honestly, that was the hottest fucking thing I've seen in a long ass time. You can come stake your claim on Scratch anytime you want. We could use some entertainment around here."

Phantom snickered. "He's not wrong. And I'm with Renegade. You need anything, we'll be there. You just gained a bunch of big brothers who will gladly beat the shit out of anyone giving you crap. Make sure you get all our numbers from Scratch."

"Shit," I muttered. "I never got her a phone."

"I'll take care of it," Renegade said. "I'll drop it by tomorrow morning. I think you two need some alone time tonight."

The other two smirked and I flipped them off before helping Clarity into the truck. They were assholes, but I knew they would protect her with their lives if necessary, and that was all that mattered. I'd deal with their taunts and teasing, for a little while at least. Then I'd have to remind them who they were fucking with.

I climbed into the truck and started the engine. Clarity reached over and put her hand on my thigh.

"I like them," she said. "I thought they'd make me nervous, but I'm comfortable around them. But the club sluts I can do without."

"Noted." I smiled at her. "For what it's worth, I don't think any of those women will come anywhere near me now. You as good as peed on my leg."

"Funny," she muttered, but her cheeks were turning a bright pink. "I've never lost control like that before."

"Sometimes the situation warrants a little more force. This was one of those times. You just gained the respect of every brother in there, and the Prospects. Pretty sure the whores will be giving you a wide berth next time they see you. You just showed them you're in a position of authority and not to fuck with you."

"You sound proud," she said.

"I am. Damn proud." I lifted her hand and kissed it. "You're the perfect old lady for a VP. Don't change a damn thing about you, kitten. All soft and sweet at home, and badass when we're around the club. The perfect combination."

"Take me home," she said softly. "Then you can show me just how much you liked that little show."

I put her hand over my zipper. "That's all for you, kitten. And you can have it anytime you want."

"Home, Damon. I'm not adventurous enough to have sex in your truck, especially in the clubhouse parking lot. I don't think you want your brothers seeing that much of me anyway."

"Fuck no!"

I put the truck into gear and headed for the house. The woman at my side completely amazed me, and I was lucky as fuck to have her. I just hoped she knew how much I cared about her, how devoted I was to her and Caleb. I'd lay down my life for them, and I'd love them until I breathed my last. Maybe Darian was right and I was already in love with Clarity. The pint-sized woman next to me already had too much power, more than she realized. I'd tell her how I felt when the time was right.

Epilogue

Clarity
Three months later

I was nice and toasty with Damon pressed up against me, his arms holding me close as I slowly woke up. The sun was barely streaming through the window and as I became a little more alert, my stomach twisted and turned. I clamped a hand over my mouth and ran for the bathroom, barely making it before I retched into the toilet. I heard Damon stumbling around, and then he was holding my hair back.

"I thought you were calling the doctor," he said, still sounding half asleep.

"I went to the doctor," I said.

Taking a few deep breaths, I looked up at him. He still hadn't put it all together yet, clueless man. Throwing up at all times of the day, my breasts were more sensitive than usual and a bit bigger, and I couldn't handle certain foods or smells.

"I'm pregnant, Damon. Not sick."

He blinked a few times, and then the light bulb came on. He fell to his knees next to me, pulling me against his chest.

"Pregnant?" he asked.

I nodded. "The doctor said I'm about two months along. Didn't take you too long to knock me up."

"Damn." He placed a hand over my belly, and the look of awe on his face nearly made me cry.

"I was hoping you'd go to my appointments with me. I was referred to an OB-GYN and my first appointment is next week. I know you missed out on everything with Darian. I'd like you to be there every step of the way with this one."

"I'd like that, kitten." He kissed the top of my head. "You've made me really fucking happy."

"Guess it's a good thing the club arranged a wedding for us last week. Now the baby will have your name without extra paperwork. Do I even want to know how Shade got a marriage license without me having to go to the courthouse and apply with you?" I asked. "It's not that I'm upset about it. Getting to marry you was the best day of my life, and I'm really glad we share the same name, and that you're adopting Caleb."

"Probably don't want to know. There are things we just don't ask when it comes to Shade. He's good. Damn good. Whenever we go see Darian, I'll introduce you to Wire. He's with the Dixie Reapers and is way more badass than Shade. I think even the government is a little afraid of Wire. As for Caleb, now that we're married, adopting him should be easy. Then we'll all have the same name."

I smiled. "He sounds like an interesting person to meet. I'd love an introduction to the Dixie Reapers. If they're half as nice as Bull, then I think I'll like them."

"Bull is family, but the Reapers will treat you well, and I'm sure they'd all like to meet you. Darian has already told her friends about her stepmom who's younger than her. Ridley, Bull's daughter, thought it was fucking hilarious. She asked if Foster was going to call you Grandma."

I nearly choked I laughed so damn hard. "Grandma?"

"Ridley had a lot of fun getting her kids to call my daughter Grandma. You should see the looks Darian gets when she's out somewhere with all the kids. She's given Ridley some death glares. Bull finds it amusing as hell, though."

"Grandma," I muttered and giggled again. "I think it would be funny to see the looks on everyone's faces if

Foster did that while we're out in public, especially if Darian is with us when it happens."

"Yeah, I picked the right woman," he said, his laughter rumbling in his chest.

"Damon?" I looked up, all laughter gone. "There's something I need to say. Should have said it before now."

"What is it, kitten? You feeling okay? Baby's all right?"

"I'm fine. We're fine. No, it's…" I reached up and ran my fingers through his beard, something I loved doing. "We're married and have been living together a few months now, but I've never told how much I love you."

"Love you too, kitten. So damn much."

"I…"

Small footsteps thundered down the hall and Caleb came bursting into our bedroom, quickly finding us in the bathroom.

"Momma. Daddy. Want pancakes!"

Damon held me tighter. I knew he loved it when Caleb called him daddy. Over the last few months, Caleb had started talking more. We'd consulted a child psychologist and she'd helped us break through his shell. He went to something called play therapy twice a week and had improved so much. I only hoped that what he'd witnessed, and the abuse he'd suffered, wouldn't have lasting effects.

I'd been assured the club had made sure Mary and the monster she'd been dating would never be found. I didn't know the details, and I didn't need to know them. Though I suspected the day Damon had come home with blood spatters on his jeans that he'd had a little "talk" with one or both of them. The violent side of him and the club might frighten some people, but it made me feel safe because I knew they would never hurt me or my family, but anyone who fucked with us was fair game.

"What kind of pancakes?" Damon asked.

"Mouse pancakes," Caleb said, trying to squeeze himself between us.

"Mouse pancakes? You mean the pancakes with the round ears?" I asked.

He nodded enthusiastically. "Mouse pancakes!"

Damon nodded. "All right. Let's give your momma a minute to herself and we'll head down to the kitchen and get started. Think you can stir the batter for me?"

Caleb clapped and latched onto his daddy. Damon gave me a wink as he headed out of the bathroom and carried Caleb downstairs. I brushed my teeth and splashed some water on my face, then joined them.

Mornings like this one it was almost hard to remember what life had been like before I'd been claimed by the VP of the Devil's Boneyard. I was happy, my son was happy, and we were both loved by so many people. Falling asleep in that shop doorway was the best decision I'd ever made, because it brought me to the love of my life and the father of my kids.

I couldn't wait to see what the years would bring for us, but I knew the future held many happy memories for us. Now I just needed to find a way to bring that happiness to others in the Devil's Boneyard. Jackal had Josie, and Scratch had me. Maybe it was time to find a happily-ever-after for the others. A little matchmaking never hurt anyone, right?

Havoc (Devil's Boneyard MC 3)
Harley Wylde

Jordan -- I spent a year in prison for a crime I admittedly did commit, but I had a good reason. I was supposed to serve a longer sentence, but a handsy guard and a pissed-off warden who wanted me to keep quiet meant I got out early. My brothers have abandoned me, and there's nowhere for me to go. Until the hottest man I've ever met decides to be my knight on shining Harley. He only thinks he knows me though, and if he ever finds out I was locked up for a violent crime he might walk away. For some reason, the thought sends me into a panic. Havoc isn't at all what I'm used to, but maybe he's just what I need.

Havoc -- No way the pretty blonde was doing hard time for anything bad. Just looking into her eyes, I can see how sweet she is. There's a vulnerability there that makes me want to wrap her in my arms and never let her go. When I find out the same prison that nearly killed me was trying to cover up another incident, one involving the woman I can't stop staring at -- the goddess with the body of a porn star -- fury flows through me. Whatever it takes, I'll keep her safe, because if there's one thing I've learned it's that what happens in that prison doesn't stay there. Whoever hurt her will be coming, and I'm going to be ready for them. No one touches what's mine, and Jordan may not realize it but I'm not letting her go.

Chapter One

Jordan

Being the only girl in a house full of boys had taught me a few hard lessons. For example, guard your food when you eat, or it will be stolen from you. Punch first and ask questions later. And never, ever let your brothers know that you think their friends are hot. That last one had been a painful lesson to learn, and I was certain I'd be scarred for life. The second one is what landed me in a ton of trouble, and the first one had kept me from starving while I'd been locked up. If I'd known the prissy blonde who was running her mouth about my youngest brother was the daughter of the District Attorney, I might not have broken her nose and called her a whore. Then again, I'd never been known for holding my temper. Or at least I hadn't before.

Being locked up for assault had taught me a new set of rules. Make friends with the right people, always watch your back, and never find yourself somewhere alone inside the prison. It wasn't the inmates I worried about quite as much as the male guards. Not that some of the inmates weren't scary as hell, but I'd heard enough horror stories about the guards that I'd tried to stay away from them, and I'd mostly succeeded. I'd been released early after a guard had tried to force himself on me. I'd made sure he wouldn't be having children anytime soon, and the warden had fired him, then made sure my release papers were in order. As long as I kept quiet, of course.

I hadn't realized that freedom would be so fucking scary, though. I'd been locked up for a year, only a fraction of my sentence, but it was long enough that I felt a little like a caged animal being set free. I wanted to run and feel the breeze on my face, but I didn't trust it. I found myself scanning the area, a nervous energy thrumming inside of me as I waited for the Boogeyman to jump out and pounce on me. Stupid maybe, but I'd heard they called it *fear of freedom*. Just hadn't thought it could happen after only a year inside, or that it would happen to me at all.

My next to youngest brother, the one I fondly called Dopey, was supposed to pick me up. I should have known better than to trust he would keep his word. He'd never been on time for anything in his life, so why would today be any different? Our parents were gone and all I had left were my brothers. Only one of the four had come to visit me while I'd been locked up, and he'd only come twice in the very beginning. I hadn't heard from any of them since then, until I'd asked for a ride home, and even then I'd only been able to reach one of them.

I honestly didn't even know where I was going. I didn't have a home anymore. The only brother who had answered the phone hadn't offered me a place to crash, and I didn't have friends after what had happened. Staring down the long stretch of road that led to the prison, I wondered if I could make it to town before nightfall if I started walking right now. I wasn't quite sure I liked being out in the open, but I sure as hell didn't want to step back through the gates. With my luck, the warden would change his mind, revoke my early release, and lock me back up. Since I hadn't gotten out of prison in a typical way, I hadn't even met with a parole board.

All I had were the clothes I'd been wearing when I was arrested, my ID, a useless bank card, and twenty-two dollars. My bank card hadn't expired but it wouldn't do me much good since I was sure my account would have been closed in my absence. If it hadn't, I probably had overdraft fees or some shit to take care of, because I had no doubt my brothers hadn't bothered to call the bank on my behalf and tell them I'd been locked up. I hadn't exactly had the time to wrap up any loose ends before losing a year of my life. They'd tossed me into jail and kept me there until my hearing. I'd gone straight from that court room to the prison. My trial hadn't even taken a full day.

My jean shorts were frayed at the hem and seemed to be a little tighter than I'd remembered. I doubt it had anything to do with my diet the past year, but I had gained some muscle. One of the women who had watched over me was big on fitness. I'd hit the gym equipment with her every day that we were permitted to use the space. I still had curves, but I also had some toned muscle to go with it. And apparently more junk in the trunk than when I'd gone inside.

While I'd been locked up my Nikes had mysteriously vanished. I'd been given prison issued flip-flops to wear home instead. Not only were they hideous, but I could feel every damn pebble in the road as I walked toward what I hoped was the nearest town. The prison I'd been sentenced to wasn't near my home area, and I honestly didn't have a fucking clue how to get back without someone picking me up. My money wouldn't buy me a bus ticket, or much else for that matter. I seriously doubted that motel rooms had dropped in price enough for me to get one, which meant I would be sleeping outside if I couldn't find a way to reach one of my bonehead brothers, and hope the jackass actually came to get me. Unlike Dopey.

The sun beat down on me and sweat trickled down my spine. I could feel my hair sticking to my neck and wished I had a way to pull it up. I hadn't gotten it cut while I was locked up and it was now nearly down to my waist. As I looked off in the distance, the road looked a little hazy and I wondered just how fucking hot it was today. Summer in Florida was no fucking joke. I paused when I heard a rustle off to my right and my gut clenched. *Please don't be a hungry gator.*

A rabbit bounded out of the brush and darted across the road, making me sigh in relief that it wasn't something about to make a snack out of me. I kept walking, but it felt like I wasn't getting anywhere. Looking over my shoulder, I saw the prison in the distance and figured I'd probably walked two or three miles. Nowhere near far enough, since I still didn't see any sign of a town on the horizon.

The longer I walked, the drier my throat became. My legs felt like they would give out at any moment, but I trudged onward. It wasn't like I had much of a choice. If I was lucky, Dopey would finally show up at the prison and someone would tell him which direction I took. I wasn't entirely sure he'd come after me though. My brothers acted like it was entirely my fault I'd been in prison. And maybe I did need to control my temper better, but I'd been defending my family! That should have counted for something, right? Apparently not.

I could feel my body swaying and dots were swimming across my vision. Had it gotten even hotter? My mouth felt like it was stuffed with cotton, and my limbs were getting heavier. The next step I took, I went down hard on the pavement. As much as I fought to get up, I just couldn't do it. Instead, I fell forward and just lay there, panting and wondering if I was about to die after having survived a year in hell.

A roar filled my ears and made my eardrums vibrate. I wondered if it was a common sound to hear when you were dying. The sound came closer, got louder, then shut off. I heard someone say a string of bad words that would have a made a sailor proud, then heavy steps came toward me.

"Miss? Hey, you all right?"

Whoever he was, his voice was deep and rich. I struggled to open my eyes, but everything was a big blur. I got the impression of a rather massive man dressed in black, and that was about it. Before I could say or do anything, I could feel myself slipping away again. The man cursed once more, then I was lifted into his arms. I heard more bikes and what sounded like a loud truck or SUV. I tried to focus on the voices, but I couldn't keep up with the conversation.

Something cool and wet was placed against my lips and I eagerly slurped the water.

"Easy," someone said. "Don't want to get sick."

They took the bottle of water away and I whined, wanting more.

"Let's get her into the truck. The AC has been running and we need to lower her body temp. She's burning up," said another voice.

"I didn't see a vehicle broken down anywhere. You think some asshole kicked her out of their car?"

Now that voice I recognized. The man who had first stopped to help me. My savior. Well, I hoped that's what he would be. If they had something nefarious planned for me, I honestly didn't have the strength to fight them.

The icy air coasted over my skin as someone laid me across the seat of the truck. Eventually, I was able to open my eyes and focus a bit more. A group of big bikers were staring into the vehicle. One of them helped me sit up and drink some more water.

"How long you been out here, sweetheart?" a giant with red hair asked. It was the man who had stopped to help. The one with the voice I could listen to all day and never grow tired of.

"Don't know. Since ten o'clock?" I said, my voice croaking a bit.

"Ten?" an Asian man asked, his eyebrows shooting upward. "Damn. That was five hours ago. Where the hell were you going on foot?"

"Town."

"Sweetheart, town is another ten miles down the road," the redhead said. "Why are you on the side of the road? Some asshole kick you out of the car?"

"My brother was supposed to give me a ride. He never showed."

The men shared a look then the redhead's gaze sharpened on me. "A ride? From where?"

I licked my lips and looked away, but he reached out and forced me to look him in the eye. Something about his gaze made me want to answer his question, like I needed to obey.

"The prison," I said. "They released me today and my brother was supposed to pick me up."

"Shit." One of them stalked off then came back. "How long were you inside?"

"A year." Which was the truth. It just hadn't been the full sentence I was supposed to serve. I wasn't about to volunteer that information, though. I hoped they didn't ask why I'd been locked up. All I wanted was a ride to town, and maybe a way to call my brothers and see if one of them would come get me.

"Just a year?" the Asian man asked. "Drugs?"

"No. I've never taken or sold drugs."

"Prostitution?" the redhead asked.

I stared at him. "Really? I look like a whore? Thanks."

He shrugged then his gaze landed on my bare legs. I felt my cheeks warm, but my face was probably so red from the sun it wasn't noticeable. Even if he wasn't painting me in a flattering light, he was probably the most gorgeous man I'd ever seen. Not in that pretty boy kind of way, but in a rough, rugged, and manly type of way. His red hair gleamed in the sunlight and the full beard along his jaw made me wonder if it was as soft as it looked. When he lifted his blue gaze from my legs, I knew I'd remember that heated look of his for a long-ass time.

"What's your name, darlin'?" one of them asked.

"Jordan. If you guys could just give me a ride to the next town, I'll try to call one of my brothers for a ride."

The Asian arched his eyebrows and looked at the others before returning his gaze to me. "I'm Phantom, and the guy who can't stop checking out your legs is Havoc. He's the one who found you. The other two are Renegade and Irish." He pointed to each one as he named everyone.

I blinked a few times then stared. "Um, did your mothers not like you?"

Renegade snickered. "They're road names, baby girl."

He turned and I saw a rather scary winged skull on the back of his leather vest, it had demonic horns and seemed to hover over a pile of bones. The words *Devil's Boneyard MC* was stitched across the top. Huh. I'd pegged them as bikers just based off the motorcycles I could see parked on the road, but I hadn't realized they were the hardcore kind. Were they like that show that had been popular a while back? I wasn't about to ask.

The one called Havoc was staring at my legs again. I wasn't entirely sure what was so fascinating about them. Being on the short side, it wasn't like they were miles long. They were toned though, and maybe that was enough to make him keep checking them out. If he hadn't assumed I was a prostitute, I might have been tempted to see where things would go. I tried to avoid assholes though, and he was coming across as one, even if he had stopped to help a stranger passed out on the side of the road.

Renegade smacked the back of Havoc's head. "Dude, it's not like you haven't seen a woman's legs before. You're going to make her think you're some sort of creeper."

Havoc looked away, then moved further back. He crossed his arms over his chest and turned his gaze anywhere but at me. Renegade took his place, giving me a sympathetic look.

"Ignore him," Phantom said. "We can give you a ride to town, if that's what you want. Since you didn't know how far it was, I'm going to assume you aren't from here. Where are you going to stay while you wait for your brothers?"

"I-I don't know. I have a little cash. Maybe I can get a meal somewhere and borrow a phone."

Renegade pulled a cell from his pocket and handed it to me. "Here. Call them and tell them you'll be at the Devil's Boneyard compound. If you live within fifty miles of this place, then they should know where that is and how to find you."

I accepted the phone. Phantom made me buckle my seatbelt, and then the one they'd called Irish slid behind the wheel of the truck. Everyone else got onto a bike, and then we were pulling away. I hoped I hadn't made a mistake getting into the truck with a strange man, or by putting my life in the hands of a bunch of bikers. They seemed nice enough, but I wasn't the best judge of character.

I tried calling my eldest brother first, and went down the line. The first two numbers I called were out of service, which made me feel like there was a lead weight in my stomach. Had they changed their numbers and not let me know? Did they even still live at the same places they had before? Dopey's no-show had me wondering if my brothers were cutting me out of their lives.

No one answered any of my calls. I left a voicemail and told them where I'd be, but something told me none of them would come for me. I'd never been completely on my own, not in the outside world anyway. Prison had been an eye-opener for me, and I liked to think it had changed me for the better, but it didn't seem like my brothers would let me prove that to them. I'd never gotten into trouble with the police before the day I attacked that stupid bitch, and I'd been defending my family. It seemed one sin was too much in their eyes.

I gripped the phone tight, willing it to ring, but deep down I knew it wouldn't. Once we arrived at their compound, whatever that was, I'd thank the motorcycle guys for helping me, then I'd set out and try to find my own way. I'd need a job, and with a record I didn't think that would be easy. My future was looking bleaker and bleaker the more I thought about it. Maybe it would have been better if I hadn't been released, or hadn't ever made it out of that place. What was the point if my only family wanted nothing to do with me?

I stared out the window at the passing scenery, but I didn't find any joy in it. Freedom seemed more like a curse than a blessing at the moment. I'd survive because I didn't have any other choice. I wasn't a quitter, even if lying down and not getting back up would be much easier. Looking at the phone in my hand, I forced myself to relax my grip and I set it down. The phone wouldn't save me, and no one else would either.

When the town came into view, Irish drove through the streets and stopped in a place that looked a little like a warehouse. There was a closed gate and someone on the inside opened it to let us through. Irish pulled to a stop in front of the large building and got out, then opened my door. I hesitated a moment before stepping down from the truck. I swayed for a second, then managed to stay upright.

"Thank you. For helping me," I said, tucking my hair behind my ear. "Will you give Renegade his phone back?"

Irish tipped his head toward the bikes pulling through the gate. "Give it to him yourself."

I picked it up off the seat and waited for the bikers to shut off their engines. When Renegade stood up, I walked over and handed his phone back to him. His gaze locked on mine, and in that moment, I wondered if he could see right through me, see everything I was thinking and feeling, and I wasn't sure I liked it.

"Thank you for letting me make a few calls," I said.

The gate at the front of the driveway slid shut and I saw someone lock it.

"Um, will he let me out?" I asked.

Renegade glanced toward the gate before looking back at me. "Where are you going? Your brothers meeting you in town somewhere?"

"I just thought I'd go find a diner and get a bite to eat," I said, only lying a little.

"They didn't answer or call her back," Irish said.

Renegade folded his arms over his chest. "So, where were you going? The truth this time."

"I don't know. I'll figure it out."

I heard a deep sigh and turned to see Havoc, his head hanging down and his hands braced on the back of his neck. He suddenly turned and stormed in my direction, making me tense and wonder if I should run. Before I could process what he was doing, he bent down and pressed his shoulder against my stomach, lifting me over his shoulder.

Too stunned to do much but hang there, I found myself staring at a rather awesome ass cupped in denim. Not a bad view. Some part of my brain was insisting that I should be putting up a fight, hitting him or at least struggling in some way. Honestly, the feel of his hand against my bare thigh and the other one grabbing my ass seemed to have short-circuited my brain. It felt way too damn good.

He stomped up some steps and then into the warehouse-like building. When my world turned right side up again, I realized I was sitting at a bar, and the inside of the building was nothing like the outside. The other three came inside and eyed us, but none of them approached. I looked up at Havoc then glanced at the others, wondering why he'd carried me in here. With the way he'd treated me before, I would have thought he'd be glad if I walked away.

"Jordan," he said.

I snapped my gaze back to his. The commanding tone he'd used hadn't let me do anything else. He was a big man to begin with, the type who probably expected to be obeyed.

"You're not walking through those gates without having a place to stay or a way to take care of yourself," he said.

"I can manage," I said. "It's not like I'm some kid. I'm a hardened criminal, remember?"

He snorted. "Yeah. I'm sure you were doing time for something really bad, like murder or some shit."

Not murder, but assault. I didn't think I should volunteer that information though. Right now they seemed to think I was a helpless female. I didn't know what they would do to me if they learned otherwise.

"Where's your release papers?" he asked.

I swallowed hard. I didn't have the standard paperwork since the warden was trying to cover up his guard's misdeeds. It was just a piece of paper saying I'd served my time. I'd folded it up and shoved it into my pocket. That wasn't what made me hesitate. I'd only glanced over the document the warden had given me. What if it listed my crime? Or said something about the sentence I was supposed to have served? He'd promised I didn't have to go through parole or anything like that. I didn't know what strings he'd pulled to make it happen, but I was grateful. Sort of.

Havoc arched an eyebrow and held out his hand.

I pulled the paper from my back pocket and gave it to him. I watched as he unfolded it, skimmed over the lines, then his lips thinned, his jaw hardened, and his gaze clashed with mine. The fury in his eyes made me tremble and wonder if maybe I'd been a lot safer in the prison than here with him.

"You only get this kind of paper when something bad went down," he said. "What the fuck happened in that prison?"

I shrank from him and would have climbed right over the bar to get away, if he hadn't grabbed my arm in a tight grip. My heart hammered so hard, I thought it might beat right out of my chest. This wasn't good. It really, really wasn't good.

Chapter Two

Havoc

I'd seen a paper like this before. It had happened when they released me from the same fucking prison, except I hadn't been in there for a small crime. I should have stayed locked up until I was too damn old to care about being free. But the guards had fucked up. Three of them had stood by and laughed as a gang tried to take me out. They'd beaten the shit out of me with a lead pipe, and the guards had even given them a knife. I hadn't exactly made friends inside, but I think the guards helping is what made things go in my favor in the long run. The entire thing had been caught on film and when the warden had seen it, I'd been given a choice: remain inside and serve my time, or walk away a free man -- as long as I kept my mouth shut about what'd happened. I wasn't fucking stupid. Staying would have meant a certain death.

So for Jordan to have this paper, it meant something had happened in that prison, something they wanted to keep quiet. And she'd likely been the victim. It pissed me the fuck off that someone would try to hurt a sweet woman like her. Just looking in her eyes, I could see she wasn't some hardened criminal, could see how vulnerable she was. Whatever crime she'd committed, she hadn't belonged in a hell hole like that. I also knew one other thing with a certainty... whatever guard had fucked up this time, they'd be coming for her, just like they had with me. I'd had my brothers at my back and we'd buried those fuckers, but Jordan? She wouldn't make it on her own, no matter how tough she tried to appear.

"I won't ask again, baby. What the fuck happened in that prison? And don't try to tell me 'nothing' because I fucking know better."

"Easy, Havoc," Renegade said, placing a hand on my shoulder. "You're a big motherfucker and you're scaring the shit out of her."

I closed my eyes and took a breath, then focused on her again. Renegade was right. She looked scared shitless, and I'd put that look in her eyes. It made me want to kick my own ass. I might do a lot of bad shit, kill people when the need arose, but I'd never hurt a woman and I never would. Well, not one who didn't deserve it anyway. There were some evil, twisted bitches in the world, like the woman who had abused Scratch's kid, and stood by while her fucked-up boyfriend filmed kids in her apartment to sell on kiddie porn sites. That bitch had deserved a shallow grave.

"He's not going to hurt you," Renegade said. "None of us will."

Renegade took the paper from me and looked it over, then we shared a look. Yeah, he knew what that paper meant. Every man in this club did, or at least the ones who had been around back when I'd been released. I'd been a free man for ten years, but sometimes it felt like yesterday that I was in that cement cage, having my every move dictated.

It was hard to picture Jordan having to live that life. I knew it wasn't easy on the inside. Even if she hadn't had enemies when she went in, she'd have made some during her stay. There were fuckers in there who thought they had to prove something, and liked to pick on those they thought were weaker than them. I didn't know how she'd survived without becoming hard, but somehow she'd managed it.

"What happened inside, Jordan?" Renegade asked, his voice softer than mine had been.

She licked her lips and her gaze darted around the room before settling on his. I didn't like that. Didn't like her focusing on him and not me, but I tried to hold back my snarl. She wasn't mine, but for some reason, I didn't like the thought of her being with any of my brothers. Or any guy who wasn't me for that matter. Fuck! We hadn't even spoken more than few words to each other and already I wanted to toss her over my shoulder and carry her back to my place. What the fuck was wrong with me?

The VP was down the bar a ways, but I felt his gaze on me. I looked over and he had a smirk on his face as he glanced from me to Jordan and back again. Yeah, that asshole knew I wanted her. Fuck. This wasn't good.

"One of the guards tried to…" Jordan stopped and pressed her lips together.

"What did they do?" I asked, trying to contain my anger.

"He tried to rape me," she said softly. "I fought him off, then I stole the stick thing he kept on his belt. I nailed him between the legs and managed to run. Another guard found me and took me to the warden."

"And they pulled the footage from that area, saw what happened, and bribed you to keep quiet," I said. "By giving you freedom in exchange for not pressing charges or shedding light on the prison."

"Right," she said. "I had another two years."

"What the fuck did you do to get three years in that place?" Renegade asked.

"Assault," she said, dropping her gaze and twisting her hands in her lap.

I couldn't help it. I belted out a laugh, drawing the attention of everyone in the room. The thought of this pint-sized woman going to prison for assault, then taking out a guard who had tried to hurt her, just amused the shit out of me. Not that she'd been in that position, but that she'd managed to get the upper hand on anyone.

Especially one of those asshole guards. They only hired big, mean motherfuckers. Or at least they had when I was inside.

Her gaze shot up to mine and her mouth dropped open. "It's funny?"

Renegade was even smiling. "Honey, you look like you weigh a hundred pounds soaking wet. The thought of you doing enough damage to someone to get sent to prison, much less taking out a guard? Yeah, it's kind of funny."

Her lips twisted and she looked away, but not before I'd seen the flash of anger in her eyes. Seemed the pretty little angel had some fire in her. It just turned me on even more, but then I was a sick fucker. I liked that she could apparently fight and hold her own. Part of me wanted to see her in action.

"I weigh more than that," she said. "A lot more."

My gaze skimmed over her. "I don't see how. You were light as a damn feather when I picked you up."

"You mean when you brought me in here like a sack of potatoes slung over your shoulder?"

"How else was I supposed to grab your ass without being obvious?" I asked.

Her cheeks pinked and she bit her lip. So fucking cute.

Renegade snorted. "In case you hadn't noticed, our Sergeant at Arms is fascinated with you. Especially your legs. And your ass."

She opened and shut her mouth a few times, but never said anything.

"Your asshole brothers still haven't called back," Irish said, coming over to join us. "While some of our phones have blocked numbers, our personal ones don't. I heard you leave a message for them. Do they usually ignore your calls?"

"They didn't used to," she said. "I... I think my two oldest brothers changed their numbers. It said the numbers I called were out of service. It was the younger two I left messages for, and one of them was supposed to pick me up when I was released. He didn't show."

"And they didn't fucking tell you? Just ghosted on you?" I asked. The thought of her family abandoning her made me want to kick the shit out of them. I didn't care that she'd gone to prison. It wasn't like it made her a bad person. She probably had a good reason for assaulting someone, like the dickhead guard who'd thought to take what wasn't offered. Brothers were supposed to watch out for their sisters. It seemed hers hadn't gotten the message. I would be only too happy to enlighten them about that with my fists.

When I thought about her walking down that stretch of highway from the prison, the way she'd passed out on the side of the road, it pissed me off even more. If we hadn't come along, she could have died out there. Her fucking brothers needed to have the shit kicked out of them. My crew might not care much for laws, but there were rules we adhered to, and not abandoning a woman who belonged to us was a big fucking rule. You just didn't do that shit. If any of my brothers had pulled that stunt, every last one of us would have pounded him into the fucking ground.

"You could have died," I said. "Do they even care that someone could have hit you, or that you could have passed out and dehydrated out on the road? Did they stop to think what would happen if no one picked you up today?"

"I haven't seen any of them in a while," she said. "Only one came to visit, and he didn't come more than twice in the very beginning. I haven't had a visitor in at least ten months."

I crowded her, bracing my arms on the bar on either side of her, and leaned into her space. Her eyes flared, but she didn't flinch.

"Your piece of shit brothers might have abandoned you, but you aren't alone, Jordan. I'm not letting you walk out of here knowing that you have nowhere to go, no job, and would end up on the streets."

"What are you saying?" she asked.

I heard booted steps and could see Scratch out of the corner of my eye.

"Yeah, Havoc. What are you saying? Because she's not club pussy, and she's not an old lady. You live inside the compound gates, which means…"

"I don't give a shit," I said, glancing at my VP. "I'm not letting her walk out of here to an uncertain fate. And you know damn fucking well the guard who assaulted her will come looking, see if he can find her and shut her up for good. Maybe even pick up where he left off. I know you aren't going to stand for that shit any more than I will."

Scratch shrugged a shoulder and cracked his neck. "Do you remember who you're talking to?"

"Yeah, VP. I get it. You're in charge when Cinder isn't around, but let me ask you something. Just how welcoming will your wife be if she hears you kicked out a woman in need?" I asked.

Scratch looked from me to Jordan, and I could see his gaze soften. "You're about my wife's age, aren't you? Early twenties? I couldn't turn her away, and I don't suppose I'll be turning you out either."

"She's going home with me, VP. I'm not asking," I said.

Scratch's gaze locked with mine and I wondered if I'd been wise to assert myself. He might dote on his wife and kids, but I knew he'd put his fair share of bodies in the ground, and I didn't believe for a second that he'd think twice about adding mine to the list. Brother or not, there were some lines you didn't cross. Just because there was a good dose of silver in his hair, didn't mean Scratch was any less of a badass. From fighting at his side previously, I knew he could be a scary motherfucker.

"You take her home, she's yours," Scratch said. "Think on that long and hard. I have a spare room she could use, and she could keep Clarity company. I'll give you a minute to think it over. Might want to discuss it with her too. She seems like the type that might take you out if you make decisions for her."

He winked at Jordan then went back down the bar to the beer he had waiting.

"What does he mean I'm yours if you take me home?" she asked.

"You'd be his old lady," Renegade said.

Her nose scrunched and her brow furrowed.

"You'd be his. That's all you need to know. You wouldn't be leaving unless he was by your side or you had permission and protection," Renegade said.

"You mean like a girlfriend?" she asked.

"More like a wife," Irish said, then gave me a grin when I glared at him.

"Wife?" she asked, her voice squeaking her eyes going wide.

This was fucked up. I didn't like the idea of her walking out of here. Even if she did stay with Scratch, what would stop the guard from coming after her? At least if she stayed with me, she'd be locked behind a gate with round the clock protection. And did the VP even think about the danger to his wife and kids?

"She could stay in one of the rooms upstairs," Irish said.

"With the Prospects?" I asked. "Yeah, because that sounds like an awesome idea. You know those jackasses can't keep it in their pants."

"I can take care of myself," Jordan said. "You don't have to keep me here under lock and key. I'll be fine."

My gaze locked on hers and I saw the hint of fear and uncertainty, even though she was trying to sound all brave and tough. Her lip trembled slightly and it was all I could do not to lean forward and kiss the hell out of her. I'd be willing to bet she tasted sweet. What the fuck was I going to do with her? I couldn't just claim some random woman, but the VP had backed me into a damn corner.

Scratch came back toward us, then snatched her release papers from Renegade. His eyebrows shot up and he stared hard at the woman I was fighting the urge to keep.

"Jordan Withers?" Scratch asked. "Any relation to Jameson Withers?"

"My oldest brother," she said.

Scratch's gaze locked with mine and his jaw tightened a minute. "Shit just got more difficult."

"Why?" I asked, not having a fucking clue who Jameson Withers was.

"I've kept up with the VPs of Hades Abyss and Devil's Fury after what went down with Wraith's woman. I mentioned our latest prospects last time I was talking to Slash. Devil's Fury has two new prospects. Denver Casey and Jameson Withers," Scratch said.

I heard Jordan gasp and when I looked, she had paled and swayed on the stool. I reached out to steady her and she melted against me. Damn but she felt too fucking perfect.

"What's the problem?" I asked Scratch.

"I need to talk to your girl," Scratch said, his voice lowering as he gazed at Jordan, and I could tell by the look in his eyes that whatever he had to say, it wasn't good news.

She clutched at me and I didn't think she was letting go anytime soon, but the others backed off and gave us some privacy. Scratch moved in closer and reached out to smooth his hand down her hair. He looked like he'd rather be anywhere else right then, and I wondered if the news he had would break the woman in my arms.

"Jordan, your brother Jameson did change his number. Your other brother, Stuart, did not. And there's a good reason your other brother didn't pick you up today," Scratch said.

"Where are my brothers?" she asked, her voice subdued and all the fight having gone out of her.

"Jameson is with a club called Devil's Fury. He's a Prospect, which means he hasn't patched in, but he's trying to earn his place. Stuart... Stuart's dead, sweet girl. I'm sorry to be the one to tell you that. He got mixed up in some stuff he should have left alone, and he ended up shot," Scratch said.

"Why didn't Dopey come pick me up?" she asked.

Dopey? I looked at Scratch and he seemed to be fighting back a laugh.

"Dopey," he said, "or CJ as the rest of us know him, was on an errand that I sent him on earlier today. He said he had somewhere to be, but didn't elaborate. It's my fault you weren't picked up."

Wait. What? CJ? Our Prospect CJ? Scratch gave me a nod. Yep, I was fucked.

"CJ is one of you?" she asked, her brow furrowed.

"He's a Prospect," Scratch said. "Jameson tried to get him to go to Devil's Fury with him, but CJ had been hanging out with some of us already and felt more at home here. He's been prospecting about six months now."

"And what about my other brother?" she asked.

"From what little I know of your youngest brother, he's probably been out partying all night and is dead asleep. He may very well come for you when he wakes up, or knowing that CJ is here, he may decide you've already got the help you need," Scratch said. "Either way, that makes you part of two clubs. You can stay here with us, and we'll protect you, or I can call the VP of Devil's Fury and tell him what's up and see if they want you over there."

"I don't... I don't..." She shook her head, then buried her face in my chest.

I tightened my hold on her and pressed a kiss to the top of her head. Her life had been turned upside down, after having already lost time on the inside of hell, and I could only imagine how she felt right now. Whatever she needed, I'd see that she had it. Scratch was right. With CJ being one of our Prospects, that made Jordan family, or prospective family. Either way, she was mine to protect. I just hoped she'd let me.

The clubhouse door slammed into the wall and a harried looking CJ stormed inside, then drew up short when he saw Jordan in my arms.

"What the fuck are you doing with my sister?" he demanded.

Yeah, this was going to be fun. Hope Jordan didn't hold a grudge if I had to beat her brother's ass.

Chapter Three

Jordan

CJ sounded pissed off as he entered the clubhouse and found me in Havoc's arms. Honestly though, being held by the ginger made me feel safer than I ever had in my life. With his size and strength I would have thought him to be rough, but his touch was gentle, and his voice both soothed me and made me want things I shouldn't.

I tried to pull away, but Havoc held me tight.

"I'm fine, Dopey," I said, making my brother wince as he approached us.

"Do you have to call me that?" he asked.

"Right. You're a big, badass biker now," I said. "Any other changes I need to know about?"

He looked away, but not before the I saw the pain in his eyes.

"They told me about Stuart," I said softly. "Why didn't any of you come and tell me what was going on?"

"You had enough to deal with," he said.

"Is that why no one came to see me?" I asked. "Colby came twice, and then I didn't hear from any of you again. I thought…"

"She thought you fuckers had abandoned her, asshole," Havoc said. "And you sure as fuck did. I found her passed out on the side of the road between the prison and here."

CJ paled. "I'm sorry. Scratch sent me on an errand, and I tried to get back on time."

"Have you even been to the prison or called to check on her?' Havoc asked.

"No, I was going to drop off the stuff I was sent to pick up, and then I was going to go get her." He looked at me, but what I saw wasn't reassuring. I didn't believe him.

"With CJ being her brother, we can permit her to stay in a room here at the clubhouse," Scratch said. "But she may not like all the things she sees. The offer still stands to come stay with my family."

I didn't want to release Havoc, but Scratch's words played in my mind. If I went with Havoc, that meant I was letting him claim me, and I didn't want that. And I was almost certain he didn't want it either. Yes, there was an attraction between us, but we hadn't even known each other an hour. Surely they didn't just go around claiming random women they'd never met before.

"In light of who her family is and everything she's been through, maybe we should let her decide what she wants, VP," Havoc said. "I think she's had enough stress for the day."

Scratch rubbed a hand across his beard before nodding. "All right. Jordan, where do you want to stay? Or if you would prefer to go to Jameson's club, I can make a call and have it arranged."

I looked at my brother. To everyone else, he probably just seemed concerned about me, but I could see beneath that. He didn't want me here, and he wasn't pleased that I wasn't still locked up. No matter what he said, he'd kept everything from me for his own reasons and not to save me. I didn't know who Dopey had become while I was locked up, but I didn't think I much cared for this version of him.

"I want to stay with Havoc," I said. "But I don't want…"

I bit my lip when I felt Havoc tense. Maybe he didn't want me to stay with him. I should have just asked to go stay with Jameson. That would have been the smarter thing to do. It was obvious that CJ didn't want me, and Havoc sure as hell didn't want to claim me. I tried to pull away, but he wouldn't let me.

Scratch moved in closer. "You don't want what?"

"You shouldn't make him claim me. It's not right. We're strangers and may end up hating each other," I said.

Humor flashed in his eyes. "I seriously doubt Havoc is going to hate you. If anything, you may get sick of his overbearing ways and want to kick him in the balls."

"I do have experience hitting men where it counts," I said. "Maybe he should be worried about that."

Havoc started laughing, and I wasn't sure what to make of it. He didn't seem the least bit worried about me hurting his family jewels, or any other part of him. Guess I could see why. The man was huge, and I doubted that many men, let alone women, decided to take him on. He shouldn't underestimate me though. If I had to fight to protect myself, or someone I loved, then I'd do it. I thought I'd proven myself capable of handling things if the need arose.

"Wait," CJ said. "Claim? Like in…"

"Havoc is going to make your sister his old lady, if he takes her home with him," Scratch said.

"No fucking way!" CJ's face flushed red and fury came off him in waves. "That's complete bullshit! I've been busting my ass around here for six months to prove myself, and you just pick her up on the side of the road and she's automatically a part of the club?"

Scratch and Havoc both went still and focused their gazes on my brother. I wondered when it would click in his pea brain that this was an "oh shit" moment for him, and he should probably start groveling for fucking up. Neither man seemed to be the type to take that kind of shit, especially from someone who wasn't officially part of their club. I'd noticed Scratch's leather vest said VP and

Havoc's said Sergeant at Arms, while the others just had their names on it. And in the case of my brother, not even his name was on his. Which meant he was at the bottom of the totem pole and had likely just fucked up big time.

"What did you say to me, boy?" Scratch asked, his voice a low growl.

CJ tensed and I watched as the red faded from his skin and went nearly albino white. "I didn't mean... Sorry, VP."

"Something wrong with your sister being part of this club?" Havoc asked.

He hadn't let go of me yet, and I wondered if that was all that had saved CJ from getting knocked on his ass. Havoc seemed like the type who might hit first and ask questions later. At least with other men.

"No, sir," CJ said, taking a step back. "It's just... she's a criminal! She's not like Clarity or Josie."

I looked up to see how Havoc felt about that and he had arched one of his eyebrows. Releasing me, he took a step toward my brother, then another until he was right in CJ's face.

"If you have a problem with people who have done time, then I'd suggest you turn in that cut right now and haul your ass out of here as fast as you can," Havoc said.

Cut? What the hell was he talking about?

CJ clutched at his vest and I figured that's what Havoc had meant by cut. I'd never really paid attention to biker shows before and it seemed I had a lot to learn.

Scratch put himself between me and my brother, which was sweet but unnecessary. Even if CJ did come after me, I could hold my own against him. We'd been fighting amongst ourselves since I was big enough to be a pain in all four of my brothers' asses. Jameson was twenty-nine, Stuart would be twenty-eight if he were still alive, Dopey was twenty-six, and Colby was twenty-five. I was the baby at twenty-one, and definitely an "oops" since Mom had thought she couldn't have more kids. She'd had her tubes tied after Colby, but apparently they'd grown back, and I came along four years later.

"No problem, Havoc," CJ said.

"Or didn't you know that quite a few men in this club had done time?" Havoc asked. "Myself included. I spent quite a bit of time in the same hellhole as your sister."

Havoc had been in prison? Before my life behind bars, that would have sent me running the other way. Now, not so much. I'd met some really great women inside. Some were doing time for crimes they swore they hadn't committed, others like me had done the crime but for reasons we thought were legitimate, and then there were those who had no remorse and would likely be locked up again shortly after they were released. If they ever got set free to begin with.

It also explained how he knew about the letter I'd been given. Had he received the same thing? I didn't like the thought of something bad happening to him inside, but he seemed to be fine now. Whatever had happened, it seemed to be firmly in his past, which is where I was hoping to leave my time served. Even though I knew it would haunt me the rest of my life, every time I applied for a job or if I wanted to finish college. I'd screwed up my life because of my stupid temper.

"I didn't mean anything by it," CJ said. "Just thought you deserved someone better."

I gasped as Havoc hauled back his fist and slammed it into my brother's jaw. Part of me felt like I should rush to CJ's side, but the fact Havoc had just defended me against my own flesh and blood sent me scurrying over to him instead. He was reaching for CJ, likely to pummel him some more, when I wrapped my hand around his bicep. Or tried to. Really, what the hell did the man do for a workout?

"Havoc," I said softly, drawing his gaze down to me.

His jaw tensed. "I won't apologize for hitting me."

"I don't want an apology," I said. I pressed myself closer to him. "Thank you."

His eyebrows shot upward. "You're thanking me? For hitting your brother?"

"You were defending me." I leaned up and tugged him down so I could whisper in his ear. "And it was really hot watching you do that. Maybe I can thank you properly?"

His gaze heated as he tossed me over his shoulder again.

"VP, if this means she's mine, so be it. We're going home," Havoc said, slapping my ass and carrying me outside.

I could hear the others inside laughing and my brother cursing. Just like that? No real conversation between us? Not so much as a kiss, and he was okay with having to keep me? I still didn't quite grasp what being an old lady meant. If it was like a wife, did that mean there was some sort of biker divorce if things didn't work out between us?

Havoc set me down on my feet and the world spun for a moment. It had been a while since I'd had anything to eat, and that bottle of water was long gone. He gripped my waist with his hands to steady me, and I could see the concern in his eyes.

"What's wrong, baby?" he asked.

"Just a little dizzy." My stomach chose that moment to growl, loudly. My cheeks flushed and his lips thinned.

"I'm not taking very good care of you, am I?" he asked. "Can you manage a short ride on the bike?"

"I think so."

He climbed onto the silver and black Harley Davidson, then nodded for me to climb on back. I wrapped my arms around his waist and he leaned over to position my feet.

"Don't want you to get burned on the pipes," he said. "Jeans and boots are better for riding."

I didn't exactly have either of those things. Hell, I didn't have anything anymore. I didn't know what my brothers had done with my stuff, but if Dopey's reaction to me was anything to go by it had likely been sent to Goodwill or burned. I didn't understand how he could hate me so much. And how the hell did two of my straight-laced brothers end up affiliated with motorcycle clubs? It baffled the hell out of me.

Havoc started the bike and eased out of the parking lot in front of the clubhouse. There was a road that stretched in either direction inside the gates and he headed left. I could see a few houses, and I wondered if everyone in the club had a house here. Then I remembered hearing that the VP lived outside of the gates. So not everyone then, but Havoc did, and probably some of the others.

He stopped in from a yellow clapboard house with black shutters and white trim. It seemed so... cheerful, and not at all what I would have thought the biker would choose for a home. Or maybe it had just been given to him without input. Either way, I thought it was cute, and I could easily picture some flowerbeds out front filled with brightly-colored blossoms. It seemed like a nice home to raise a family, not that I had any intention of having a family. I was definitely not mother material.

I climbed off the bike and Havoc took my hand, leading me inside. The little walkway leading to the front door looked rather plain, but I could imagine it with some cute little lights on either side. If he was seriously claiming me and this would be my home, maybe he'd let me add a few things here and there. Like plants and lights.

He pushed open the door and we stepped inside. The entry was small, just a tiled section that was a probably six feet square, if that. A hall lay ahead of us and I could see four doors, all of them shut. The living room was to my right, and a kitchen and dining area were to the left. The house was small, but nice. And surprisingly clean.

"I like your home," I said.

"Your home too, if Scratch was serious."

"Does that bother you?" I asked.

He shrugged, then his gaze swept over me from head to toe. "Not really. I've never been tempted to claim someone before, but the thought of you being permanently mine doesn't make me want to run away."

Not exactly a glowing endorsement, but I'd take it.

"Well, I guess I should tell you that the thought of being with you for more than a night doesn't make me want to run screaming into the night either."

He smirked and led me over to the small table and chairs. He pulled one out and nodded for me to have a seat. While I scanned the room to get a feel for what kind of man Havoc was, he pulled stuff from the fridge and cabinets.

"I hope spaghetti is okay. It's just sauce from a jar, but I add meat to it," he said. "It's the quickest thing I can make other than a sandwich, and I thought you might need something more filling than a few pieces of meat and some bread."

"I love pasta," I said, and it was true. I'd eat pretty much any type of pasta he put in front of me.

He grinned and turned back to the stove. It wasn't long before the scent of seasoned meat teased my nose, and I could hear the water starting to boil for the noodles. He drained the meat and added the sauce, then turned down the temp on the stove. After he added the noodles to the boiling water, he turned to face me, folding his arms over his chest.

"I'm going to guess that your brothers are all older than you," he said.

"Yeah. I'm the unexpected baby of the family," I said. "Turned twenty-one while I was locked up."

"If I had any damn sense, I'd send you back to the clubhouse and let someone else watch over you," he muttered and looked away.

"Why?"

"Because I'm too damn old for you," he said. His gaze locked with mine. "I'm thirty-nine, Jordan. I've seen more shit and done more shit than you can even imagine. I was locked up for a while, but before that I served six years with the Marines. I prospected for Devil's Boneyard for about a year, and was patched in. Six months later, I did something I shouldn't have and got caught. They locked me up indefinitely, but I got out after three years served because some guards thought it would be funny to let some other inmates try to beat me to death. So I'm not a good man, Jordan. You deserve a lot better than me."

"A bad man wouldn't have stopped to help me. He would have left me there, or violated me while I wasn't able to fight back."

I saw his biceps bulge and knew he didn't like the thought of that happening to me, but it was the truth. Especially if that guard had been watching and waiting for me. If what Havoc said was true, then the man would be coming for me, probably when I least expected it.

I pushed my chair back and walked over to him, putting my arms around his waist. "You're an honorable man, Havoc. Even if you don't see it."

"I follow my own set of rules, baby. Just because I don't like hurting women doesn't make me a nice guy."

"So a man who follows the law, never gets so much as a speeding ticket, but then decides to ignore a woman saying no and forces himself on her is a nice guy, but someone like you who may have done bad things but wouldn't hurt me is considered bad?" I asked. "Not by my standards."

"Then you're setting that bar too low."

"Havoc." He looked down at me. "You make me feel safe. I haven't had that in a long time. Please don't make yourself out to be some monster. No matter what you tell me you've done, you'll still be the man who saved me."

"Call me Ryan. When we're alone," he said.

"Ryan?"

He nodded. "Ryan Campbell, even though I haven't used that name in a long time."

"But you want me to use it?" I asked.

"Yeah." His gaze held mine. "I think I like the way it sounds on your lips. And just so you know, I haven't let a woman call me Ryan since I patched in and earned the name Havoc. So don't go thinking just anyone gets that privilege."

It warmed me from the inside out that he was giving me a part of himself that no one else had. I didn't know what it meant exactly, but it made me feel special.

"Go sit, baby. I'll finish up the pasta and we can eat."

I sat back down at the table and my stomach growled again as he slid a plate in front me a few minutes later. The sauce might have come from a jar, but there were chucks of bell pepper and onion mixed in with the meat he'd cooked. It smelled really damn good, and it was easily the best thing I'd tasted in the last year. Maybe even before that. We didn't talk much while we ate, and I focused on filling my belly. He'd given me a glass of water, which was probably a good idea since I was likely still dehydrated. By the time I was finished, I was starting to feel icky from the dried sweat on my skin, and I doubted I was looking my best.

I pulled at my shirt and frowned. Even if I did take a shower, it wasn't like I had anything clean to wear. Without my clothes, all I had was what I was wearing. I didn't feel up to a shopping trip, and I doubted my twenty-two dollars would buy much, but I needed at least one change of clothes. Even it was just a pair of knit shorts, a tee, and some clean undies. I could wash my bra and let it dry overnight if I had to.

"What's wrong, baby girl?" he asked.

"I need a shower, but I don't have anything else to wear."

He rubbed his beard and leaned back in his chair. After a moment, he pulled out his phone, tapped on the screen a few times, then slid it across the table.

"Enter your sizes in there, and make sure you include shoes. I'll go pick you up some things while you shower. You can put on one of my shirts when you're done if I'm not back yet," he said.

I stared at the Notes app. "Um, I only have a little over twenty dollars."

Havoc reached across the table and tipped my chin up. "You're not paying for this shit, I am. And no arguments. You've been through hell, and something tells me that even before you went inside it had been a while since someone took care of you. I'm not about to let you go without the things you need."

"Havoc, I..."

He pinched my chin and I shut up.

"If you argue with me about this, I will turn you over my knee and paddle that sweet ass of yours. Are we clear?"

My cheeks flushed and I nodded. Was it wrong that my panties were suddenly damp and it wasn't from me sweating? I'd never had a guy threaten to spank me before, but it was oddly arousing. Maybe I'd read too many romance novels, but I really wanted to know what it would feel like to have his hand crack down across my ass.

"Good girl," he said. "Now enter your sizes. For everything. If you have a shampoo and soap preference, put that in too."

I typed in my clothing and shoe sizes, including what size bra I wore and that I liked an underwire. Of course, he probably had no clue what the hell an underwire bra was, but maybe he could figure it out. I chewed on my lip a moment before putting in my favorite scents for hair and bath products, and added some lip balm to the list. As badly as I would have liked to have make-up, I knew a guy would never pick out the right things. Although, at this point, I'd be happy with some dollar store mascara.

I slid the phone back across to him, and he pocketed it without even looking at my list. Then he helped me up and led me down the hall. He paused outside one of the doors, then kept walking to the one at the end. Havoc opened the door and I knew immediately it was his bedroom. He stopped at the dresser and pulled out a gray T-shirt before herding me into the bathroom. It wasn't an overly large space, but he had a separate tub and shower, and I noticed the tub had jets. It had been so long since I'd been able to enjoy a relaxing bath, but no way I was going to soak in the nasty water that would result from my sweaty body. Definitely a shower this time.

"Use anything in here that you need," he said. "Except my razor."

I eyed his beard.

"I keep my neck shaved," he said. "And it hurts like a bitch to use a razor after a woman has used it. I'll buy you one at the store."

For some reason, I felt insanely jealous that he knew what it was like to shave with a razor a woman had used. Did that mean he used to have someone steady in his life? Someone he'd lived with? Had she lived here with him? I looked around, searching for any sign a female had ever lived in this house or shared this bathroom with him.

"Baby?"

I snapped my gaze back to his.

"It was my sister who used my razor back in high school," he said.

"I didn't…"

He smirked and I shut up.

Havoc bent down into my space and our gazes locked a moment before he pressed his lips to mine. I gasped at the contact and he deepened the kiss, nearly making my knees buckle. My body came to life and he wasn't even touching me with anything other than his lips. The way he nearly devoured me made me think maybe he really did want me as much as it had seemed. When he pulled back, I found myself leaning toward him, wanting more.

"Never lived with a woman until now," he said. "And that bed in there hasn't had anyone but me in it. So whatever you're thinking, you can stop. I'm not a monk by any means, but no one's ever rated high enough to come home with me. I sure as fuck haven't ever been tempted to keep someone before."

It made me wonder just where he had sex with them then, but I wasn't about to ask. I dumbly watched as he walked out of the room, and I knew that my life was about to drastically change. The man was a force to be reckoned with, and while I'd never lost my heart to someone, something told me that Ryan Campbell might just be the man to storm my defenses and claim me in every way possible.

It was enough to both frighten and excite me.

Yeah, I was screwed. Probably both metaphorically and literally.

Chapter Four

Havoc

"Why do you want me to come with you?" Renegade asked. "I don't know shit about women's clothes and shoes."

"More like I was hoping you could ask Nikki for help," I said, thinking of Renegade's little sister.

He gave me the side-eye. "You want me to voluntarily bring Nicole along to go shopping for women's shit? You been sampling the products?"

I snorted. "No, shithead. I didn't fall into the weed. I just want to make sure I get the right things for Jordan. It's been a year since she's had shit that wasn't state issued. If anyone gets how that feels, it's me. And her dickhead brothers probably didn't keep any of her things when she went inside."

He sighed. "Fine. But you owe me for this. And don't go blaming me if she hits on you."

Nikki was easily handled. Besides, I wasn't the one she had her eye on. She flirted with everyone, and some of the guys always flirted back. The kid was sweet, but there was a curvy blonde back at my house who had me tied into knots. A damn Victoria's Secret model could walk in front of me wearing next to nothing and I wouldn't be the slightest bit tempted.

I tuned out Renegade as he called his sister and browsed the clothes. I didn't have a clue what women liked, especially young ones like Jordan. I grabbed some shirts with thin straps and some shorts that looked comfortable for around the house. Standing in the middle of the women's department left me feeling like a fish out of water. I didn't have a clue what any of these styles were called. A shirt was a shirt and shorts were shorts, right? Apparently not, according to the tags hanging on the clothes.

"She'll be here in ten," Renegade said. "She was nearby when I called."

"Great. While we're waiting, I'll check out pajamas and shit. Surely I can manage that much without help."

"Depends. Are you buying stuff you want to see her wear or stuff she'll actually like?" he asked.

I shrugged. "Maybe both."

I tossed some slinky nightgowns into the cart I was pushing, and was staring at the other crap in that section when Nikki came bounding up to us like an eager puppy. The broad smile on her face spelled trouble. And if that didn't, then the sparkle in her eyes definitely did. I had a feeling she was enjoying the fact I was buying crap for a woman. She'd hit on me several times and I'd always brushed her off, completely uninterested. Not that she'd ever taken it personally. Flirting was just the way Nikki operated. I didn't think anything ever tore her down. If someone could be sunshine and goodness twenty-four-seven, it was Nikki.

"I do love me a ginger!" She pressed a kiss to my cheek.

"Nikki," I said, a hint of warning in my tone.

"I know, I know. You've found a woman you actually invited to your house. I had my brother repeat himself like twenty times because I was certain my hearing was going. No way Havoc would ever let a woman into his house," she said, a grin on her lips.

"Knock it off, Nikki," Renegade said. "Jordan's a sweetheart. Besides, her brother is prospecting for us."

"For now," I said. "If the asshole doesn't straighten up when it comes to Jordan, I have no problem booting his ass out the door."

"Scratch seems to like your girl, so I'm sure he'd agree," Renegade said.

Nikki's jaw dropped. "She's met Scratch, and he approved of her?"

"Invited her to move in with him and Clarity," Renegade said. "Not that Havoc was going to let that happen. I think he decided she was his the second he saw her."

Nikki's lips twisted and there was a wistful look in her eyes. "I wish that would happen to me."

"Your time will come. In about ten more years," Renegade said.

"Cory Adams, I am *not* waiting until I'm thirty-three to find my Mr. Right! You better take those words back right now!"

He glared when she used his real name, and I tried to contain my laughter.

"Focus, Nikki," I said. "I need to outfit Jordan from the skin out."

She peered into the cart and rolled her eyes. "Really, Havoc? Satin and lace nighties that cover nothing? Do you know how damn uncomfortable those are to sleep in?"

"Who said I planned on her wearing them for sleeping?" I asked.

Nikki's cheeks flushed and she looked everywhere but at me. "Right then."

I followed along behind her as she checked the sizes on my phone, then started tossing things into the cart. We hadn't even made it out of the clothing department before we needed a second shopping cart, and I had a feeling Jordan was going to lose her shit when she saw how much stuff I was buying. It wasn't as high quality as I would have liked, but the big box twenty-four hour store was the only place I could think of that would have everything we needed without running all over town.

When we reached the shoe department, Nikki dug through the clothes in the cart before tossing in two different types of sandals, tennis shoes, and about four pair of flip-flops. Since it was summer, there was no way we were finding boots at this place, but I'd stop by the Harley Davidson store when I had more time and outfit Jordan properly for her next bike ride because I was damn sure getting her on my bike for a longer trip than going from the clubhouse to my home.

I didn't know how long I'd been gone by the time we approached the register. The poor cashier had a deer in the headlights expression when she saw two nearly overflowing carts. By the time everything was bagged and I'd paid, I was ready to never see the inside of a store again. At least one that carried clothes. I would make an exception for the Harley Davidson store, though. It was on a different level from regular store shopping, and I could stay in there for at least an hour or more. Something shiny always caught my attention. Usually the new bikes.

Thankfully, I'd snagged the club SUV or I wouldn't have had a way to get all this shit home. Renegade rode to the house with me so he could return the SUV when I was finished. I'd have to walk to the clubhouse later to get my bike. I could have ridden with Renegade, but I didn't want to be away from Jordan for another second. I was honestly waiting for her to have a breakdown of some sort, after having to walk from the prison and then her brother acting like a dick, and finding out that one of her brothers had died while she was locked up. She hadn't had an easy day.

I set all the bags inside the door, then went to find the woman who was dominating my thoughts. The sight of her curled up in my bed made my chest feel tight. I took off my boots and stripped down to my boxer briefs, then climbed into bed next to her, pulling her into my arms. She fit perfectly against me and immediately snuggled closer. She smelled like my shampoo and shower gel, but under that was her own sweet scent. I got hard just breathing her in, but fuck if I would try to do anything about it right now. She needed rest, not me pawing at her.

Jordan wedged her leg between mine and pressed even closer. Her hands clutched at me, like she was worried I'd take off. After what she'd lost today, I could understand it, but I wasn't going anywhere. Not unless she kicked my ass to the curb, but if Scratch followed through on his threat, then we were stuck together indefinitely. The club didn't believe in divorce. I knew some clubs that had stripped their old ladies of their patches and kicked their asses out when the guys were tired of them, but we didn't operate that way. After seeing the way the Dixie Reapers were with their women, it had made some of us want the same thing.

The Devils had been in a shit ton of trouble for a long-ass time, but we were pretty clean these days. We still sold pot, a lot of it, and did some gun runs, but the assholes who had tried to take us out weren't an issue anymore. We would no doubt make more enemies over the years, but for now, things were pretty peaceful. We helped some of the other clubs when the need arose, and I had no doubt they would be here if we had trouble. Depending on how things went with the guard who had attacked Jordan, we might have to call in reinforcements sooner than we'd like. Or maybe we could just hire some extra muscle. Our accounts were more than flush thanks to Scratch's wife.

Jordan whimpered in her sleep and I ran my hand up and down her back, trying to soothe her and chase away whatever nightmare she was having. She settled back down and her breathing went back to being even and deep. I wondered when she'd last slept well. Prison could be a bitch to deal with, and she seemed so soft and sweet I was surprised the system hadn't chewed her up and spit her out. It still amused me to no end that she'd not only been arrested for assault, but that she nailed a guard where it hurts most. Some men might have taken a big step back, but to me she was like one of those cute little purse dogs that would bite the shit out of you, and I had no doubt if I compared her to one of those dogs out loud that she'd do her best to hand my balls to me. Yep, cute.

My phone vibrated in my pocket and I grabbed my jeans off the floor and pulled it out and saw Scratch's name on the display.

"Everything okay, VP?" I asked when I answered.

"Maybe. Jameson knows his sister is out of prison and that she's here." He paused. "He also knows you took her home with you."

"So should I expect a visit from a pissed-off Devil's Fury Prospect sometime soon?" I asked.

"Possibly. I think Slash is trying to rein him in. He didn't know baby sis was getting out early, and doesn't seem pleased that he's not only the last to find out but that she's not there with him."

Fuck my life. "Well, he can come for her if he wants, but I'm not letting her walk out of here. That dickhead didn't even bother to make sure she knew how to reach him, or where he was. Who does that shit to their own flesh and blood?"

"I think that's part of the problem. Guilt," Scratch said. "I'll keep you posted."

"Can I ask you something?"

"What?" Scratch asked, sounding tired.

"If things get dicey and that guard comes after Jordan, are we calling in other clubs or dipping into funds to hire some extra men to keep an eye out?"

He chuckled. "You mean dig into that massive inheritance my wife refuses to touch and signed over to the club? Yeah, I could see Clarity being fine with using some of it for that. I know Cinder put down a chunk on the new compound and he plans to add more houses over the next year or two as we expand, but that won't even put a dent in what she gave us."

"I still can't believe she didn't want it."

"I convinced her to hold onto half a million for the kids to use when they get older for college or whatever the fuck they want to do with their lives. We've invested it so by the time they're old enough to need it, who knows how much will be in that account."

"Your doing or hers?" I asked.

"A bit of both. She's smarter than she gives herself credit for," Scratch said.

I stared at the woman sleeping in my arms. "You like all that daddy shit, don't you?"

"Yeah, I do. And don't you say a fucking word to anyone, but we think Clarity might be pregnant again. She'll know for sure after her appointment tomorrow. She's been a little moodier lately, and you know how damn sweet and even tempered she usually is."

I snorted. "Yeah, as long as a club slut isn't touching you."

He chuckled. "That's the truth. I think she scared the shit out of them. I haven't had a single one come on to me since that incident. And they make sure to warn the new girls."

I grinned, thinking about Jordan taking down one of those women. It would be hot as fuck to watch her in action. As much as I didn't want her in danger, I wouldn't mind seeing her kick the shit out of someone.

"How's Jordan?" Scratch asked.

"Sleeping. She took a shower while I ran to get her some clothes and other crap women need, and when I came back she was passed out in my bed."

"Did she know it was yours?" he asked.

"Yeah. Why?"

I heard him crack his neck and braced for whatever was coming.

"Listen, I wasn't really going to make you claim her. Just wanted you to stop and think with the head on your shoulders and not your dick, but I think you may actually be what she needs right now. I know you're worried about that guard showing up, but I think CJ might be a bigger problem, and he's inside the compound with you."

I frowned. "Yeah, but he was pissed I would claim her. I think actually doing that would backfire and just make him even madder."

"So let her live there with you for a bit. Help her assimilate to civilian life again, make sure she knows that you have her back and so does the club. I think she needs a good support system right now, and obviously her brothers are a bunch of fuckups when it comes to taking care of her. If she seems to want more, then you have my permission to make her yours in whatever way you want. No club vote needed. The guys who met her already think she's Devils material."

"Thanks, VP."

"Go take care of your girl. Clarity wants to meet her whenever Jordan is up for it. I'm sure Josie will want to as well once she hears you brought a woman home."

I snorted knowing he wasn't wrong. Josie had felt outnumbered for a while, until Scratch had found Clarity. Those two were thick as thieves, but Clarity's practical nature usually helped keep Josie in check. I didn't know what would happen when we threw Jordan into the mix.

"Call if you need anything," Scratch said, then he disconnected the call.

I set the phone on the table next to the bed and tried to just enjoy holding Jordan. I was glad to hear my club had my back and Jordan's. If for some reason I wasn't nearby, she could go to any of them for help and I had no doubt they'd step up. CJ could be a problem though. The comments he'd made when he saw Jordan at the clubhouse still bothered me, especially when he realized she was going home with me.

Jordan began shifting around again, and soon her eyes opened. She looked confused for a moment, then smiled softly when she realized who was holding her. She buried her face in my chest and I heard her take a deep breath.

"Does this mean you aren't going to kick my ass for getting into bed with you?" I asked.

She rubbed against me then reached between us and cupped my cock.

"Depends. Are you going to do something with this?"

"At the risk of losing my man card, are you sure about this? You've had the day from hell and I didn't get into this bed expecting to do more than hold you."

She pressed her lips to mine in a brief, soft kiss. "It's because I've had the day from hell that I need to feel you inside of me. Besides, in case you've forgotten, I've been locked up in a prison with a bunch of women for a year. What was the first thing you did when you got out?"

I chuckled. "Downed a few beers and screwed anything female that came within arm's length of me."

"So it's okay for a man to do that and not a woman?" she asked, arching a brow.

"Depends."

"On what?"

"On if you plan to only screw me or if you're going to try to take a ride on every dick in the compound."

She bit my bottom lip, making my cock jerk. "Only yours."

"Then I'd say we're wearing too many clothes."

She pulled back and tugged my shirt over her head. Her body was even more beautiful than I'd imagined. Her skin was pale from not getting much sun the last year, and even though she was curvy as fuck, she had some muscle tone too. I could see how she could take down a man twice her size. I admired her body another moment before I pulled off my underwear and tossed it aside.

Her gaze went wide as she stared at my cock.

"Did you think I wouldn't be size proportionate?" I asked.

"I just… I've never seen one that big before."

I nearly choked as I tried not to laugh at the expression of awe on her face. I'd seen plenty of impressed women over the years, but none of them mattered. The way Jordan eyed my cock made me feel like a fucking king. I moved lightning fast and had her pinned to the bed within seconds. She blinked up at me then smiled slowly.

"And what are you going to do with me now?" she asked.

"Taste every inch of you."

I kissed her long and hard before I sampled every dip and curve. Her breasts weren't that big, but they were a tempting handful. Her nipples were so fucking responsive I wondered if I could make her come just by sucking on them. I figured she had a lot of orgasms coming to her, and I intended to be the only man giving them. I licked and sucked at her nipples some more, then lightly bit one. She cried out and her body bucked under me.

With a groan, I teased her pussy with my fingers and felt how fucking wet she was. Christ! She really had come just from me playing with her nipples. I bet she'd go off like a rocket when I ate her pretty little pussy. There was only one way to find out. I kissed my way down her body until my shoulders spread her thighs wide. The hair covering her mound was trimmed really damn short. I looked up at her, knowing the prison hadn't let her do that.

"I may have borrowed your trimmers," she said. "But I didn't touch your razor."

I closed my eyes and just breathed a moment. Now every time I touched the damn things, I'd know they'd been used on this delectable pussy. I spread her lips and gave her a long, slow lick. When my tongue touched her clit, her body tensed and she made a low keening noise. My gaze fastened on her face as I sucked the little bud into my mouth, and fuck if she didn't come again. I'd never had a woman respond so fast before, or so easily.

I made her come twice more, lapping up her cream each time, before I braced my weight over her and pressed my hips to hers. My cock brushed against her wet folds and I was so fucking tempted to just sink inside, but I was just sane enough to remember I needed to wrap my dick first. I'd never been inside a woman bare before, and had never been tempted until now.

When I opened the bedside table drawer I froze a second, remembering Scratch say he'd knocked up Clarity when a condom broke. I stared at the box in the drawer and tried really fucking hard to remember when I'd gotten it, or where. I never brought women here, but every now and then I'd stash a box of condoms here just in case it ever happened. Usually, I grabbed a condom out of the community supply at the clubhouse.

"What's wrong?" she asked.

"Not sure I trust the condoms I have stashed here."

"I'm clean," she said. "If that's what you're worried about."

"More worried that you'll kick me in the balls if I knock you up."

She tugged on my beard until I looked down at her. "Put the damn thing on, then get inside of me. I'm not waiting while you go get more."

I glanced at the condoms again. "What if they break? Or maybe they're defective?"

"I believe in fate," Jordan said. "If we use protection and I end up pregnant, then it's meant to be. Maybe that baby will grow up and cure cancer or something."

I looked down at the sexy woman lying under me. "You serious?"

"It's not like I'll make you step up and take care of us. I'll get a job and figure things out."

I growled and nipped her on the jaw. "You get pregnant, you better damn sure believe I'm taking responsibility. Fuck, Jordan! I already want to keep you in my damn bed. You think I'm kicking you out if I knock you up?"

"No," she said softly. "You seem like the honorable kind of guy who would do the right thing. Ryan. Shut up and fuck me. Either put on the damn condom or don't, but don't make me wait anymore."

I stared into her eyes and it was like I was looking at my future. The way she looked up at me so trustingly, the way her body had responded to my touch... I probably wasn't in the right frame of mind to be making monumental decisions, but fuck it. I sank into her wet heat and locked my gaze with her as I filled her. She moaned and her eyes dilated as I sank balls deep inside of her.

As much as I wanted to pound into her, I used slow, easy thrusts, enjoying the hell out of her expressions and her rapid, shallow breaths that told me she was already fucking close to coming again.

"That's it, baby. Let me feel you come on my cock."

She gripped my biceps, her nails biting into my skin, and she came apart under me, her pussy damn near strangling my cock, I knew I couldn't hold back anymore. I took her harder and faster, not stopping until I came with a roar. My cum slicked her tight little pussy as I came harder than I ever had before. My muscles trembled when the last drop left my balls and I breathed heavily as I stared at the beautiful angel lying under me.

"You're mine, Jordan. Fuck giving you a choice or giving a shit what anyone else thinks. After that, I'm damn sure not letting you walk out."

She threaded her fingers in my hair and pulled me down for a kiss.

"I'm right where I want to be," she said against my lips.

My cock was already getting hard again and I had a feeling it was going to be a long day and night, because I wasn't sure I'd ever get enough of her.

Chapter Five

Jordan

"Did you buy out the entire store?" I asked as I stared at what had to be close to twenty sacks of clothes, shoes, and bathroom crap. "I figured you'd buy me one or two things to get by for now."

He smacked my ass. "Nope. Wanted to make sure you had everything you needed."

I grinned and grabbed his cock through his jeans. "Everything I need is right here."

His eyes heated. "Keep that up and you'll end up bent over the nearest piece of furniture, and I know you're sore."

He wasn't wrong about that. We'd had a sex marathon well into the morning hours, only stopping long enough to eat or take a short bathroom break, then we were back at it. I'd never felt the way I did when I was with Havoc. He made my body sing, but it was more than that. I felt like we were connected, almost like we were supposed to have found each other. Crazy probably, but I couldn't deny that I was addicted to him already.

"Get dressed and I'll make breakfast for us. Then I need you tell me everything you can about the guard who assaulted you," he said. "If he comes for you, I want to be prepared."

"You really think he'll try to track me down? How could he even find me here?" I asked.

"You can't stay behind the compound gates forever, baby. Sooner or later, someone will see you around town. He could live here. If he sees you with any of us, then he'll know where you are."

"Right." I blew out a breath. "I'll just put on something real quick and head to the kitchen."

He kissed me hard. "I'm going to keep you safe. You hear me?"

"Yeah, I hear you." I smiled. "My big, bad biker won't let the boogeyman get me."

"Damn straight." He winked at me before walking out of the bedroom.

We'd showered separately since we couldn't seem to keep our hands off each other, and while I'd gotten cleaned up, he'd hauled all my new things into the bedroom. I had no clue what to do with everything. We hadn't exactly discussed the logistics of how this would work. For now, I just dug through the sacks and pulled out panties, a bra, a tank, and some denim shorts. Quickly putting everything on, I ran my new brush through my hair and braided it, then tied it off with the elastics he'd bought as well.

I eyed the sacks again. There was no way that big, burly man had chosen all this girly crap. I could see him selecting the sexy stuff, but the rest? It smacked of a woman helping him, and for some reason that made me feel insanely jealous. Not that I had a right to be. Or did I? He'd said he was keeping me, but I wasn't entirely clear on what he meant by that. We hadn't really talked much, mostly just fucked like bunnies.

The fact he hadn't used a condom even once made me press a hand to my belly. I'd told him if he knocked me up then it was meant to be, but at the time, I'd thought it would be a one-shot deal. He'd filled me with his cum at least a half dozen times. Was he trying to get me pregnant? We definitely needed to talk at some point, and about something other than my predicament. I needed to know what place I held in his life before I said or did something that landed me in a heap of trouble.

The smell of bacon frying teased my nose as I got closer to the kitchen. He stood at the stove, shirtless and barefoot, and I had to admit it was the sexiest thing I'd ever seen. He'd towel dried his hair, but hadn't combed or brushed it yet, and it stood up in disarray, making him look like we'd just been fucking. I must have let out the sigh I felt building because he turned and smiled at me, giving me a wink.

"If you're a vegetarian or something, better tell me before I make a run to the store tomorrow," he said. "Until then, you're stuck eating whatever I have left in the house. Not that you've complained so far when I've fed you meat."

"Nope. I like meat," I said, eyeing his ass in those tight jeans. It was like the denim was made just for him the way it molded to his thick thighs, and everywhere else important.

He snorted and I looked up, realizing he'd caught me checking him out.

"Behave," he said.

"But we have so much fun when I don't."

"Seriously, baby. As much as I'd love to spend the next week in bed with you, there are things we need to take care of, like making sure you're safe."

Speaking of safe... "Are you trying to get me pregnant?"

His shoulders tensed then he slowly looked at me over his shoulder. "Maybe I am."

Huh. Hearing him admit it made me feel... I didn't know what the hell I felt. "Why?"

"If you're pregnant, you won't run far."

I rolled my eyes. "Ryan, do I look like I'm running? If I do run, it's only to take a leap straight onto your cock. I don't think you have to worry about me slipping away in the middle of the night. It's like you're crack and I'm an addict."

He smirked then turned back to the stove. I pulled out a chair and sat. I felt useless, but I still didn't know where he kept everything, or if he even wanted me rummaging around in his kitchen. Seemed kind of silly considering his mouth had been all over my body, but I knew some people were particular about others digging through their things.

I didn't say anything more as he finished making breakfast, then set a plate of eggs, bacon, and toast in front of me, and another plate for himself directly across from mine. He poured two cups of coffee then sat down, sliding one of the mugs over to me. I'd never been a huge coffee drinker, except for my guilty pleasure which was a white mocha once a week, but I sipped at the brew and was pleasantly surprised.

"It's not that cheap shit you get at the store," he said.

"I didn't say anything."

"You looked shocked when you took a swallow." He smiled. "I get it from this company that is veteran owned and operated. Have to order it online, but it's worth it."

"It's really good," I said, taking another sip.

"Eat up and then I want to hear everything, from start to finish. Including why you were arrested to begin with."

I felt my face pale and wondered if he'd think my temper was so cute when he heard why I'd been locked up. Most men didn't want a girlfriend who lost her shit and got arrested for assault. I didn't think even a guy like Havoc would be all that thrilled.

I ate as slowly as I could, even when he was finished and staring at me with his arms folded. It made me feel a little like I was in trouble, except he was far from being my parent, even if he was probably old enough to have a kid my age. Age was just a number though, and I honestly didn't care how old he was. It was refreshing that an older man liked me, since the college and high school boys I'd dated up to this point were all dismal failures. I'd only had sex with one other person in my life, and it had been horrible. He definitely hadn't known what the hell he was doing, but Havoc did. Maybe I'd seen one too many romantic comedies, or read too many books, but surely there wouldn't be so many stories out there about how amazing sex was unless there were guys who could actually please a woman. I'd always wanted to find one.

When I stuffed the last bite of food into my mouth, I knew I was out of time. Whatever bliss I'd experienced since Havoc had brought me home yesterday would be gone soon enough. Men didn't want violent women in their lives, right? Yeah, they might talk a good game, but I doubted that deep down they really wanted someone like me. Hell, just the fact I'd been in jail would run most guys off. Maybe not Havoc since he'd said he'd done time. That should probably bother me, knowing he'd been in jail and possibly still did illegal stuff, but he made me feel so safe and so special it honestly didn't bother me.

"So, I guess you want to know why I was sent to prison," I said. "I told you it was for assault, but I didn't tell you what happened."

"That would be a good place to start. Some college ass get too handsy?"

"Um, no. There was this blonde girl; you know the type. The ones who think they're perfect and God's gift to man, that their shit doesn't stink. She was mouthing off about my youngest brother and I took exception to some of the stuff she was saying. I broke her nose, called her a few names. Next thing I know, police are putting me in cuffs because she'd pressed charges. It seems her daddy was the District Attorney."

He winced.

"Yeah. I didn't have a snowball's chance in hell of getting out of that one. So I was sentenced to three years. I'd been in about thirteen months when one of the male guards cornered me in a dark area. Maybe he didn't realize there were cameras there, or maybe he didn't think it mattered if he was caught. He groped me, then pinned me to the wall and started pulling at my pants while he unfastened his belt."

Havoc's muscles tensed and his cheeks flushed. I could tell he was pissed just hearing about it. Too bad my own flesh and blood didn't seem to give a shit what had happened to me.

"The guard's name was Mark Slater. He had my pants down my hips and stuck his hand between my thighs. When he pulled back enough to unzip his pants and get his cock out, I managed to grab the baton thing in his belt. He just laughed and asked what I was going to do."

Havoc stared but didn't interrupt. I could see the fury in his eyes though.

"I nailed him between the legs with it, and since his cock was partially exposed… Yeah, it wasn't good. I don't know if it will ever work right again, and I don't care. If he goes around raping the inmates, or any other woman, then he deserved what he got. The warden must have felt the same. He fired Slater and offered me a chance of freedom, if I kept my mouth shut. Guess I'm voiding that now, which means he could send me back inside."

Havoc shook his head. "I'm not going to go blabbing to anyone, not outside of the club anyway. They're family and will protect you. I'll see what Shade can find on Mark Slater, ex-prison guard, and we'll go from there. If there's dirt to dig up, he'll find it. And if not, we have friends we can call in."

"Dig up?" I asked.

"Shade's a hacker, but one of other clubs has the number one hacker in the country, possibly the world. If Shade can't find anything useful, he can call Wire and see if the Reaper has any better luck."

Devils. Reapers. Just what kind of world had I tumbled into?

"So what do we do now? Are you going to kick me out?" I asked.

"Kick you out?" His brow furrowed. "Why the fuck would I do that?"

"Because I hit that blonde just for talking shit about my brother. They considered it an unprovoked attack and said I had anger issues. I was supposed to get help inside, learn to control my temper, but I never saw a counselor. I did learn to control myself better. I think. That was more out of necessity though."

He nodded. "Yeah, small as you are, pissing off the wrong people wouldn't have been smart. Since you didn't have ties to any gangs inside, you were probably a sitting duck."

"A woman took me under her wing. She was doing twenty years and was old enough to have been my mom. If it weren't for her, I'm sure my time inside would have been a lot worse. She's why I'm in such good shape. She'd been into weight training before her arrest and she used the prison gym on a regular basis, which meant I did too."

Havoc smiled. "I think it paid off. You have to be the sexiest woman I've ever seen, and as you can tell, I've had trouble keeping my hands off you."

"If you're not kicking me out, what do we do now? Just sit and wait?"

"Want to meet the other ladies in the club? I have to warn you, they both have small kids so either house is probably in total chaos. Neither of them live inside the compound though."

"So it's not a requirement?"

He shook his head.

"You just choose to live inside the gates?" I asked.

"Something like that. All officers had first pick of the few houses that went up when we bought this place. Most of the money went into fencing the property, but six homes were built right off. More will go up over time."

"And you're an officer." I remember his Sergeant at Arms patch. "What is it exactly that you do?"

"Think of me as an enforcer. Someone needs to be reminded of their place, I handle it. Shit gets bad, I make the problem go away. When I said I would protect you, I meant no matter the cost. If I have to get my hands bloody, I'm all right with that. Truth be told, I like putting bad men and women in the ground."

"Just the bad ones?" I asked.

He shrugged. "I guess it's subjective. What I consider a bad person someone else might not. Anyone who hurts women and children is fair game. Someone double-crosses the club, I handle it. Anything else is a case by case basis."

"Why were you in prison?" I asked.

"Killed a man." He watched me, but I just waited to see if he would say more. "I'd served time in the military so when I killed that man, even though I hadn't used a gun or knife, they decided I had used unnecessary force. Something about me being a trained weapon. So they sentenced me to twenty-five years, no possibility of parole. I served ten."

"Ten years?" I asked softly. "In that same prison that held me?"

He nodded.

"What happens to me now?" I asked.

"I guess that depends on you." He reached across the table and took my hand. "You're mine, baby. I'm not letting you walk out of here. That being said, I'm not going to keep you prisoner. You want to take college classes or get a job, I'm okay with that."

"No one will let me near a school or decent job with a record. I fucked up my life that day."

"Maybe not. The club owns a few businesses. You could always work at one of them, but don't feel like you have to do anything. Money isn't an issue."

"Just be your kept woman?" I asked, smiling a little.

"Scratch called this morning. Gave me permission to make you mine. Officially. No club vote needed." He grinned. "Not that Scratch or Jackal asked for permission to claim their women either. We might as well throw that idea away. Seems that when a Devil falls for a woman, we don't give a shit if our brothers approve or not."

"Does that mean by your club standards we're married now?" I asked.

He tipped his head to the side and studied me. "You want a ring or something?"

"I think most little girls dream of walking down the aisle one day. Wearing some pretty dress, flowers everywhere, her best friends standing next to her. I think that dream died for me a year ago. I lost my friends, apparently lost my brothers, and a big wedding just seems stupid."

He squeezed my hand a moment. "Need to tell you something."

"What?"

"Jameson found out that you're not in prison anymore. He's pissed you aren't with the Devil's Fury, says you belong there with him. Since he's just a Prospect, he doesn't really have any clout in the club, but the VP over there gave Scratch a heads up that your brother might try to cause trouble. So, at least one of your brothers does give a shit about you."

"Doesn't explain why he never visited. And I damn sure know he wasn't part of some biker gang when I was arrested."

"Club," Havoc said. "Not a gang. Although, anyone the AMA considers a one-percent club isn't sanctioned."

"AMA?" I asked.

"American Motorcycle Association. The legal clubs are sanctioned through them. We aren't."

I wondered if I would ever understand all the lingo, or ever truly grasp what it meant to be with a member of the Devil's Boneyard. Then again, maybe ignorance was bliss and I didn't really want to know everything. I knew without a doubt that if Havoc needed me, in any capacity, I would be there, no question asked. He'd saved me when he could have left me to die, or called it in and let someone else handle the passed-out lady on the side of the road. I owed him, and as insane as it was, I was already starting to feel things for the rough biker.

I knew insta-lust was a real thing, but maybe the books weren't far off and love at first sight was a thing too. While I wanted to climb him like a tree and let him do wicked things to me, it went deeper than that. I felt like I owed him my loyalty, and by extension the club. The thought of being his, staying with him indefinitely and being his wife or old lady, didn't send me running off. Maybe I craved that sense of belonging, or just liked the thought of someone like him wanting to keep me long-term. Whatever it was, I knew this path I was on was the right one. My life had been derailed a year ago, or so I'd thought. Now I wondered if maybe it was just a way to set me on the course destiny had in mind all along.

"Something else you need to know," he said.

"What?"

"The clubhouse isn't all quiet and tame when the sun goes down. We party hard, and a portion of that includes women who like to fuck bikers. We refer to them as club sluts or club whores. They'll do anything we ask, and have no trouble fucking multiple guys a night, sometimes more than one at a time."

My gut tightened. "And do you partake of their services?"

"Used to."

"You used to?" I asked.

He nodded. "Only woman I want is you, baby. But it won't stop them from trying to get into my pants. Being an officer, they'll covet finding favoritism with me. Think you can handle that? Some naked woman begging me to fuck her?"

The tightening turned into a burning anger as I thought about anyone touching him, putting their breasts in his face and begging for his attention. Yeah, I wasn't going to handle that shit well. Did I lie and tell him it didn't bother me? Was it a deal breaker? I didn't have a clue what he wanted from me right now. What was the right answer?

"Tell you what. Tonight they'll be partying like always. I usually head down for a beer or two, even on the nights I don't stick around." He leaned back in his chair, releasing my hand. "You decide what you want and come let me know. For now, I'm going to call Scratch and Jackal, see if we can meet up at one of their places so you can get to know the ladies."

"All right," I said.

"Don't worry about the dishes. I'll put them in the washer while I make my calls. Go put your things away. The right half of the dresser is yours, and there's half a closet available. I've never kept much shit in the dresser and it only took a minute to shove my clothes over in the closet. If you need more room than that, we'll figure something out."

I nodded and pushed my chair back. By the time I'd put up everything I could, Havoc was drinking another cup of coffee and scrolling through something on his phone. He seemed relaxed at the kitchen table, and I wondered if he was worried about how I would react later tonight. If he was, it didn't show. Either he had a great deal of faith in me, or it didn't matter to him either way, which fucking hurt to think about.

"Josie and Clarity are anxious to meet you," he said, his gaze locking on me. "Seems neither of them thought I'd ever settle down, so they're curious about the woman who tamed me."

I snorted. Tamed. Right.

He grinned. "Come on, baby. I don't want you riding the back in those shorts and without the proper shoes, so we'll take a club vehicle for the day. While we're out, we'll make a stop for the proper riding gear for you."

Just what I wanted, for him to spend even more money on me. I didn't think he would care if I complained, though. I'd likely just get one of those looks that said to shut up and follow orders. A lot of women would be over the moon about a guy spending so much money on them, but I'd never been one of them. I liked being able to earn my own things, probably because my parents had made me get a job at the age of fifteen for all the extra crap I kept asking for. Looking back, I really owed them for that. I'd appreciated the things I'd paid for way more than all the stuff they'd given me, and since it fell to me to pay to replace broken shit, I'd taken better care of my things.

The thought of meeting the ladies of the club scared the shit out of me. What if they didn't like me? What if they thought I wasn't good enough for Havoc, or they were worried when they found out I'd done time? My stomach was knotted as we drove out of the compound, and I hoped like hell I didn't embarrass myself and puke. That would make an awesome impression.

Was it too late to change my mind?

Chapter Six

Havoc

Jackal had offered to watch not only his kids but Scratch's kids too, which meant the ladies were gathered in the living room of the large Victorian house Scratch owned without a kid in sight. The VP and I leaned against the doorframe, watching the women. Clarity and Josie had both welcomed Jordan without question, even though I could see my woman had been scared shitless about meeting them.

"She fits in with them," Scratch said.

"Did you doubt it?"

He didn't answer right away. "Being locked up probably changed her from the woman she was before all this shit went down. My Clarity has a big heart and I knew she'd welcome her, but Josie was a little iffy. You know how she gets when it comes to the club and what she calls her family. I think she adopted all of you as her brothers when Jackal brought her home. Probably makes her miss Tank a little less."

"Any news on Allegra?" I asked. Josie and Jackal's little girl had been through hell, and had some developmental delays. I knew they'd been taking her to some specialists in hopes of having a breakthrough. The kid was three and a half and was still barely speaking.

"The speech therapist has been working with her, but the kid just refuses to talk. I don't think it's so much that she can't, but that she doesn't want to. I have a feeling it will take something special to make her open up. Josie said she'll say something here and there. Like calling Jackal daddy, but as for everyday shit she won't say a word."

"What about counseling?" I asked.

"They're trying that now. Family sessions with all four of them, even though Levi is only a year. He's talking more than Allegra is and it's worrying Jackal and Josie."

I nodded. "I'm sure she'll talk when she's ready."

Scratch watched the ladies a few more moments before nodding toward the hall. We left them alone and I followed him to the kitchen. He leaned back against the cabinets, crossing his ankles and folding his arms.

"You think you're doing the right thing?" he asked.

"About what? Keeping Jordan?"

"No. Testing her tonight," he said. "What if it blows up in your face?"

"I have no doubt she'll show her true colors, which is exactly what I want. She's trying to suppress who she really is, probably because of her arrest and the fear she felt behind bars. I want her to realize she's completely safe with the club and with me, that I welcome her true nature. Am I hoping she'll put a club slut in her place? Hell yeah. But if she doesn't, then I'll know that we have some work to do."

Scratch shook his head. "You're a crazy motherfucker, aren't you?"

"Did you ever doubt it?"

"Not really." He sighed. "I guess I should have known the most hardcore member of this club would need a crazy woman. Just be careful. No one inside the gates will dare have her arrested, but if she loses it out in public then we could have a mess to clean up."

"I'll handle it if that happens. I'm not letting her get locked up again."

Scratch snorted. "No, I guess you wouldn't. You're already trying to knock her up, aren't you?"

"What makes you say that?"

"The way you watch her. I saw the look in your eyes when you walked inside the clubhouse with her yesterday. I knew then you wanted to keep her, and would do whatever it took. Just remember that kids are a lifelong commitment. Don't get her pregnant as a way of hanging onto her, not unless you're prepared to change diapers and get up at three in the morning to help take care of your kid. Being a daddy isn't for everyone."

"Never wanted kids. Never wanted a woman for that matter, not for longer than it took to get off. Jordan's different."

"Seems the Devils have a big problem," Scratch said.

"What's that?"

"We see a woman we want, and that's it. We're done. Head over ass in love and ready to slay any dragons that stand in the way. Just remember that forever is a long fucking time."

"Not long enough."

He smiled. "No, it isn't. Not when it comes to the ladies in the other room. I'm sure Jackal feels the same, now that he's not running scared. I'm surprised Tank didn't rip him to shreds when he showed back up two years after knocking up Josie."

"I can tell you right now if I ever have a daughter and some asshole gets her pregnant and runs, there will be nowhere for him to hide, and he'll be in a shallow grave before he can draw another breath. Unless he wises the fuck up and realizes what's important in life, and that my daughter is a damn angel."

"More like a demon," Scratch said. "Between your personality and Jordan's, you'll probably need a lot of bail money before she's even eighteen."

I laughed, knowing he wasn't wrong. No, whatever kids we had were going to be strong, and be fighters. Girl or boy, I'd make sure they could hold their own and wouldn't take any shit off anyone. I hoped like hell we had a daughter as fierce as Jordan. Maybe several of them, although the thought of multiple teen girls in my house wasn't all that pleasant. I'd heard they were even crazier than me and twice as hormonal as an adult woman with PMS.

The ladies visited until dinnertime, then I took Jordan out for a steak. She was nervous and constantly checking her surroundings, but I didn't know if it was a holdover from prison or if she was searching for Slater. I'd messaged Shade while she putting up her shit earlier, and he was already seeing what he could dig up. With some luck, I'd have something to hold over the asshole's head before long. Not that it mattered. If he came for Jordan, he wouldn't be breathing for much longer. Plenty of land for hiding a body when the need arose, and there were always gators.

The clubhouse already had loud music pouring from inside when we pulled through the gates after dinner. Jordan tensed next to me and I wondered how tonight would go. As much as I wanted to pull her close and assure her that I would never stray, I needed to see if she could handle this life. It wasn't for everyone. Only the strong ones could make it, and while I knew she was strong, I needed her to see herself that way. She talked about her temper like it was a bad thing, but if she channeled it and let it loose at appropriate times, then she'd make the ideal wife for someone like me.

I dropped her by the house with a quick kiss and then headed out for a beer with my brothers. I didn't think she'd disappoint me, but only time would tell. Hell, she might not even show up. The sex between us was epic and I liked being around her. Just the same, we were strangers who'd only known each other for a day and a half. If she decided she wanted to go to Jameson and Devil's Fury, I wouldn't stand in her way, but I wouldn't like it either. As far as I was concerned, that woman was mine. Even if she ran, if I ever found out that she was pregnant with my kid, I'd haul her ass back here. Unlike Jackal, the thought of being a dad didn't scare the shit out of me. It wasn't something I'd ever thought I would have, a wife and kids, but it felt right when the woman was Jordan.

The Prospects were manning the bar and making sure shit stayed clean. My brothers were already cutting loose. A few of the single ones were getting their dicks sucked or were balls deep in pussy. That had been me just a few days ago. Now I didn't feel shit when I looked at the women parading around in various states of undress. My cock didn't even get a little bit hard. Guess Scratch was right. When a Devil found his woman, he just knew, and he didn't want anyone else.

I saw Irish with two women hanging on him and amended that to 'most of us'. Everyone knew that a little teen had broadsided Irish a few years ago and he'd never been the same since. I was waiting for the day that girl grew up and came looking for him, if she didn't find someone else to settle down with first. If Janessa did ever come here, I wanted a front row seat when she saw what a manwhore Irish had been. I had no doubt she'd set him straight pretty quick, or her daddy sure as fuck would.

"Beer or shots?" Reed asked from behind the bar.

"Just beer."

He nodded and grabbed a bottle of my favorite brew, popped the top, and passed it to me. I took a long pull and felt a small hand on my thigh a little too close to my dick. As the whore's hand slid higher, I grabbed it. It was one thing to see how Jordan would react, and another to let someone other than her grab my cock.

"Missed you," Rachel said, her lips brushing my ear. "You've been gone for days."

"Had a run to make," I said.

She ran a nail down my chest all the way down to my belt buckle. "I've been waiting for you. Knew you'd show me a good time."

"Sorry, Rach. Not interested."

Her hand tensed and I could see anger flash in her eyes as I glanced at her. Yeah, there was the bitch I knew had been hiding underneath. She was all sugary goodness around my brothers, hoping someone would claim her used up ass, but none of us wanted her for more than a quick release. She wasn't the type of woman you kept around long-term.

"I thought we had something special," she said, smiling again. "You know no one can make you feel as good as I can."

"Honey, you're not that good. You were just a place to stick my dick. Same as with everyone else here."

Her lips tightened and I wondered if she was about to show the entire club her true self. I felt warmth on my other side and hoped it wasn't another damn club slut trying to get a piece of me. I wasn't in the mood for this shit tonight.

"He said to fuck off," Jordan said.

I turned to look at her, my eyebrows going up. She didn't seem even a little bit pissed. There was a bored look on her face as she stared at Rachel. Guess she decided to keep me around after all. Which was a damn good thing because I'd have eventually hauled her ass home if she'd left.

"No one asked you, bitch," Rachel said. "You're new so I'll give you a break, but this one is mine. Go fuck someone else."

Jordan sighed and sat on the barstool next to mine. Turning away from Rachel, she looked at Reed and ordered a daiquiri.

"Virgin," I said. "Don't give her fucking alcohol."

Jordan focused on me but didn't say a word.

"You could be pregnant," I reminded her.

She rolled her eyes. "Only if you have super sperm."

"What the fuck?" Rachel asked. "You slept with that bitch?"

Reed brought some frou-frou-looking red drink over and slid it to my woman.

"You must be the Jordan I've heard so much about," he said.

"That would be me," she said, then took a sip of her drink and wrinkled her nose. "It just tastes like a fruit slushy without the alcohol."

"I'm not going against his orders," Reed said with a nod in my direction. "You want alcohol in it, you'll have to come back here and fix it yourself."

"Not unless you want your ass spanked," I told her.

"Seriously?" Jordan asked.

I leaned into her space. "Baby, if there is even the slightest chance you have my kid in your belly, you're not drinking alcohol."

"Havoc," Rachel said, a whine to her voice. "Who is she? Why is she here?"

Reed snorted. "You don't stand a chance, Rachel. From what I hear, she's tough as shit, and two of her brothers are Prospects. CJ is here and her other brother is with Devil's Fury, so unless you want two clubs to kick your ass, I'd give her a wide berth. And Havoc claimed her."

"I can fight my own battles," Jordan said. "But thanks for the backup."

"Claimed?" Rachel asked. Her eyes went wide. "You made that slut your old lady?"

"I think someone needs a vocab lesson," Jordan said. "Because I've been with two guys, and one of them is sitting next to me. And I'm sure you've been used by everyone here often enough everything's so loose downstairs their dicks fall out of you. Can they even tell if it's in?"

Rachel blinked and I could tell she hadn't processed the insult, but I couldn't hold back my laugher another moment. I laughed so fucking hard I damn near fell off my stool, and Reed wasn't faring much better.

Jordan calmly sipped her drink and acted like she hadn't a care in the world. Damn! If I hadn't been falling for her before this, I sure as fuck was now. I'd never met her equal before, and something told me I never would again. She was one in a million, and I was holding on tight.

The clubhouse doors flew open and CJ practically rolled inside, blood smeared on his face and his Prospect cut falling off. I put myself between him and Jordan so I could see what the fuck was going on and decide if I needed to get her to safety. A guy who had to be her other brother barreled into the clubhouse and started kicking the shit out of CJ.

"Motherfucker! You didn't tell me she was getting out! Then you just left her there!" Jameson nailed CJ in the ribs again and I wondered if our Prospect was about to puke.

"Jameson?" Jordan asked, edging from behind me.

He froze and turned toward her, then ate up the ground in long strides until he reached his sister. She was in his arms a second later, and as hard as he was hugging her, I wasn't sure she could breathe. I gave them a moment since I knew they'd been separated for a year, then I pulled her away and wrapped my arm around her waist.

Jameson looked from my arm to my face, then his gaze landed on my cut. "She yours?" he asked.

I gave a nod, then waited to see what else he had to say. I could tell he wasn't pleased that Jordan was with me.

"Because I don't give a shit who you are. If you're going to fuck her over, I'll still knock your fucking teeth down your throat," Jameson said.

He had some stones, that was for damn sure. Most men cowered when faced with me. Not Jameson. Too bad he was trying to patch in with Devil's Fury. I wouldn't have minded having him here. CJ groaned and I saw Shade helping him up.

"If anyone kicks his ass, it will be me," Jordan said. "As soon as I know for sure he didn't knock me up already."

Jameson stared at her, then a slow grin spread across his face.

"Why the fuck didn't you come see me?" she demanded of her brother. "I was inside a damn year and not one word from you."

"I couldn't handle seeing my baby sister locked up. It was shitty of me, and I'm sorry. If I'd known you were getting out, I'd have personally picked you up. But I guess if I'd done that, you wouldn't have met Havoc." He arched a brow. "Is that a good thing or a bad thing? Because I didn't bring backup, but we could make a run for it just the same."

Jordan snorted then started laughing. "You're an idiot, but thanks. And yeah, being with Havoc is a good thing. Most of the time."

Her gaze slid to Rachel who still looked fucking confused, and probably still didn't grasp the insult Jordan had lobbed her way. Jameson winked at his sister then strolled over to Rachel and looked her up and down.

"Word of advice, don't piss my sister off. She'll hand your ass to you, both verbally and physically. So unless you have some fighting skills other than hair pulling and slapping, trust me when I say you're outmatched. And you're sure as fuck outclassed,"

Jameson said. "Can't think of anyone more perfect for the Sergeant at Arms than my ticking time bomb sister."

"I..." Rachel clamped her mouth shut and hurried off. I knew one of my brothers would console the poor thing. Just hoped he wrapped his dick twice because I now had no doubt Rachel was gunning for a property cut.

"So you're not going to haul me out of here like a naughty two-year-old?" Jordan asked her brother. "Because I haven't had a good fight in a while. Although, your club might kick you out when they see a girl can kick your ass."

He winked at her. "You only wish you could kick my ass."

Jordan moved toward him and I tightened my grip on her, pulling her back. He might be taunting her, but I had no doubt she'd take him down if she put her mind to it. As humorous as that might be, she wasn't wrong. His club would laugh their asses off, and might consider him weak. They didn't realize my woman was a fighter and fearless.

"Don't tease the possibly pregnant woman," I said. "Otherwise I'll let her loose and then film her kicking the shit out of you and send it to every club in a two-hundred-mile radius."

The humor slipped from Jameson's face. "You'd do it too, wouldn't you?"

"Yep. Hell, might be the best entertainment I've had in ages."

"Shit." Jameson wiped a hand down his face. "You're as bad as her. You may just be the perfect fucking couple, both sadistic fucks."

"Play nice," I told him.

Jameson stared at his sister. "You haven't told him about all the shit you used to do to us, did you?"

She shrugged. "Been busy."

He winced and held up a hand. "I seriously don't want to hear it. I'd have to bleach my brain."

Cinder came out of the back of the clubhouse. His lips were firm and his jaw taut, and I had no doubt he was pissed. He looked at a bleeding CJ, a Devil's Fury Prospect who looked a little too at home, and the woman in my arms. After staring at the ceiling a moment, he huffed out a breath. "Fuck this shit. All of you want to act like kids, have at it. I'm going home if anyone needs me. And, Havoc? Patch her before someone else decides to." He pointed to the cameras in the corners of the room. "Heard and saw it all. She's the female version of you. Don't be a dumbass and lose her."

"You got it, Pres."

Jordan tipped her head back and whispered loud enough for everyone around us to hear. "So, is sexiness a requirement to be a Devil? Because I've never dug a silver fox before, but damn."

I bit my lip so I wouldn't laugh, but I did clock Cinder by the door, shaking his head as he made his way outside. Something told me that Jordan was going to keep everyone on their toes. Fuck me. If our kids were anything like her, I'd probably never sleep again. I had a feeling if anyone dared hurt them, they'd handle it before Jordan or I had a chance. I almost felt sorry for anyone who dared claim a girl who took after my woman. They'd need balls of steel, and a sense of humor.

"What are you doing?" Jordan asked. "You look both amused and angry at the same time. How the hell can you pull that off?"

"Just thinking about our kids. I think I almost pity whoever they end up with."

"Can you wait and see if I'm even pregnant before you marry our kids off? For all you know, we'll never have any."

"Like you said, super sperm." I winked at her. "Trust me. We'll have a house full."

"Uh, no we won't. You'll either get fixed after two, or I will. I'm not chasing fucking kids for the rest of my damn life, especially a herd of them. If they're anything like you, I may cut you off after one."

Jameson slapped me on the back. "Good luck. You're going to need it."

"Why don't you grab a room upstairs and stay overnight?" I suggested. "You can visit your sister some more in the morning before you head back. Have someone direct you to the house around eight o'clock and you can join us for breakfast."

"Thanks. And welcome to the family. It's fucked up, but I have a feeling you'll fit right in."

"Mom and Dad already set the bar pretty low when they had you," Jordan said. "Anyone else joining the family is an improvement."

Jameson turned his gaze to me. "Can we send her back?"

She tensed and I watched the blood drain from her face.

"Shit!" He reached for her, but I turned to keep him from touching her. "What the fuck did I say?"

"We'll talk tomorrow," I said. "Just don't ever say a damn word about sending her back to that prison. Not even as a joke."

Jameson nodded. "Got it. Sorry, Jordan. I didn't mean anything by it. You know I'm glad you're out."

"CJ!" I yelled across the room. "Show your brother to a room, then make sure he has anything he wants or needs. You two fuckers start fighting again, and you'll answer to me."

CJ nodded.

"Come on, baby. Let's go home," I murmured to Jordan.

I picked her up and carried her out to the truck I'd be using until I could get Jordan something of her own. If there was even the slightest chance she was pregnant, I didn't think she should be on the back of my bike. I'd love to feel her pressed against me again, but I knew accidents happened, and being on a bike was dangerous. Cars had a tendency to not see us, and being out in the open made it easy for a rival to take a shot. I'd never forgive myself if something happened to Jordan.

I smoothed her hair back as she buckled then kissed her softly. "Home and a hot bath. Then we can do whatever the hell you want, okay?"

She nodded.

"I'm really fucking proud of you."

I got a slight smile, and I knew I'd do whatever it took to make her happy again. Her jackass brother had flipped a switch in her head, and it made me wonder if she had PTSD. Wouldn't surprise me in the least. I'd have to watch her carefully, maybe get her to see someone to talk things out. Counseling was supposed to help. Hadn't done shit for me, but might work for her. Whatever she needed, I'd make sure she got it.

Yeah, I wasn't falling for her. I'd already fallen, ass over ears. Fuck me.

Chapter Seven

Jordan

The next few days passed without anything big happening. I didn't get into any fights, Jameson went back home, and CJ actually came to apologize for his behavior the day I was released from prison. The way Havoc was watching him, I had a feeling he had something to do with that apology, but I'd take it. I still hadn't heard from my youngest brother, but I knew he'd come around when he was ready. At least two of them were talking to me. My heart ached over the loss of Stuart, but I hadn't really had time to process the fact he was gone. I no longer felt like my family had abandoned me.

Havoc and Shade were in the kitchen with papers spread all over the table. I didn't know what they were discussing, but I had a feeling it was about me since they shut up every time I went in there for something. The dumbass probably thought he was protecting me, but he was hobbling me. If I knew what was going on, then I could prepare myself. I might not be some big badass like him, but I hated being in the dark. Still, I wasn't going to confront him in front of one of his brothers. I knew respect was a big deal for the men in his club, and I didn't want to make him look bad.

On what had to be my fifth trip to the kitchen, because now I was just fucking with them, I leaned against the counter and stared Havoc down. He folded his arms over his massive chest and arched a brow at me. Yeah, not happening. I wasn't fucking moving until I was ready. I might not confront him in front of Shade, but it didn't mean I had to make shit easy for him.

"For fuck's sake. Would you please let her sit in on this so she'll stop coming in for bullshit reasons?" Shade asked. "Do you really think she needs that many damn drinks in an hour? Her bladder would have exploded if she'd consumed everything she's hauled out of here."

Havoc still stared at me, silent.

"If you're trying to intimidate me, it's not working," I said.

"I think Cinder was right. She's the female version of you." Shade smiled. "The two of you are going to make things interesting around here. You're like Dexter and Hannah."

"You think I'm capable of killing someone and not getting caught?" I asked.

"Okay, not the best example, but Bonnie and Clyde didn't fit either. The point is that you both kick ass first and ask questions later," Shade said. "You're exactly the type of woman he needs."

"Are you two finished bonding?" Havoc asked.

"Maybe. Do I get to hear what you're planning? Because you've made it pretty obvious it's about me," I said. "How the hell am I supposed to protect myself if I don't know what the fuck is going on?"

Okay, so I sucked at the no confrontation thing.

"She's not wrong," Shade said. "I think she's proven she can hold her own when she needs to. Your call though."

"Sit down," Havoc said, nodding to the chair next to him. "If I don't let you stay, you'll just be a pain in the ass and come in here every ten minutes."

"You're a fast learner, aren't you?" I asked as I pulled out the chair.

Shade coughed to cover his laughter. I smirked at Havoc, but the heat in his eyes promised he'd get me back in interesting ways later, the kind of payback that would leave me sore and begging for more.

"Fill her in," Havoc said.

"So, I did some digging on that guard at the prison, the one who tried to…" Shade pressed his lips together. "Moving on. He was living two towns over, until the day you were released. He's now renting an apartment over on the rough side of town. The intel I've gathered suggests that he's watching for you. Someone leaked the information that you're at the compound."

"No one knows I'm here except your club and my brothers," I said. "I don't see anyone in either group letting that asshole know where to find me. Not even when CJ was pissed would he have turned me over to a rapist."

"Not quite." Shade pulled some more papers out, and a picture. It was the skank from a few nights ago, and she was leaning in close to the asshole guard. "It seems Rachel didn't take too kindly to being shown up, or having you take Havoc. I think she believed she had a shot with him."

Havoc picked up the picture and the ice in his eyes almost scared me. I knew he'd never hurt me, but I wasn't so sure about Rachel. If he got his hands on her, she might have a very limited time remaining above ground. If she'd sold me out to a rapist, I was all right with that. Hell, I might help him dig the damn hole.

"Does he have any allies in town?" Havoc asked. "Anyone he could turn to for help in getting his hands on Jordan? Besides that bitch?"

"Not that I've seen. I managed to hack his phone records. He placed some calls to the guards at the prison, but they seem to be avoiding him. The two who answered hung up after thirty seconds. The rest didn't even answer, and they haven't called back," Shade said.

"So what do we do?" I asked.

"We can wait him out," Shade said. "Or we can set a trap. I think the club needs to deal with Rachel first though."

"She's mine," Havoc said.

"If you're offing her, you're not doing it alone," I said.

He focused his gaze on me. "You're not a murderer, Jordan. And I'd never ask you to do something like that."

"She gave my location to a rapist asshole. If you want to kill her, I won't stand in your way. I just figured I'd help hide the body."

Shade snickered. "Like I said. Perfect for you."

"And if someone comes looking for her?" Havoc asked. "You have a shitty poker face, baby. They start asking questions about where Rachel is and they'll immediately hone in on you. One look and they'll know you saw or heard something."

"Right. So the fact I *know* you're going to kill her already implicates me. Might as well follow through," I said. "I never do anything half-assed."

"The two of you are going to put Cinder in an early grave," Shade said. "Remind me to bring popcorn when all this goes down. Better than a damn *Die Hard* movie."

I looked over at Shade. "In that scenario, which one of us is Bruce?"

Shade's shoulder shook with silent laughter and he held up his hands. "I'm out. Your girl is too much for me to handle. I'll hand all this over to Scratch and Cinder. I'm sure they'll be in touch."

"Am I supposed to just sit here until the big, tough men come up with a plan and take out the bad guys?" I asked.

"Yep," Shade said and winked. "Get used to it. Your other half is as alpha as you can get. Don't be surprised if he tries to keep you barefoot and pregnant."

"Not if he values his balls," I said.

Shade laughed his ass off all the way to the front door. Havoc was staring with an unreadable expression. I wasn't sure if I'd pissed him off, or if he just wasn't sure what to make of me.

"You going to say something?" I asked.

"Nope. Figure you say enough for the both of us."

I rolled my eyes. "Does that mean I'm supposed to just sit here and look pretty when bad shit happens?"

Havoc reached over and pulled my chair closer until my side was pressed against his. He gripped my chin and held my gaze. "Have I ever treated you like a China doll? Made you feel like I thought you were some pathetic, weak, breakable woman?"

"No," I grudgingly admitted.

"And I never will. I love your strength, and your sass. Watching you go toe to toe with people amuses the shit out of me. When we catch Slater, and we *will* catch him, I'll let you use my knife if you want to de-ball him. What I'd like is to keep the bad shit away from you, not because you can't handle it, but because I don't want any backlash coming your way. Anyone tries to take you from me, and I mean anyone, I will fucking end them."

"I think I love you," I said, smiling a little.

"You damn well better."

He kissed me hard, not letting me come up for air for several minutes. Yeah, I loved the asshole. Maybe instead of a match made in heaven, we were a match made in hell... because I was fairly certain that's where we'd both end up one day. Maybe we'd kick Lucifer off his throne and take over the place. I was sure there was room for improvement down there.

"Does that mean you love me too?" I asked.

"If you have to ask, I guess I'm not being obvious enough. I'll have to rectify that. What's it going to take? Name it and it's yours. As long as it's not my dick mounted on the wall, that is, because I plan on getting lots of use out of it."

"Well, as much as I'd love to stare at it all day every day, I much prefer it still attached to you. Kind of hard for you to fuck me without it. And there's still lots of things we haven't tried yet."

"Like what?" he asked, his voice getting deeper and rougher.

"I saw some handcuffs in your dresser when I was snooping, and yes, I was digging through your crap without permission. If you don't like it, you can bite me. Maybe you could give me some happy memories to associate with being handcuffed. The only time someone has used them on me was during my arrest and incarceration."

His gaze skimmed over me. "Anything else?"

"I'm sure I could make a list. You seem like the type of guy who likes lists."

"I'll be happy to check off every item. Twice."

I smiled and kissed him, gripping his hair in my fingers. "Then item number one is for you to give me lots of sexy orders, and punish me when I disobey. Marines like orders, don't they?"

"Maybe I'll tell you do things I know you'll refuse, just so I can spank that ass. I bet it would turn nice and pink."

"Ryan," I said softly.

"What, baby?"

"I'm so fucking wet right now. What are going to do about it?"

"Just hearing you say that makes me hard. Stand up, Jordan."

I pushed my chair back and stood. His gaze caressed me from head to toe, lingering here and there. I let him look his fill and waited to see what he wanted me to do next. He twirled his finger and I turned, letting out a yelp when he grabbed my ass and gave it a squeeze. I glanced at him over my shoulder and saw the hungry look in his eyes.

"Know what I want?" he asked.

"I'm sure you'll tell me. You seem to go after what you want."

"I want you naked and bent over the table, this gorgeous ass on display."

I turned to face him and slowly stripped off my clothes. When I dropped the last of them to the floor, I stood next to him and bent over the table. Havoc let out a groan and his fingers lightly trailed down my ass cheek.

"Spread your legs," he said, his voice rough and filled with need.

I parted my thighs and bit my lip as he lightly ran his fingers along my wet slit. Havoc stood, knocked his chair over, then I felt the denim covering his thighs press against me. He ground his cock against my ass then pulled away. I heard the jangle of his belt as he unbuckled it and then the rasp of his zipper sliding down. My heart was hammering in my chest as I waited, breathless with anticipation.

Havoc held me open and slammed home, not stopping until I'd taken every inch. I cried out, closing my eyes at the sheer pleasure of having him inside of me. He gripped my ass cheeks and spread them apart, then started fucking me with long, deep strokes.

"So fucking beautiful," he said. "I love watching you take my cock."

"Ryan, please… Don't tease me."

His hand cracked down on my ass, making me clench down on him. It stung and burned a bit, but I liked it.

"Don't rush me," he said. "Watching your pussy take me, seeing your cream coat my dick, is the most beautiful thing I've ever seen, and I want to fucking enjoy it."

"Ryan." His name sounded breathless even to me. He seemed to turn me into a needy mess, some wanton hussy who craved his cock any way I could get it.

He took his time, driving me crazy with his slow, steady strokes. I wanted more, wanted him to take me hard. I loved it when he lost control, but he seemed to have an iron grip on it today. Or maybe this was my punishment for interrupting his meeting. There were worse ways to be disciplined.

"You like that, baby?" he asked. "Like feeling the slow slide of my cock in your pussy?"

"God, yes! Please, Ryan. I need more."

He slammed into me hard and fast, making me cry out. "That what you want?"

"Yes! Yes! More!"

He pounded into me, every thrust driving me up onto my toes. My vision went hazy as I came, pleasure rolling through me in a never-ending wave. He hit all the right spots, making my orgasms last forever, one sliding into another until I was breathless.

Havoc roared out his release as he filled me with jet after jet of his cum, and still he kept stroking in and out of me. I trembled and twitched in the aftermath, feeling like I'd soared to the heavens then crashed hard back to earth. He pressed tighter against my ass and I smiled a little. I'd asked him the other day why he always did that afterward, and he said he was making sure none of it escaped. It seemed he was determined to get me pregnant, if I wasn't already.

It should have scared the shit out of me, but the thought of having a kid with him wasn't all that frightening. I knew that he'd watch over us, protect us. And I was quickly learning that he'd love us with his last breath. I'd been one lucky bitch the day he found me on the side of the road.

"Did that satisfy my little nympho for the moment?" he asked, easing out of me.

I gave him an indignant glare over my shoulder. "I'm not a nympho. You just have a magic dick that's bewitched me."

He winked then smacked my ass. "As long as it's only my dick you crave."

I stood up and faced him. "You know it is. Besides, I'm pretty sure the only way I'm finding someone with a bigger cock is if I hit up the porn industry, and who knows where their shit's been?"

Havoc threw back his head and roared with laughter. "Good to know I have a porn-star-worthy cock."

"As long as the pornos you're making are with me."

He pulled me closer and kissed me. "There's no other pussy I want but yours. I think I've proven that already."

His phone started ringing in his pocket and he tucked his cock back into his pants, zipped up, then answered the damn thing. It always went off at the worst possible times and he seemed adamant that he answer it, regardless of what we were doing. If his VP interrupted us one more time when I was about to orgasm, I was going to say a few words to his wife and see how he liked a case of blue balls. I might not be able to lay a hand on him, but it didn't mean I couldn't seek my revenge in other ways. Clarity seemed like the sort who might play along and help me out.

Havoc's gaze locked on mine and the tense lines in his face told me whatever was going on, it wasn't good. I quickly pulled my clothes back on while he finished his call, trying not to eavesdrop too much. It was damn hard not to listen when he was standing right in front of me though. It wasn't like I could just turn my ears off.

He finally ended the call and heaved a sigh that didn't sound the least bit positive.

"What's wrong?" I asked.

"Shade filled Scratch and Cinder in on the current issue. The club decided to round up Rachel. She's being held inside the compound."

"So? Let's go deal with that bitch."

He smiled a little. "Jordan, you're fierce and God knows I love you for it, but I want you to let me handle this. It could get messy."

"You mean bloody."

He shrugged. "Same difference."

"Are you worried what I'll think if I see you like that?"

"Taking someone's life isn't the same as giving them a good beatdown. I'm not just going to slap her around and let her go, and since I'm the Sergeant at Arms, it's my job to handle this shit. Permanently."

"Ryan, you could gut her like a fish in front of me, and it wouldn't change the way I feel about you, or how I see you. She's not some sweet, innocent woman. The bitch sold me out. Do you really think if Slater gets his hands on me that he'll be satisfied with picking up where he left off? The man was fired. I'm as good as dead if he catches me."

"I know," he said. "It's why he's next on my list."

"I'm going with you."

He rubbed the back of his neck. "Fine. But you'll need to stand back out of the way. Who knows where the fuck she's been? If her blood gets on you…"

I nodded, then stopped and stared at him. "Wait. It was all right for you to put your dick in her then fuck me, but it's not okay for me to get her blood on me? That's fucked up, Ryan. Even for you."

"Never touched her without protection."

"You should still get tested. Today preferably. If you gave me anything, I'm kicking your ass, then I'm bringing that slut back from the dead so I can kill her all over again."

He smiled and kissed me again. "It turns me on when you get all pissed and violent."

He rubbed his cock against me and I could feel how hard he was again.

"You have issues. You know that, right?"

"Everyone has their kinks. Mine happens to be watching you kick someone's ass, with words or physical violence."

"You're so weird. Good thing I love you."

Chapter Eight

Havoc

I didn't like the fact Jordan was here. She was about to see the worst side of the club, of me, and while I'd assured her that wasn't my concern with her tagging along, it was a big fucking part of it. Even if she was tougher than the other two ladies in the club, I didn't know if she could really handle what was about to happen. If she ran, I'd just have to go after her.

Rachel's hands were chained above her head and she had to stand on tiptoe to alleviate the pressure on her shoulders. Wouldn't be long before she didn't care about that anymore, or much of anything else. After what she'd done, she wouldn't be walking out of here. She'd betrayed the club, and had put my woman in danger. Neither sin could be forgiven, not in the eyes of Devil's Boneyard, and sure as fuck not in mine.

When she saw me, and noticed I was removing my cut, her eyes went wide with fear and her face paled. Someone had already set out my tools on a table nearby and I let my hand hover over each one, trying to decide the best way to start things. Jordan came closer, her arms crossed as she stared down at everything. My gaze locked with hers, and there was a hint of challenge as she stared back. Without breaking contact, she reached down and picked up some special pliers that had been used for the removal of teeth, nails, the occasional nut, and whatever else I could pull off with them.

I arched a brow as she placed the pliers in my hand.

"Why don't you start with those fake ass nails of hers? Bet she screams like a baby."

I stared, waiting to see if she was joking, or expected me to back down. Instead, she gave me a shooing motion. Was she for fucking real? I didn't like feeling as if my world had been turned upside down, but that's what was happening. I glanced at her again before I got to work. She didn't so much as flinch or try to intervene. Rachel screamed and cried as I pulled off her nails.

"Do you know why you're here?" Jordan asked her.

Rachel blubbered and didn't say anything.

"You sold me out, bitch," Jordan said. "Did you honestly think no one would find out? What? You thought when I was gone Havoc would come back to you?"

"He was s-supposed to b-be mine," Rachel said, snot starting to run down her face with the tears.

"He was never yours," Jordan said. "You're a weak, pathetic excuse of a human being."

She moved closer and it wasn't until I saw the flash of silver that I realized she'd picked up one of my knives. She cut an X across the tops of both Rachel's breasts, making me wince at the savage look on her face. All right. So I'd underestimated her. It seemed my kickass woman really did have the stones for this kind of work. Part of me was proud that she could hold her own and take care of business. The other half wanted to wrap her up and lock her in the house where she'd never be tainted from the ugly side of life again.

"What did we discuss?" I asked.

She rolled her eyes. "I'm supposed to stay out of the way in case her potentially contaminated blood gets on me."

I pointed stared at the spot across the room where I'd left her.

"Fine," she said. "You don't want me to see the big, bad Havoc doing what he does best? I'll wait outside with Killian. Heaven forbid someone with my delicate sensibilities remain in the room with you while you kill that stupid bitch."

She stormed across the cement floor and slammed out the door.

Scratch chuckled. "That went well. I'll call Clarity. She'll distract Jordan while you take care of this. They can hang out inside the compound so you don't have to worry about Jordan being outside the gates without protection."

"Thanks, VP. She's tough as shit, but it doesn't mean I want her seeing this side of me."

"I understand." He clapped a hand on my shoulder and pulled his phone out. While he arranged for my woman to stay occupied, I turned my attention back to Rachel.

"I'm sorry," Rachel said. "I'll never do something like that again."

"No, you won't." I walked back over to the table, realizing that Jordan still had my damn knife. Stubborn-ass woman.

I worked my way through the tools on the table, torturing Rachel for over an hour before I finally ended her life. Irish took a picture of her body to make sure the others learned a lesson. Don't fuck with the club, or our women. Killian helped me wrap the body in plastic, then we tossed it into the bed of one of the trucks and tied a tarp over the back, then left the compound. It was dark enough that I didn't anticipate any trouble on the road. I never dumped a body inside the gates, and I sure as fuck never used the same place twice. Too easy to get caught if you had a dumping ground.

"Where are we taking her?" Killian asked.

"We have a bit of a drive ahead of us. When we made that last run, out past the prison there were some buildings going up. KJ Construction."

"What's that have to do with anything?" he asked.

"KJ is owned by Kent Jenkins. The man will do anything for money. I've dumped a few bodies at some of his sites over the years. He'll let us drop Rachel into the foundation of one of the buildings and cover her over with cement. No one will find the body until those buildings are torn down."

Killian stayed silent for a few minutes. "I think you frighten me a little."

"I frighten most people."

"Yeah, but in all honesty, your girl scares me more. I'd be worried about falling asleep after pissing her off and waking up without my dick."

I laughed long and hard, and knew he wasn't wrong. Good thing she seemed to like mine attached. Jordan was fierce for sure, and I loved that about her. I just worried that one day it would get her into trouble. The kind I couldn't save her from, but I'd sure as fuck die trying. I never thought anything or anyone would be more important to me than the club, but if I had to choose between her and my brothers, I'd pick her.

I called Kent on my way to his construction site and he agreed to meet me with a crew who knew how to keep quiet. For a price. I'd gone into this knowing where I'd dump the body, and Scratch had shoved a duffle bag of money into the back of the truck I was currently driving. It should be enough to pay off Kent and anyone else he pulled into this mess. Anyone involved would be made aware up front that if they opened their damn mouths, they'd be the next body I buried.

"Did you ever think you'd end up doing this kind of thing?" Killian asked.

"No. My childhood wasn't fucked up or anything. I joined the Marines because I wanted to make a difference, to save lives and make sure the people I left behind could keep their freedom."

He nodded. "A protector. In a way, you still are. You just do some fucked up shit to make sure everyone stays safe."

"Yeah." I chuckled a little. "Got arrested and spent some time in the same prison as Jordan. The club was there for me, and I was willing to do whatever it took to protect them. It's why I was voted in as Sergeant at Arms. The last guy made some stupid mistakes and ended up as gator food."

"Heard about that," Killian said.

"What about you?" I asked. "No one really knows your story, except for probably Cinder and Scratch."

"My parents were Irish, and my dad was involved with organized crime in Ireland. When my mom convinced him to get out, we came to the States. I was about eleven at the time. Didn't take long for Dad to get mixed up with the Irish mob here. When he died, they came for us. It seemed dear ol' Dad had double-crossed them. They wanted to use us as a lesson to anyone else who tried the same thing. I was fifteen. I could hear Mom's screams, but she'd made sure I had a way out."

I glanced at him and Killian had a faraway look in his eyes, probably reliving those moments.

"Anyway, I lived on the streets for a while, tried to lay low. Made my way down here. I've worked odd jobs all my life, under the table kind of shit. Got into underground fighting for a while."

"How did you end up a Prospect for my club?" I asked.

"Met some of the crew from Hades Abyss, The Marauders, and Demonic Reign. Some of those bastards are pure evil, even worse than the men my dad was mixed up with. The guys from Hades seemed okay though. Hung out with them a bit and I guess it planted the seed that maybe MC life was right for me."

"But why here? Why not join Hades Abyss?"

"I like the Florida weather," he said with a smile. "Honestly, I followed my dick down this way. Didn't work out with the girl, but I saw your crew around town. Took me a few weeks to get up the balls to approach Cinder. The rest is history."

The construction site was coming up and I pulled down the road that would take us there. A few lights were on and I easily found Kent and two other men. When I got out, I grabbed the duffle and tossed it to him.

"There's enough for you and these two," I said. "They know the score?"

Kent nodded. "They won't say a word. If you don't bury their asses, I will."

"Good enough."

I tipped my head to the back of the truck and Killian helped me unload Rachel. We dumped her into what would be the foundation of one of the commercial buildings. We stood back and watched as Kent's crew filled in the space with cement, and we didn't leave until the sun was about to rise and the entire foundation was setting. My neck and back ached, and I was more than ready to see Jordan.

When we got back to town, I dropped Killian at the clubhouse and drove straight to my house. Scratch hadn't said where inside the compound I'd find my woman, but knowing Jordan, she'd want to be somewhere she felt comfortable. The sun was peeking over the horizon when I walked through the door and heard voices from the kitchen.

Clarity looked exhausted and Jordan was... pissed.

"You!" She pointed a finger at me. "No sex. Ever again."

I tried really damn hard not to smile and leaned against the doorframe. "Is that so? And how do you plan on having the daily orgasms you've come to expect?"

"I'll get a vibrator. They're reliable enough. Just add batteries. They won't tell you that you're not strong enough to handle shit."

Clarity stood from the table and patted my arm. "Good luck. You're going to need it."

I gave her a quick hug. "Thanks for keeping her company."

Clarity glanced at Jordan, who was still glaring at me. "I like her. She's tough, and she has the temper from hell, but I can tell she loves you."

Clarity walked to the front door and I followed.

She dropped her voice a little. "I think she's a little scared."

"What?" I looked down at Clarity thinking I'd misheard. Because Jordan didn't seem the least bit scared. Ready to remove my balls? Check. Scared? Not even a little.

"You chased her off," Clarity said softly. "She's worried that you don't think she can handle this life, or your true self. You haven't marked her, Havoc. She isn't certain of her place. Saying she's yours is one thing. But she's seen my property cut and Josie's tattoo. She doesn't have either of those things, just your word that she's here to stay."

Well fuck me. I guess I had a few things I needed to fix before I could crash for a few hours.

"I'll take care of it," I promised.

I gave Clarity a hug and locked the door behind her. Then I went to face the she-demon in my kitchen, hoping she didn't launch shit at my head. She was seething when I stopped beside the table and I clocked the cast iron skillet behind her, the butcher block of knives within her reach, and a dozen other weapons she could use.

"Miss me?" I asked.

"Miss you?" Fire snapped in her eyes. "*Miss you?*"

Maybe not the right thing to say given the situation.

"Baby, you know why I didn't want you to get your hands dirty. We talked about this."

"I'm not a fucking delicate flower!" she screamed.

"No, you're not." I moved in closer, watching to see if it was safe to get my dick within striking distance. When she just vibrated with anger and didn't try to maim me, I pulled her into my arms. "What you are is the most important person in my life. The woman I love, and possibly the mother of my child. I have no doubt that you can handle yourself. But it doesn't mean I want you to be in a position where you have to deal with that shit. It's my job to protect this club, and it's sure as fuck my job to protect you."

"Ryan."

"Hush and listen. I love you, Jordan. I would give my life for you, put you before my brothers. What I won't do is let you submerge yourself in the ugly side of my life. You want to smack some club sluts around, go for it. Someone tries to hurt you or talks shit about you? Hand them their ass. I'm all for it. But the darker shit? That's all on me, okay?"

She sighed and melted against me, the anger draining from her. "Fine. Just as long as we're clear that I could have buried that bitch."

"Crystal clear, baby. You get any sleep?"

She shook her head.

"Come on. We'll take a quick shower then crash for a bit. When we get up, I'll work on cornering Slater. I want you to walk around this town without fear that he could jump out from the shadows."

"If you need bait, you know I'm going to volunteer. I trust you to keep me safe, Ryan, you and the club. And if I'm armed, there's no reason I can't put the dickhead in his place myself."

"You still have my knife, don't you?" I asked dryly.

"Yep. You're not getting it back. I did disinfect the shit out of it though."

My body shook with silent laughter. Fuck, I loved this woman. I had a feeling she would constantly surprise me. The next thirty years should prove to be entertaining at the very least. Assuming we lived that long. In this life, it was never a guarantee. My club was mostly legit these days, not really dabbling in anything that would cause a lot of violence, but it didn't mean a war wouldn't come to us like it had before. I should handle Slater and set Jordan free, but I wouldn't. She was mine, and I was holding on tight.

"Come on, baby. You can wash my back and I'll wash yours."

"Is that code for your dick will accidently fall into my pussy?" she asked.

"If I weren't so damn tired, yeah that's what it would mean. Right now? It means we're going to wash each other and get some sleep."

"Sounds good. I'm tired as hell."

I kissed the top of her head then led her to the bedroom and master bath. After a hot shower, we climbed into bed naked and I fell asleep with her curled against my body.

Chapter Nine

Jordan

Havoc, Shade, and one of the Prospects had been keeping tabs on Slater for the last two weeks, trying to find a pattern so they would know when to strike. When Havoc wasn't working on my little issue, he was doing his damnedest to make sure he planted a baby inside me. Not that I was complaining about that part. I loved feeling him inside of me, loved how close I felt to him in those moments, and even after. Who'd have guessed my big badass was a cuddle bunny? Of course, if he ever heard me call him that, I'd likely not be able to sit down for a week.

No, it wasn't the fact he was trying to get me pregnant that bothered me, or that he couldn't keep his hands off me. It was the fact I'd woken to find Havoc gone. His side of the bed had been ice cold, so he'd left quite a while before I'd woken up. No note, nothing. I tried not to let it piss me off but I had no doubt he'd gone after Slater. Alone. Or at least without me. I hoped he had some of the club with him. I should have known something was up. He'd been more tender last night than usual. If the idiot got hurt trying to protect me, I'd kick his ass.

I sipped a cup of coffee as I looked out the window over the kitchen sink. It was pretty outside and should have been a great morning. Instead, I was just hoping that Havoc made it back in one piece from wherever he'd gone. Not my best morning since being released from prison, but something told me I'd have more days like this one. If he thought he could sneak out without telling me, he'd do it. Mainly so I wouldn't try to tag along.

I could see the road that wound through the compound and recognized Josie's SUV heading toward the house at what seemed like a greater speed than usual. It wasn't like her to be careless, especially if the kids were with her. My stomach clenched and I began running through the worst-case scenarios. Had one of the kids gotten hurt? Did Jackal do something that had gone horribly wrong?

Making my way to the front door, I pulled it open in time to see a panicked Josie run straight for me.

"Hey! Josie, what the hell?"

"Inside, now!" She pushed at me until I stepped back and shut the door.

Josie locked the deadbolt and put a hand to her chest. I could see the rapid pulse beating in her throat. What the fuck was going on? I hadn't seen the redhead look this damn scared before; not that we'd interacted much, but she hadn't seemed like the panicking type. I'd even heard the story about how she and Jackal had met, and she seemed like the type to kick ass and take names. Or she had before having kids mellowed her.

"Josie, where's Jackal? The kids? What happened?"

"The kids are the clubhouse, along with Clarity and her kids."

"Okay, so if the kids are fine, why are you so upset?" I asked.

"Jackal went with Havoc, Renegade, and Phantom to take care of that guard. They left before the sun came up," she said. "I got a call from Jackal about twenty minutes ago. I heard an explosion in the background and he was screaming at me to get the kids and run. I called Clarity on my way here in case she needed to get to safety too."

Josie sobbed and sagged against the wall.

"Wait. What?" What the hell was she talking about? Why would there be an explosion? And why were she and the kids in danger?

"Pack a few things. Scratch is declaring a state of emergency," she said, calming a little. "You, me, Clarity, and the kids are all being put on lockdown. It's... Havoc is missing. And Renegade was badly injured. None of them have returned, and I can't reach Jackal. I'm so fucking scared that I'm ready to pull out my hair."

It felt like the world was tipping and I realized I was falling. I landed hard on the floor, my coffee cup shattering and the liquid going everywhere. Havoc was missing? Black spots swam across my vision, and I could hear Josie yelling at me but it sounded like she was down a long tunnel. She started shaking me and a quick slap to my cheek snapped me back to the present.

"Missing?" I asked.

"Come on, Jordan. We have to move!"

I numbly nodded and went to get a few things I'd need, not even caring about the broken mug on the floor or the mess my coffee had made. I hauled myself off the floor and went to the bedroom, Josie on my heels almost as if she were afraid I'd run. I pulled down a bag off the top shelf of the closet, a camo-colored one that belonged to Havoc. It was empty and I shoved my stuff inside, then let Josie push me into her SUV and drive me to the clubhouse. When we stepped inside, Scratch was standing next to Clarity, his hand on her shoulder and one of his kids cradled in his other arm. He looked worried, and that scared the fuck out of me.

"Jordan, I know you have questions, and you probably want to charge out of here and find Havoc, but I'm putting you on lockdown. It's what he would want," Scratch said.

"What's going on?" I asked.

"I'll tell you, as soon as I have all of you someplace safe."

"And where's that?" I demanded. Probably not wise to get snippy with the VP, but I wanted Havoc. I didn't give a fuck right then if I was being disrespectful. I'd never admit it, but I was scared shitless.

"With the Devil's Fury," Scratch said. "Your brother and his crew are going to watch over you. They've called in backup from the Dixie Reapers and Hades Abyss, and each club is sending help here too. If this is bigger than we anticipate, then there are some more allies we can contact. We're going to find Havoc, and when it's safe, you can come back home. All of you."

My brother, CJ, came over and placed a comforting hand on my back. He softly kissed my temple, and I was a bit surprised at the tenderness after he'd been such an ass the day Havoc found me. Maybe he really had meant that apology a couple weeks ago. I'd thought Havoc had just twisted his arm but perhaps I'd been wrong.

"VP, everything's set," CJ said.

"Everything?" I asked. What the fuck did that mean?

"Convoy," Scratch said. "You'll ride with Josie, her kids, and Shadow. I'll be with Clarity and my kids. Cinder is going to hold things down until I get all of you settled, then I'm coming back to make sure this shit gets handled."

"I'll be taking up the rear with Stripes," CJ said. "And Irish and Killian will be up front."

I frowned. "Does that leave anyone here? If Phantom, Jackal, and Renegade were with Havoc..."

"Shade's here," Scratch said. "And there are a few brothers you haven't met. I've made sure they'll be present as well. When all this is over, I'll introduce you to Gator, Ripper, and Ashes. They tend to keep to themselves."

"Just..." I bit my lip so I wouldn't fucking cry in front of them. "Bring Havoc home."

Scratch winked at me. "Won't stop until he's back safe and sound. Whatever it takes, I'll bring him back to you. First, I need to be able to assure him you're safe and out of harm's way. Can't do that if you're still in town."

"Fine. I'll go without a fight. But I want updates."

"I'll assign someone to keep you up to date," Scratch said. "I know you and Havoc have gotten close, and this probably isn't the time..."

He nodded to someone behind me and I turned to see Killian heading over with a cut in his hand. He gave it to Scratch, who handed his kid off to Clarity then faced me fully. Opening the cut, he showed me the back and the front, and tears misted my eyes. It was a property cut like Clarity and Josie had, and mine said *Property of Havoc*.

"He ordered it a week ago, but said he was waiting for the right moment to give it to you. I'm not sending you off somewhere without a way to show all those fuckers you're taken. Havoc would kick my ass if someone made a move on you while he was gone," Scratch said. "And no, I'm not ashamed to say that beast of a man would try to stomp me into a mudhole."

"Thank you," I said softly, shrugging it on. I ran my hands over the black leather and tried really fucking hard not to cry.

"Everyone load up," Scratch said. "The sooner I get all of you out of here, the quicker I can return."

I heard booted steps heading toward us from the back of the clubhouse and turned to see Cinder coming our way. He looked tired, but power still rolled off him. Even without seeing the President patch on his cut, anyone with eyes would know he was in charge of things, and it wasn't because of his silver hair. The man had a confidence I hadn't seen that often, and a look in his eyes that made men twice his size back down. I knew that even Havoc wouldn't dare go against Cinder, and not much of anything scared him. The way he carried himself, and the fuck you attitude, was enough to make everyone give him a wide berth.

Cinder eyed my property cut and smiled faintly. His gaze locked with mine, and I could see the concern there, but also resolution. No matter what it took, I knew he'd bring Havoc home to me. I didn't know his background, but it wouldn't surprise me if he'd ever been in the military or done some other work for the government. Probably dark shit no one was permitted to hear about. He seemed like the type of man who could get anything done, no matter the odds. And I was counting on that right now.

"Looks good on you, Jordan," he said, patting my shoulder. "We'll get Havoc back for you."

"Thank you," I said.

"You're not going to fight us, are you?" Cinder asked. "I know you want to go after him yourself. Even if we haven't spent time together, I've heard enough to know you aren't a woman who likes to stand aside and let the men handle everything. Wouldn't expect anything less of Havoc's woman."

"I don't want to cause problems," I said. "I know that if I stay, you'll be more focused on me than on finding Havoc. It's better for him if I go, even if I don't want to."

"Good girl," Cinder said, patting my shoulder again.

The smartass half of me wanted to bark and ask if I was supposed to sit. Wisely, I kept my mouth shut. I doubted he'd appreciate my sarcasm right now. Or at any time for that matter. Cinder didn't seem like the type of man who would tolerate a woman being anywhere other than in her place. And while Havoc liked my sass, I didn't think the President of the Devil's Boneyard would be as impressed with it, especially if it were aimed at him.

I followed Josie and her kids out to an SUV with blacked out windows. She nodded for me to take the front and she climbed in back with the kids. Shadow was already behind the wheel with the engine running, and the tense lines around his mouth and eyes said enough about how dire this situation was. I hadn't had a chance to spend much time with any of the Boneyard members, but even I could tell that everyone was tense and ready for whatever may come next.

Josie spoke softly to the kids as the SUV pulled forward. The one ahead of us looked identical and I'd seen Scratch get into it with Clarity and their children. It was unbelievable that something so bad could happen that we'd have to leave the compound. Wasn't this place supposed to be safe for us? Hadn't that been why Havoc had insisted I not leave the gates unless I was protected? My stomach cramped and I felt my throat burning.

"Pull over!" I yelled.

Shadow jerked the wheel to the side and the vehicle hadn't even stopped before I opened my door and threw up. I'd never been the type to scare easily, and I'd certainly never gotten sick from it before. My heart was pounding and booted feet appeared at the edge of my vision.

"Jordan, you okay?" CJ asked.

"Fear can make a woman sick," said Stripes in his Russian accent.

"I've never seen Jordan get sick from being scared before," CJ said. He moved in closer and rubbed my back. "Any chance you're pregnant?"

My gaze shot to his. "Pregnant?"

He nodded. "You've been with Havoc for a few weeks now. I heard you say something to Jameson. It's possible, right?"

"Y-Yeah." My brow furrowed. "Wait. What do you know about pregnant women?"

CJ shrugged. "That's a story for another time. Right now, we need to get you back on the road. It's not safe to sit out here like this."

"Your brother is right," Stripes said as he scanned the area.

"I think I'm okay now," I said, pressing a hand to my stomach.

"Here, rinse your mouth then sip on this," CJ said, giving me a small bottle of water.

"Thanks."

He helped me get situated in the SUV again, then shut the door. We were moving again a minute later and I hoped I could hold it together. I knew that Havoc had done his best to knock me up, and it was a definite possibility, but the idea of pregnancy and being faced with it were two different things. I'd heard stories of women trying for months or even years before they conceived. It hadn't occurred to me that it would happen practically overnight. How likely was it I was pregnant after a few weeks?

The drive to the Devil's Fury compound would have gone smoother if I hadn't had to stop twice more to throw up. If this was pregnancy, I wanted to ask about returns because I wasn't sure I wanted any part of it. I'd never done well with being sick. Guess it was too much to hope I'd be one of those beautifully pregnant women who glowed and loved every second of their pregnancy. If that's what this even was. I could have just as easily picked up a bug.

Jameson greeted me with a hug then ushered me into what I assumed was their clubhouse. I only saw one woman and she didn't look like a club whore. The way one of the men had his arm around her waist, I figured she must be his old lady, even if she wasn't wearing a property cut.

The pretty woman came toward us, a smile on her face. "I'm Adalia. Welcome to the Devil's Fury."

Jameson coughed and gave her a pointed look that had the woman rolling her eyes.

"I'm Badger's wife and my dad is the President of the club," Adalia said. "I've had no end of grief over leaving my property cut at home today, not that every member of this club doesn't know who I am."

"I'm Jordan," I said, shaking her hand.

"She's my sister," Jameson said. "And the old lady of the Sergeant at Arms for Devil's Boneyard it seems."

He was eyeing my property cut and I smiled at him, though it felt forced. I wasn't sure I could call myself that if something had happened to Havoc. What if he never returned? What if the explosion did more than just injure him? Did I still have a place with Devil's Boneyard if Havoc was dead?

The room started spinning and I felt sick again.

"Bathroom!" Josie yelled. "Get her to a bathroom."

Jameson scooped me up and went running toward the back of the clubhouse, which wasn't the best move since it jostled my stomach. He kicked open a bathroom door and set me down just in time for me to dry heave. Whatever coffee and water I'd had in my stomach was long gone, and when we'd stopped for food, I hadn't been able to bring myself to eat anything.

"Are you sick?" Jameson asked.

I glared at him from where I still knelt in front of the toilet. "No, I'm throwing up because everything is just peachy."

"Smartass," he mumbled.

"She might be pregnant," CJ said, deciding to join us.

It almost made me feel like I was back home in middle school. Every time I tried to get alone time in the bathroom one or all of my brothers would push their way inside, being the nosy fuckers they are.

"Only one way to find out," Jameson said. "I'll go pick up one of every pregnancy test I can find, and we'll see what they say."

"It's only been a few weeks, jackass," I said. "I doubt those things will work that fast."

CJ shrugged. "You'd be surprised. Some of them can tell from the first day of your missed period."

"I still want to know how you know so much shit about pregnancy," I said as I slowly climbed to my feet.

"He knocked up a girl six months ago," Jameson said. "She was hit by a drunk driver. She died when she was only three months pregnant."

I eyed CJ and could see the one thing he wanted to keep hidden from everyone. He was hurting. Whoever that girl had been, even if he hadn't loved her, it was obvious he'd wanted that baby. Maybe he'd planned to be a happy family with the two of them. I hated that I was just now hearing about it. What else had they hidden from me while I serving time?

"I'll get her situated if you want to grab whatever tests you think are best," Jameson said.

"Where am I staying?"

"We have a few guest houses," Jameson said. "Sometimes other clubs stop by for a few nights. Those who have old ladies tend to skip the partying and want a quiet spot. Each of you will have your own house while you're here, mostly because three women and four kids won't fit into just one of them. Not without you tripping over each other."

"Fine. Take me to my temporary lodgings," I said.

Clarity and Josie were already gone when I stepped back into the main part of the clubhouse, and I noticed their kids were absent too. Scratch was nowhere in sight, and Shadow was gone. I knew Scratch was going back home and I wondered who else would be leaving. I could only imagine how scared Clarity and Josie must be. Scratch might be okay right now, but who knew what he was going back to? And Jackal… My heart hurt for Josie. She still couldn't reach him, and I hoped that didn't mean he was missing also, or worse… dead.

Guilt weighed heavy on me. I'd brought this to their door. If I'd refused Havoc's help, if I'd just walked away that first day, then none of this would have happened. Yeah, I would possibly be dead right now, but how many others were going to lose their lives? Jackal and Scratch both had families. If something happened to them, their women and kids would be alone. I hated myself a little. I should have been stronger.

The house Jameson said would be mine while I was with Devil's Fury was cute. It was a two-bedroom, one-bath bungalow that had a lot of windows. A sun porch ran across the back of the house, and I knew I'd spend a lot of time out there. If I stayed. What if I gave myself up to Slater? I pressed a hand to my stomach again. No. If I was pregnant, then I had to protect my child at all costs. But if I wasn't…

When CJ showed up with a sack full of pregnancy tests, I opened each box and read the instructions. Each one said it was best to take it first thing in the morning. Neither of my brothers were listening though, so I found myself peeing on three of the sticks then waiting to see the results. I'd saved two for the morning just to make sure.

Jameson and CJ crowded me as we stared at the sticks. The results showed up one after the other, and it felt a little like the world was tilting. The room spun and Jameson had to wrap an arm around me to keep me upright.

"So, looks like we're going to be uncles," he told CJ.

And that's when the dam broke. I sobbed harder than I ever had before. Havoc should have been here for this moment. It should have been him waiting with me to see the results, the one holding me. If he were here, we could have celebrated. All I felt was anguish that my child might never know their father.

"Stress isn't good for her," CJ said. "We need to calm her the fuck down."

That just made me cry harder, mostly because I'd been convinced CJ hated me. But he was being sweet and supportive. There were times in the past he'd shown he cared for me, even if most the time we fought like siblings tend to do. Then I'd been sentenced to prison and it was like everyone had turned their backs on me. Knowing he was there for me now felt really damn good.

"I'm calling Adalia," Jameson said. "She'll know what to do."

Eventually, the tears dried up and all I felt was pain. If Havoc didn't come home, I didn't know what I'd do. No, we hadn't been together all that long, but he'd quickly become the most important person in my world. I loved him, and I knew that even if he didn't come back, I would love him every day the rest of my life. There would never be another man for me.

Where are you, Havoc? Please come home!

Chapter Ten

Havoc

Motherfucking Slater! When I got my hands on that piece of shit, I was going to rip him into pieces with my bare hands. The spineless coward had hooked up with some of the worst scum, but it had backfired on him. Yeah, he might have managed to take a few of my brothers down, myself included, but he'd also pissed off the people who supposedly had his back. I glared at him as he pathetically leaned against the cell wall next to mine. Only bars separated us, and if he were close enough, I'd reach through and smash his head against them a few hundred times.

I mourned the brothers who had been with me when that bomb went off, but even worse, I worried about what would happen to Jordan. If I didn't get back to my club soon and they thought I was dead, would they kick her out? We didn't exactly have a precedence for something like this since Scratch and Jackal were the only ones with old ladies. Until now. I'd never even had a chance to give Jordan the property cut I'd had made for her.

She was going to be fucking pissed when she realized what I'd done. Never had I regretted something as much as I regretted not telling her goodbye, or saying I loved her one last time. At the very least, I should have left a note. I'd just worried she'd try to follow me, and I hadn't wanted her in the middle of shit. If I ever saw her again, I'd probably get an earful.

My body ached from head to toe. The blast had thrown me into a wall, knocking me the fuck out. And now I found myself cooling my heels in a cozy cell. I hadn't seen Jackal, Phantom, or Renegade. If they'd survived, I was certain they would have been locked up alongside me. Which meant they probably were gone. Josie and the kids would be alone now, and it was my fucking fault. I'd known that it seemed too easy.

"Boss wants to speak to you," one of the guards said, stopping in front of my cage.

"Then I guess he'd better get his ass down here."

The man snorted. "Yeah. You're coming with me. Try anything, and I'll put a bullet in you. Boss prefers you alive, but I don't give a shit."

"Fine. Let's go talk to the man in charge."

I stepped out of the cell when he unlocked the door, and he immediately pressed a gun to the back of my head. It was almost too easy, which meant I should probably just follow orders and see what happened. I could get his gun from him and try to make my way out of this hellhole, but at what cost? I didn't have any clue about their numbers or where the guards were stationed. I'd probably end up shot anyway.

We passed several more cages, and I didn't see any of my brothers locked up. The man with the gun prodded me up the stairs and into what seemed to be some sort of fighting arena. We passed three rings with bare-knuckle fights going on, then went down a dark hall. A door marked *Office* was straight ahead, and the guy shoved me inside.

"You didn't come cheap," the asshole said from behind the desk.

"You're not Demonic Reign," I said, knowing for damn sure I'd seen them with Slater before that bomb had gone off.

"No. They were only too happy to make a trade though. You and Slater in exchange for a tidy sum, and their promise to leave the area without causing more trouble."

"Who the fuck are you?" I asked. "And where am I?"

"My name is Raul Silva, and you're in my domain now. You're a big one." He smiled. "Here's how this works. You want your freedom, you're going to work for it. Do as I say, when I say, and in six months I'll let you walk out of here."

Six months? It was a long ass time to be away from Jordan, and for my club to not know where the fuck I was. And there was no guarantee this dickhead would keep his word. What if I played along and then in six months he decided I had to stay longer?

"Never heard of you," I said, hoping he'd volunteer more information.

"You're in South America, Mr. Havoc. I run a few establishments down this way. Illegal fights mostly. That's where you come in. I need a champion."

I didn't understand what the fuck was going on. How had I gotten to South America, and how had this asshole found me?

"I see you're confused," Silva said. "Demonic Reign made an agreement with Slater to take you out of the equation so he could get his hands on the little whore who got him fired. I've been after Slater for a while now. We had an arrangement. He filtered my drugs into the prison system in the States, and in exchange he got a hefty sum."

"And when he got fired you didn't have a way to do business," I said.

"That's only part of it. It seems that Mr. Slater thought to pocket the rest of my drugs and sell them himself, cutting me out completely. Loyalty goes a long way with me, Mr. Havoc."

"I don't understand how Demonic Reign fits into this," I said.

"They work for me from time to time, and knew I wanted Slater. So they made an arrangement with him. My fight rings down here are legendary and when they saw you, they knew I'd want you. Money changed hands, and now you're mine," Silva said.

"And my brothers?" I asked.

"Not my concern," Silva said.

"You ensure the safety of my club, and see my brothers are sent back home, and I'll do what you want. But I want it in writing that in six months I walk out of here a free man, with passage back to the States."

"A shrewd businessman. I like that, Mr. Havoc." He looked at the man still holding a gun to my back. "See that he's given adequate quarters, proper meals, and access to the gym. I need him in top form."

"Yes, Boss," said the asshole at my back.

I was shown to a room one floor up. It was sparse, but adequate. Bathroom, bed, dresser. I didn't really need anything else.

"There's a gym down the hall," he said. "This floor remains on lockdown at all times. So don't get any ideas about slipping away. Kitchen is four doors down on your right. If there's something you need that we don't have, add it to the list on the fridge."

"Will he keep his word?" I asked.

The man hesitated. "Probably."

"What the fuck does that mean?"

"It means if you win, he'll want to keep you. You lose, and he'll kill you." The guy shrugged. "I'd suggest winning and hope he holds to the agreement. And signing something won't mean shit."

I hesitated a second, not wanting to show any weakness, but I couldn't leave my club and Jordan in the dark.

"Is there any way to get a message to someone?" I asked.

His dark eyes focused on me. "Look, we all have families to support. If you have a girl back home, or kids, I'd keep that shit to yourself. If Mr. Silva thinks he has leverage against you, he'll use it. For the next six months, you eat, breathe, and live for fighting. Clear your mind of everything else, or you'll end up dead."

The guard walked off, leaving me to contemplate my fate. I slid my cut from my shoulders and stared at it a moment. For the next six months, I wasn't Sergeant at Arms, wasn't Devil's Boneyard, wasn't the man who loved Jordan. I'd shut that shit off, take care of business, and then go home.

I put my cut into the top dresser drawer and closed it, sealing away that part of my life until it was time to wear it again. I wasn't going to wear my colors while I was here. It seemed disrespectful, especially since I hadn't even tried to find a way out of this shit.

If I didn't have Jordan at home, I might have tried. Ending up dead wasn't high on my to-do list though. She might be a tough little thing, but she needed me just as much as I needed her. Since Jackal, Phantom, and Renegade weren't with me, I was alone and needed to proceed with caution. It was the first time since leaving prison that I didn't have my brothers at my back.

There was a knock at the open door and I turned to find a small woman standing uncertainly at the threshold. There was a stack of clothes in her arms and a towel draped across her shoulder.

"Mr. Silva said to bring these to you," she said, entering the room.

I took them from her and noticed that she trembled and wouldn't meet my gaze. I put the clothes and the towel on top of the dresser and when I turned back to her, she was starting to remove her clothes.

"Whoa! Hey, don't do that," I said, reaching for her.

"Mr. Silva said I'm to do whatever you want, be good to you."

"The clothes and towel and fine. I don't want or need anything else from you. Not now, and not in the future," I said.

She took a shuddering breath and finally looked up at me.

"Can you keep a secret?" I asked.

She nodded.

"I have a woman back home. I'm not about to cheat on her, for any reason. I don't want Silva knowing about Jordan or he'll use her against me, but I'm not going to accept your offer either."

She licked her lips. "I could… maybe tell him that you don't fuck and fight? That you need to focus? We once had a fighter like that."

"Yeah, that's good. If he asks, just tell him that. Maybe it will keep him from sending anyone else to me either."

She paused. "Your woman. She's lucky to have you. I hope you get back home to her."

"Me too," I muttered as she walked out of the room.

I grabbed the towel and clothes, then showered the filth off me from however much time I'd lost since going after Slater. I wasn't sure I wanted to know. The fact they'd gotten me to South America meant they'd either drugged me, or I'd hit my head hard enough to be out for days, if not longer.

The hot water eased the aches in my body, and when I was finished and dressed, I went in search of food. Adding some items to the list on the fridge, I decided to explore the floor that was now my prison for the next six months. I found three more bedrooms, but only one looked like it was being used. It made me wonder how often Silva purchased fighters, or backed people into a corner so they had no choice but to accept his offer. The floor was vacant, and when I checked the door that led downstairs, it was locked and I saw a handprint keypad next to it. The guard hadn't used one to let me onto the floor so I wondered if it had been disengaged since the place was empty.

I prowled the second floor and ended up working out in the gym until my body ached again. It didn't feel like anything was broken, but I'd noticed some bruising when I'd showered. Nothing I wouldn't survive. I'd had much worse in the past, not just in prison but before that too. With four Devils missing, possibly dead, I knew Cinder and Scratch would keep digging until they figured out what the fuck happened, and possibly even my current location. Having never heard of this asshole, Silva, it was doubtful they'd find me, but I could hope.

The door opened and a man stepped through, dripping with sweat. A butterfly bandage was holding his eyebrow together, his lips were split in two places, and he looked about ready to drop. He sagged against the wall when the door locks engaged and met my gaze.

"Whatever you do, don't accept any drinks from them down by the ring. Ever. Keep your head down, fight when they tell you to, and pray you get the fuck out of here," the man said with an accent. He held out his hand. "Andre Phillipe."

"French?" I asked.

He nodded. "I have eight months left on my sentence with Silva. You?"

"He asked for six months, but if you have eight left, I have a feeling he fucking lied to me."

"Wouldn't surprise me," Andre said.

"We the only two fighters on the floor?" I asked.

"Yeah. One served his time and left. The other..." He shook his head. "He decided not to play by the rules.

Haven't seen him since. They either put a bullet in his head, or sold him to someone else."

"Fuck."

"Yeah. Like I said, follow the rules, but don't drink anything near the ring. Not unless you bring it yourself and entrust it to someone who won't fuck you over."

"In other words, no one?"

"Letti would hold it for you."

"Who?" I asked.

"Little Hispanic woman they probably sent to take care of you. Told her I was gay."

"Are you?" I asked.

He snorted. "No. I just don't rape women and there's no way she's doing this because she wants to. Wish I could get her out of this place, but she's as stuck as we are. What about you? Take her up on the offer?"

"No." I didn't volunteer more than that, not knowing if I could trust this guy. I'd only confided in Letti so I wouldn't hurt her feelings. Now that I knew she was just as much a victim in all this as the fighters, I was determined to get her the hell out of here when I left. Just didn't know how to pull it off yet.

Andre smirked. "A man of few words. I like it."

"How's this work?" I asked.

"We eat, work out, rest… and when they're ready for us, we fight. You'll either have one big fight, or a few smaller ones. As big as you are, I'm sure he'll throw you into the center right first off."

"Downstairs?"

"*Oui*. All fights are held here. Silva not only places bets on his fighters, he also gets a cut. A door fee of sorts, I suppose. I heard him talking to another man shortly after I arrived and realized they were negotiating costs for a fight."

"Any idea what else he's dabbling in?" I asked.

"Drugs. Guns. Women. The man has his hand in every illegal activity in these parts."

"How did you get mixed up in this shit?" I asked.

"Wrong place, wrong time." Andre sighed. "My woman broke up with me and my friends brought me here to forget her. They wanted to party and bought drugs from the wrong person. Things went to shit and I was picked up with one of my buddies. He didn't make it. I'm determined to make it home."

"More than eight months because of drugs?" I asked skeptically.

"I started winning. A lot. It was supposed to be three months."

I didn't like the sound of that. It meant Silva would likely back off his deal if I won, but like the guard had said, if I didn't I could end up dead. I was fucked one way or the other.

Wait for me, baby. I'll be home when I can.

No matter the cost, I'd go home to Jordan and I'd make things right. I'd fucking marry her if that's what she wanted, and I'd damn sure not take as many risks. Too bad that hindsight was 20/20.

Chapter Eleven

Jordan
Three Months Later

Unbeknownst to my brothers, or anyone else except for one person, I'd been doing a bit of digging. Havoc was still missing. Renegade had been found, along with Jackal and Phantom. Thankfully, they were able to heal from their wounds and seemed to be doing fine, though the few times I'd seen them, none would hold my gaze. I knew they blamed themselves for Havoc being gone. Truth was, my stubborn ass of a man had tried to be a hero, *my* hero. Which meant I was going to save his ass, one way or another.

Outlaw was the Devil's Fury version of Shade, and once I'd told him what I needed and why, he'd been happy to help. All right, so happy might be stretching it. I'd threatened to geld him if he didn't give me everything he had on the events leading up to Havoc disappearing, and anything they'd found since. I'd found that pregnancy made me more feral than usual and most of the guys were giving me a wide berth. Probably wise since I was ready to tear everyone to pieces.

Havoc had found Slater, but it seemed he'd gotten more than he bargained for. I knew the Devil's Boneyard had picked up a member from another club. Demonic something or other. The asshole wasn't talking so Cinder had sent the guy here, to the Devil's Fury compound. I wasn't supposed to know that, but I'd gotten good at eavesdropping. They just thought their Church doors were soundproof, but they weren't. I really didn't think they'd tried all that hard to make the man talk. I had no doubt that Havoc would have had the man singing like a canary within minutes. Maybe the Boneyard crew was feeling his loss as much as I was, but Cinder and Scratch had seemed capable enough of getting this sort of thing handled.

Devil's Boneyard seemed to think there was still a threat to their women and kids. Josie, her kids, and Jackal were still in one of the homes here. Clarity and her kids were still here too, but Scratch was back home trying to sort this shit out, along with Cinder and a handful of other Devil's Boneyard members. I'd heard they had crew there from several clubs, everyone banding together to find Havoc and bring him home. It was sweet, and I was grateful they were trying so hard, but I wasn't going to sit on my ass, twiddling my thumbs, and wait for good news.

What was that saying? Behind every great man was a greater woman? They would have been wise to listen. I knew that damn biker they were holding was the key to all this shit. They might not be able to make him talk, but I'd be willing to bet I could. I'd do anything to get Havoc back. I pushed away from the table and shrugged into my cut. Setting out on foot, I made my way to the back of the compound and the little barn I'd seen on one of my walks.

Badger was standing guard and stared me down as I approached.

"Go home, Jordan. This isn't a good place for you."

"Why? Because I'm pregnant and a delicate little woman?" I asked.

"Not a damn thing delicate about you. I think you proved that when you went batshit crazy and damn near crushed Demon's nuts."

I rolled my eyes. Demon had deserved it, and he damn well knew it. There were just some things you didn't say to a pregnant, hormonal woman who was missing her man. The slap to my ass right after might have been playful, but I'd decided Demon needed to be taught some manners.

"You can't go in," he said.

"Let me ask you something. If it were you missing, if Adalia and your kids were here alone, what would you want her to do? Sit and wait patiently for you to be found? Or act on her instincts and bring your ass home?"

"First, Adalia isn't like you. She's soft and sweet, and damn sure isn't going to kick someone's ass, much less come after me. And second..." He sighed and looked around before pushing open the door. "Try to leave him breathing. If he's dead, I'll have some explaining to do."

I kissed his cheek. "Thank you, Badger."

I entered the barn that smelled like piss and other unpleasant things. The man tied to the chair in the center looked like he'd been worked over pretty hard, several times. The fingers on his hands appeared to have been broken and healed wrong, the ones he still had, but they didn't look like fresh breaks. That little tidbit told me that he was used to torture, and probably could withstand quite a lot. When he smiled, I saw that teeth were missing, but for all I knew he hadn't had them when Cinder had picked him up.

"They send something pretty for me to play with?" the man asked.

I smirked. "No, you won't be the one playing. I will be."

He eyed me uncertainly as I removed my cut and looked over the table of tools. Not as good a selection as Havoc had, but I could make do. Someone had already removed his nails, on his remaining fingers. Someone had removed a few of his fingers already, and while they had cauterized the wounds, they still looked fresh. I hated to take what was left of his teeth. I wanted to be able to understand his stupid ass when he finally talked. The asshole was shirtless and had chunks missing from his chest and abdomen, some new and some healed over. Might have made a softer woman squeamish. Not me. This dickhead was standing between me and Havoc, and I was fucking pissed. I picked up an ice pick and stepped closer. His legs were tied tight to the chair, leaving them spread. Perfect.

"So, you're going to tell me what you know about Havoc."

"And why would I do that?" he asked. "Out of the goodness of my cold, black heart?"

"I was thinking more along the lines of self-preservation." I gripped the ice pick tighter. "Otherwise, I'm going to see how loud you scream when I stab this through your balls."

He sneered at me. "You don't have the stones, little girl."

"Oh, trust me. I do."

I brought the pick down, straight into his crotch, and the man howled and cursed as blood soaked the denim of his pants. Well, that should get his attention. I jerked the pick free and stared at him. Maybe if the clubs had gone after his family jewels, he might have talked sooner.

"Let's try this again. I want to know where Havoc is."

"Bitch!" He spat at me. "I won't tell you shit."

"Pity. Probably a good thing you shouldn't reproduce." I slammed the pick down again and felt his testicle pop. It grossed me out, but I wasn't going to be deterred. I wasn't leaving this damn barn until he squealed and told me what I needed to know. I could understand why the guys hadn't gone this far though. If it squigged me out, I could only imagine how they would feel, seeing as how they had balls themselves. I'd always noticed men winced whenever a guy got nailed in the nuts.

By the time Grizzly walked in with several other Devil's Fury members, the idiot tied to the chair was bleeding from a dozen places and was blubbering like a baby. Probably because I'd made sure he'd never use his dick again. Take away a man's cock, and it was amazing how they suddenly were able to think clearly and use the brain upstairs.

"I'll talk," he said. "Just please... keep this crazy bitch away from me."

I washed my hands at the nearby sink then listened as the whiny little bitch spilled his guts as I slipped my cut back on.

"Raul Silva has him," the man said. "He's in South America."

I arched a brow and moved in closer, making the man flinch. "South America is pretty fucking big, asshole. *Where* in South America?"

"He has a fight ring someplace in Colombia. That's all I know. I swear! I just handed your guy over to some of Silva's people. He paid cash," the man said.

"Well, fuck me," Grizzly said, eyeing me with both respect and a little bit of awe. "You did what four clubs haven't been able to do. I'm not sure if I should praise you or back the fuck away slowly."

I snickered. I didn't have a doubt the big guy wasn't even remotely scared of me, but it was nice to know he had my back and wasn't going to bitch about my methods. The grimace on his face when he'd seen the captive's blood-soaked crotch hadn't escaped my notice either. One of the other guys had grabbed his dick and turned away, as if he felt the pain himself. Men could be such babies when it came to their cocks.

"How the fuck are we going to extract him from Colombia?" Dagger asked.

"I'm going," I said, "and don't fucking tell me I can't."

Jameson leaned in closer to his crew and whispered loud enough the entire room could hear him. "She's still near the weapons. I wouldn't argue."

Grizzly let out a long, hard laugh.

"I'm being serious," I said. "You're not going after Havoc without me. Don't take this the wrong way, but the Devil's Boneyard couldn't keep him safe when he went after Slater, and none of you could get this jackass to talk. I'm not leaving his fate in anyone's hands other than mine."

"Uh, Jordan. Can you maybe not piss off some of the toughest men in the state?" my brother asked, giving me the side-eye.

"I'm not scared of them."

Demon smiled. "Of course, you aren't. Havoc chose wisely. We'll let you go, on one condition. You don't do anything that could endanger you or the baby. I'm not getting Havoc back only to have him murder the lot of us because you got hurt."

"Whatever." I folded my arms. "When do we leave?"

"We don't exactly keep passports," Grizzly said. "We have to arrange passage out of the country, grease a few palms to make sure they look the other way, and then find our way back home once we have Havoc. It won't be easy if this Silva person is coming for us."

"Then we take him out," I said.

The guy tied to the chair started laughing. "Take him out? Sure, bitch. Just waltz in there, demand your man back, and murder the toughest man in the country. Cake walk."

"Even evil assholes have men who can be bought," I said.

"That's going to take a lot of cash," Grizzly said.

"I'll talk to Clarity," I said.

"What the fuck does the VP's wife have to do with anything?" Dagger asked.

"She's an heiress and told Scratch to use her inheritance to help the club. Can't think of a better reason to dip into those funds than getting Havoc back. Can you?" I asked.

"Where the fuck do we find an heiress?" Scorpion asked.

I eyed him up and down. "I'm guessing you don't. Have you looked in the mirror lately?"

Jameson was turning red from trying not to laugh, but the President of Devil's Fury didn't have any problem laughing at Scorpion's expense. At least someone found me funny, other than Havoc. My mean side seemed to amuse him endlessly, and fuck did I miss him!

"Go see Clarity and I'll start making arrangements," Grizzly said. "Tell her to call Scratch to give us access to the funds, or send someone to meet us at the airstrip with them."

"Airstrip?" I asked. "Not airport?"

"The Dixie Reapers have a connection I'm hoping they'll let us use. Casper VanHorne has a plane that won't rouse any suspicion leaving the country or coming back. His daughter is married to the President of the Reapers," Grizzly said.

"Whatever it takes," I said. "Anything."

I stared at him hard and he shook his head.

"I'm not letting you do anything that will piss off Havoc. Well, more than letting you go to Colombia. He's going to lose his shit when he sees you."

"Let me deal with Havoc. Just get me there," I said.

"Badger will take you to Clarity." Grizzly looked at him. "Just drive really damn slow since you'll have a pregnant woman on the back of your bike."

Badger snorted. "I think I know the drill."

"Yeah, because you keep knocking up my daughter."

Badger flipped him off, which just made Grizzly smile. I followed Badger outside to his bike and climbed on back. He went so fucking slow I wanted to reach around him and twist the throttle. I was pregnant, not made of spun glass. When we reached the little house Clarity was sharing with her kids temporarily, I got off and let myself inside.

Clarity looked tired as she slumped on the couch, both kids entertained by some cartoon on TV. She gave me a smile when she saw me, and I went to sit beside her.

"Everything okay?" I asked.

"Yeah. Just miss my husband, and the kids miss him too."

"I might have a way of getting you home soon," I said. "But it's going to take some money."

"I'm listening," Clarity said, her gaze sharpening.

I told her what I'd discovered about Havoc, and what Grizzly had said. It didn't take much to persuade her to give us access to the money. Even better, the money was being hand delivered by Cinder himself, and two other Devil's Boneyard were coming with him. She no sooner hung up than she called Josie to fill her in, which turned into Josie calling her brother and arranging for Dixie Reapers to come help extract Havoc from Colombia.

"Three clubs?" I asked.

Clarity bit her nail. "You're right. We should call Laken and Ryker, make sure Hades Abyss will be there too."

My eyebrows shot up. "Just how connected are all the clubs?"

"Well, Josie's brother is Tank. He's the Sergeant at Arms for Dixie Reapers. As you know, she's married to Jackal, so that makes her part of Devil's Boneyard too.

And she recently found out she has another brother. Slash is the VP for Devil's Fury. Laken is Flicker's sister, also with Dixie Reapers, but she's married to Ryker, who is the son to the President of Hades Abyss. Then there's Saint. He had a daughter with the sister of another Hades Abyss member, even though she's dead from what I hear. Scratch's daughter is married to Bull, who is a Dixie Reaper. Then there's you. You have one brother prospecting for Boneyard and one for Fury, and you're the old lady to the Sergeant at Arms for the Devil's Boneyard."

"I think I need a drink to process all that," I muttered.

"I'll make sure to have one ready for you after the baby is born and you're done breastfeeding."

I blinked. "Um, no. Just, hell no. I know breast milk is supposed to be all that, but this kid is going to be fed with a bottle. If I have to incubate it, then Havoc can sure as fuck help feed it. Plenty of kids are bottle fed and turn out just fine."

Clarity snickered.

"So what do we do now?" I asked.

"Wait."

Great. I hated waiting. Now that I knew where Havoc was, I wanted to go after him. I didn't know what kind of condition he'd be in, or what the hell Silva was forcing him to do. Fight rings didn't sound so bad, but I'd heard some underground fights led to a lot of deaths. If Havoc wasn't still breathing when I got there, I'd gut Silva myself.

Clarity smiled a little as she stared at me.

"What's that look for?" I asked.

"You really do love him, don't you? Despite the fact he practically claimed you the second he saw you on the side of the road."

"Sometimes you just know, I guess. He made me feel safe from the very beginning."

She nodded. "I understand. I felt the same with Scratch, except I wasn't quite as tough as you. I fought to survive on the streets with my son, but I didn't have your strength."

"You're strong, Clarity. It's just a different kind of strength," I said. "No way Scratch would pick a weak woman as his wife. He has an image to uphold after all."

"I guess you're right. I'm just not all fiery like you." She smirked. "Unless a club slut puts her hands on my man. Then I have no trouble kicking the shit out of someone."

"Now that I would pay to see."

"Oh, it happened," she said. "Only took once before they backed the hell off. Now the new girls are always warned to keep away from the VP unless they want me to haul their asses out of the clubhouse."

"Am I the only one who finds it funny that sweet little you beat on a club slut, and all I did was insult one when she came after Havoc?"

Clarity stared at me. Hard.

"All right, so when she betrayed me to Slater I may have wanted her blood. I think deep down I knew Havoc didn't want anyone but me. The asshole was testing me. Took me a few minutes to realize it, and once I did, I decided to have a little fun."

"You're good for him," she said. "And I think he's been good for you too. The two of you complement each other."

"Let's just hope we can get him back."

"We will," Clarity said. "Have faith, Jordan. You didn't find him only to lose him so soon afterward."

"Technically, I did lose him. I just have to hope he's still breathing."

"If he's not, just remember that jails in Colombia aren't as nice as the ones here," Clarity said. "And you sure as hell don't want to have your baby in one."

She made a good point. Would it stop me from seeking revenge? Nope. But it was nice to know someone was worried about me. I hadn't had as much time with Clarity and Josie as I would have liked, but I felt like we were forming a friendship. Even though we'd all been stuck here, hiding out, I'd spent most of my time worrying about Havoc and trying to find a way to get him back. But friendship was something I hadn't had in a long-ass time, and it was nice to have another woman to talk to when I made the time for it. Especially one who understood the world I'd ended up in.

Unfortunately for me, patience was not one of my virtues. It took everyone three days to make the arrangements to get Havoc. Three days of knowing where he was and being unable to do a fucking thing about it. I was batshit crazy by the time we boarded Casper VanHorne's plane, and more than ready to bring my man home. Only Demon would sit next to me during the flight, but I noticed he kept his nuts protected. I might have found it funny if I wasn't scared shitless over what we'd find in Colombia.

"I'm coming, Havoc," I murmured. "Please don't be dead."

Demon reached over and squeezed my hand, but didn't say anything. I liked his silent support and tried to calm myself and stay positive. We *would* find Havoc and bring him home. And then I'd chew his ass out for disappearing for three fucking months.

Chapter Twelve

Havoc

I had a fight tonight, a big one. I still had three months on my sentence with Silva, and I was starting to be sure he wouldn't release me when the time was up. I'd won every damn fight I'd been in, even sending a few of the men away in body bags. I'd spent most of my time working out and was now even bigger than before. Several of my opponents had literally pissed themselves when I stepped into the ring.

My latest challenge was damn near laughable. The guy had to be half my size, and even though I'd heard he could be lethal, I doubted I had anything to worry about. I had fury and determination on my side. No way someone was killing me, not when I had too much to live for. I still thought of Jordan every damn day, but when I was in the ring, I had to clear her from my mind. Silva had tried sending more women to me, but I'd refused them all. When he'd questioned if Andre and I had something going on, I assured him I wasn't gay, just didn't like fucking when I had to fight. He seemed to buy my excuse of needing to focus and left me alone after that.

I hadn't seen Letti lately though, and I worried he'd done something to her. Andre was concerned too, but there wasn't shit we could do about it. We were just as much pawns in Silva's clutches as Letti was, and probably a dozen or more other women. Hell, one of the ladies he'd sent to me couldn't have been more than a sixteen-year-old kid. I'd wanted to throw up when I'd seen that dead look in her eyes and knew she'd had a horrible life.

Help wasn't coming for any of us though. After all this time, I had to admit that my brothers didn't know where the hell I was and wouldn't be making a rescue attempt. I'd held out hope that first month, but after that, my hope slowly died and I realized I was in this until Silva released me. Whenever that might be. He'd recently extended Andre's time to another fucking year.

"You ready?" Andre asked from the doorway. "Be careful tonight. I know this guy is small, but he's got a high death toll. They're starting to call him the Grim Reaper."

"I can handle him."

Andre nodded. "Then it's showtime."

We went downstairs with two guards flanking us. The place was packed with tons of screaming men and women. I made my way inside the ring and faced off against the man with the dead eyes. I could see why people feared him, but I wasn't one of them. I'd done my share of killing, even if my body count in the ring wasn't as high as this guy's.

When the fight started, he charged me with a roar and I easily sidestepped, then felt his fist against my kidneys. Fucking hell! A red haze settled over me as I went to work, throwing one punch after another. The mat was stained red as I landed blow after blow, not caring what kind of damage I did. He got in a few cheap shots, and I knew I'd end up with a black eye and some bruised ribs, but I wasn't going to lose this one.

He came at me again and I landed an uppercut that knocked him the fuck out. As he crashed to the mat, out cold, the crowd went wild. Silva entered the ring with a smirk.

"And there you have it. Havoc remains undefeated. Any other challengers?" Silva asked.

"Yeah. I'll challenge him," a female voice said.

Silva chuckled. "A woman? A woman wants to take on the greatest warrior in Colombia?"

"You bet your ass I do."

As the crowd parted and blonde hair came into view, everything in me went still and I could barely fucking breathe. Jordan looked beautiful as she entered the ring, and really fucking pissed. She folded her arms and stared at me, her jaw tight and her eyes flashing.

Silva eyed her up and down. "Are you sure you want to take him on? You don't seem like you have what it takes."

"I'm pregnant, asshole, not weak," she said.

Silva's eyes locked on her belly and so did mine. Pregnant? My woman was carrying my kid in there? And she was going to fight me? What the fuck?

I looked up and caught the fury in her gaze.

"You're pregnant?" Silva asked. "And what type of man lets his woman fight a man like Havoc while she's expecting?"

"The kind who disappears and makes her travel all the fucking way to Colombia to find his dumbass," she said, advancing on me.

"Jordan, what are you..."

I didn't get to finish before she slammed her fist into my jaw. Fuck, but that hurt! She wasn't done though, not my little hellcat. She hit me in the ribs twice and right under the eye that was probably starting to swell already from my previous fight.

"Fucking hell, woman!" I wrapped my arms around her and held her still.

"Havoc," she said with steel in her voice. "You're getting blood on me."

I released her and scanned her, realizing she was right.

Silva moved in closer. "I take it the two of you know one another?"

"Yeah," Jordan said. "He's the asshole who knocked me up, decided to play hero, and disappeared for three fucking months."

"Interesting," Silva said, and I could see the wheels turning.

Shit. I needed to get Jordan out of here before things got really fucking bad. How the hell had Scratch and Cinder let her come to Colombia? And was she alone? Jesus Christ! Anything could have happened to her.

She turned slowly to look at Silva. "And you. You're the one who bought him, hauled his ass here, and what? Forced him to fight for you?"

"Do you realize who you're talking to?" he asked, his voice soft yet no less lethal. "I'm not a man to threaten, little girl. I can make you disappear as easily as I took your Havoc."

"Try it," she said.

Silva advanced on her and before I could process what the fuck was happening, she had a knife held to his family jewels and Silva's eyes were wide as his face paled.

"I have guards, they'll…"

Jordan twisted the blade and pressed it tighter.

"They won't do shit," Jordan said. "Want to know why? Because I own their asses now. Paid off every single one of them. See, that's the thing about being scum. No one has any true loyalty to you."

"Fuck, Havoc. What is it with your woman going after everyone's balls?" Demon asked as he climbed into the ring. "Mr. Silva, if I were you, I'd listen to her. Especially since she's armed. She's dangerous enough without weapons."

Demon grabbed his crotch and I wondered if Jordan had attacked the Devil's Fury Sergeant at Arms.

"Who else is here?" I asked.

"A shit ton of us," Demon said. "What? You thought we'd let her traipse down here alone? She'd likely have wiped out the entire country just trying to get to you. That is one fierce woman you have. I like her."

I chuckled. "Yeah, I like her too."

Cinder stepped into the ring, with Venom, Tank, Dagger, Phantom, and several other welcome faces. Fuck but I'd missed my crew, and the clubs who always helped whenever we needed it. We might all have different colors, but we were fucking family just the same.

"Do me a favor," Cinder said. "Next time you want to go on a mission, take your woman with you or hire about five assassins to sit on her ass."

I smiled and looked at Jordan who was still holding Silva captive with a knife to his balls. Damn but I fucking loved her. Even pregnant, she was still kicking everyone's ass, including mine. I worked my jaw back and forth and realized she'd hit me harder than the jackass I'd knocked out.

"You know how pregnant women clean house and bake cookies and shit?" Phantom asked. "Yeah, well, yours makes people bleed. If you don't want her to kill Silva in front of everyone, I'd take the knife away from her. She made a Demonic Reign member cry like a fucking baby."

My eyes widened as I stared at Jordan. What the fuck? They'd let her near a Demonic Reign? I wasn't sure if I was pissed she'd been anywhere near one of those sadistic fuckers, or proud that she'd made the man cry. And maybe a little scared as well. What had she done to bring one of those assholes to his knees?

I moved in closer and slowly reached for the knife, wrapping my hand around hers.

"Baby, give me the knife."

She glared at me. "I'm still fucking pissed at you."

"Be pissed at me all you want, but you kill Silva in front of all these people and you'll go to jail. You won't like a Colombian prison, baby. And just to make sure that didn't happen, I'd have to kill everyone here. That's a lot of blood."

She snorted.

"Come on, Jordan. Let me have the knife."

"He's whoring women out?" Venom asked, as he led a group of frightened females into the ring. "Shit, this one barely looks legal."

"She's fifteen," one of them said.

Oh fucking hell. Jordan took one look at the poor girl who seemed like she was already dead inside, and before I could stop her, she shoved the blade right through Silva's crotch. He fell to the mat, bleeding and grabbing at his dick, the blade still clutched in Jordan's hand.

"Well, that's one way to handle the problem," Venom said. "Now what do we do with all these witnesses and these women?"

"Take the women home," Jordan said. "The clubs can take care of them, give them a fighting chance."

"Take them home," Phantom said slowly.

Jordan locked her gaze on Cinder. "Congratulations. You're a daddy."

"Jordan," Cinder said with a warning tone in his voice.

She pointed at the fifteen-year-old girl. "You going to leave her here? I don't give a shit what your past is, but you have the means to take care of her and give her a decent life."

"I'll take her," Grizzly said, stepping closer to the mat. "My Adalia is all grown up and married. I have plenty of room at home for her. She'll get everything she needs, including counseling if that's what she wants."

Jordan nodded then glared at Cinder, who just glared back

Great. My woman was going to start a war with my President.

"Baby, can you drop the knife now?" I asked.

She tossed it aside then folded her arms over her chest. "I want to go home, but not until you shower. And so help me, if I find out you touched any of those women…"

"He didn't," Letti said. "He refused each of us, even though Silva kept trying. I think he wanted a way to put a leash on your man. Something to hold over him."

Jordan growled then jammed her boot heel into Silva's already bleeding crotch, making the man howl in agony. "Let him bleed the fuck out."

Four Colombian police officers stepped up to Silva, then eyed Jordan. She lifted her chin, but I could see the tremor in her hand. She was brave, but she didn't want to go back to prison, not even for defending me. And I wasn't about to let that fucking happen.

Cinder tossed them a duffle. "Fifty grand each to look the other way and let us leave the country."

One of them grinned and unzipped the bag. After showing the contents to the other three, he nodded.

"You're free to go. Mr. Silva had an unfortunate accident. A drug deal gone wrong."

"And the women?" Jordan asked, pointing to them. "They're going with us. I don't give a shit about paperwork. Make it happen."

The officer eyed her. "Of course. You are unarmed, correct?"

"For now," she said.

"Take her home," the officer said then looked at me. "And don't ever bring her back to Colombia."

"Like I want to come back to this hellhole," she muttered as she left the ring.

I caught up to her and grabbed her hand.

"There's a bathroom on the plane," Cinder said. "You can get cleaned up when we're on board."

"My cut is upstairs," I said.

"I'll get it," Phantom said. "And something clean for you to wear."

"I'll help," Letti said, her eyes locked on Phantom like he was the last piece of candy on earth. Huh. That could be interesting.

"Does this mean I'm free to return to France?" Andre asked.

I looked at the officers. "He's with me. Consider him included in your fee."

Several black Hummers were parked outside and Jordan pulled me into one of them. She kept her distance, but I thought that might have more to do with the blood on me than anything else. Slowly, I reached over and took her hand. And that's all it took for the dam to break. She sobbed so damn hard I worried she'd make herself sick, and then she was in my arms, neither of us caring about the blood and sweat anymore.

"I'm so fucking sorry, baby. I should have never left the way I did," I said, kissing her hard.

"Don't ever scare me like that again."

"I won't. You'll know my every move from now on."

She cried against my shoulder as she straddled my lap. I held her all the way to the airstrip and carried her onto the plane. Leading her into the bathroom with me, which was much larger than I'd expected, I got both of us clean. Then I held her the entire way back to the States, and didn't let go until we reached our house.

Being without her had been the worst pain I'd ever suffered, and my heart broke when I realized how much she'd hurt while I was gone. I should have been there when she found out she was pregnant, should have been by her side every fucking night. No matter what it took, I'd make sure that happened in the future. Taking risks was part of my job, but I'd be smarter about it. I had a family to think about, a woman and kid who depended on me. I wouldn't fuck up again.

Epilogue

Havoc
Two Months Later

I'd slowly settled back into my life since being home again. Things were great with Jordan, and I loved watching my kid grow inside of her. She was showing, and rubbing her baby bump was one of my favorite obsessions. I hadn't exactly mellowed and still did my job as Sergeant at Arms, but I also made sure I told Jordan I loved her every chance I had, and let her know where I was going when I left the house. I drew the line, though, when she'd asked if she could chip me like a damn pet.

Clarity and Josie had distracted her today while I got a special dinner set up for the two of us. Some of the women we'd rescued in Colombia were here, and it had turned out several were US citizens already. Paperwork was being handled for the others courtesy of Shade and Wire. One of the rescued women had cooked everything as a thank you for saving her, and she'd helped me decorate the house. The kitchen table had a tablecloth covering it with lit candles, two meals that looked really damn good, and I'd set up candles in the bedroom just in case things went as well as I was anticipating.

I heard the front door open and shut, then Jordan's boots clicked on the floor until she stopped in the kitchen doorway.

"What's all this?" she asked.

"Just wanted to have a nice dinner with you."

She eyed me like she didn't believe a word I said, but she took a seat when I pulled out a chair for her. I started to sit across from her but decided to just go ahead and bite the bullet.

I dropped to one knee and she froze. "Ryan, what are you doing?"

I pulled the ring box from my pocket. "Jordan, I have an important question to ask you."

She looked at the ring box like it was a poisonous snake. "It's not necessary for you to do this."

"I know it's not, but I want to. I love you, Jordan. You're everything to me, you and our kid. I want us to officially be a family. Not just in the eyes of the club, but I want it on paper that you belong to me and I belong to you. Will you marry me?"

"Ryan, I..." She snapped her mouth shut. "Are you sure about this?"

"Positive."

I took the ring from the box and slid it onto her finger. Her eyes misted with tears and then she flung her arms around my neck.

"I take it this means yes?" I asked, trying not to laugh.

"Yes, you idiot."

She kissed me long and hard, then I pulled away, determined we were going to have a nice dinner and then we'd celebrate later. I'd had a hard time keeping my hands off her since I'd gotten home, and I wanted to make sure she knew our relationship wasn't purely based on sex, even though that part was pretty awesome.

"Did you make this?" she asked.

"Uh, no. Meg made it," I said. "She helped me set all this up."

"How she's settling in?" Jordan asked. "Is she sure she doesn't want to go home?"

"All the women have refused to return to their homes for one reason or another. When they're ready, Cinder will help them find homes and jobs outside the compound. For now, they're welcome to stay as long as they need."

She nodded and took a bite of her food, her eyes closing in bliss. "Maybe we can keep Meg a while."

I laughed and then groaned as I ate my food. Jordan wasn't wrong. This was fucking fantastic. I tried to keep up a stream of conversation as we demolished the food on our plates, but I think we were both thinking about the same thing. Both of us naked.

The second she popped the last bite of food into her mouth, I hauled her out of her chair and carried her to the bedroom. I had us stripped and in the bed in no time. She giggled as my weight settled over her, even though I tried hard not to press against her growing belly. I didn't have all the muscle mass I'd gained in South America, but I still had enough of it that I dwarfed her. She'd always been small, but she seemed more fragile now. Not that I would tell her that. I valued my balls.

"Make love to me, Ryan," she said softly.

"I want to taste every inch of you, spend hours worshiping your body."

She reached between us and wrapped her hand around my cock. "Or you could just take me now and play later."

I smiled down at her. "Whatever my baby wants."

I sank into her, holding her gaze. I could see her love for me, and I felt my heart warm even more. This tiny, kickass woman completely owned me. I made love to her slowly, savoring every second of our time together. Her pussy clasped me tight as I thrust deep. Her breasts were bigger than before, and I'd discovered her nipples were more sensitive. I leaned down and took one into my mouth, licking the hard point then gently biting down.

"Ryan!" she screamed as she came, her pussy trying to milk me dry, but I wasn't done with her yet.

I took her harder, faster. As I drove into her, I licked and teased her other nipple, making her come twice more. She was so fucking hot and wet, and I knew I couldn't hold on much longer. As jet after jet of cum filled her, I roared out my release, pressing my hips tight to hers.

She'd once asked if I'd done that as a way to knock her up, and it might have started that way. Now I just wanted to be inside of her as long as possible. I always felt connected to her, but in these moments, I felt like we were closer than ever, and not just physically.

"I love you," she said softly. "So damn much."

"I love you too."

"Ryan, I..." A tear slipped down her cheek and my heart damn near stopped. My Jordan didn't cry easily.

"Did I hurt you?"

"No." She shook her head and laughed a little, wiping away her tears. "I'm just so happy. I never thought I'd find someone like you, never thought I'd have love or a family. You've given me so much."

"No, baby. You're the one who's given me everything. How many men can say their woman would literally kill for them? Much less track them down in another country?" I smoothed her hair back from her face. "You are the most beautiful, courageous, strongest woman I've ever met. And I'm so damn lucky I get to call you mine. I'm never letting you go."

"Good." She placed her hand on my chest right over my heart. "As long as I have you, that's all I need. You're my entire world, Ryan. Don't ever leave me again."

I kissed her slow and tender. "I won't. Promise. You're stuck with me. Forever."

"Forever isn't long enough, but I'll take it."

I rolled to my side and wrapped my arms around her. I didn't know how I'd managed to find the most perfect woman, but I'd never take her for granted. I'd cherish her every day for the rest of my life, her and our child. I'd been existing before, having fun but not having true meaning to my life. She'd given me that, and so much more. I was a lucky bastard and I knew it. Putting my hand on her belly, I hoped that our baby would be just as amazing as their mother. And God help me if it was a girl because I didn't know if I had the strength to keep with Jordan and a mini-Jordan. They might send me to an early grave.

"What are you thinking?" she asked, sounding drowsy.

"That if we have a daughter and she's like you, I may not survive."

She laughed softly and snuggled closer. "You'll do just fine, daddy. Besides, you have an entire club to help keep her in line. Several, actually."

She wasn't wrong. Devil's Boneyard had my back, and I knew Devil's Fury, Dixie Reapers, and Hades Abyss would be there if we needed them. Whatever life threw at us next, we'd handle it. Together.

Harley Wylde

When Harley is writing, her motto is the hotter the better. Off-the-charts sex, commanding men, and the women who can't deny them. If you want men who talk dirty, are sexy as hell, and take what they want, then you've come to the right place!

An international bestselling author, Harley is the "wilder" side of award-winning sci-fi/fantasy romance author Jessica Coulter Smith, and writes gay fantasy romance as Dulce Dennison.

Harley on Changeling: changelingpress.com/harley-wylde-a-196

Jessica on Changeling: changelingpress.com/jessica-coulter-smith-a-144

Dulce on Changeling: changelingpress.com/dulce-dennison-a-205

Changeling Press E-Books

More Sci-Fi, Fantasy, Paranormal, and BDSM adventures available in E-Book format for immediate download at ChangelingPress.com -- Werewolves, Vampires, Dragons, Shapeshifters and more -- Erotic Tales from the edge of your imagination.

What are E-Books?

E-Books, or Electronic Books, are books designed to be read in digital format -- on your desktop or laptop computer, notebook, tablet, Smart Phone, or any electronic ebook reader.

Where can I get Changeling Press e-Books?

Changeling Press ebooks are available at ChangelingPress.com, Amazon, Barnes and Nobel, Kobo, and iTunes.

ChangelingPress.com

Printed in Great Britain
by Amazon